Praise for *Scrapper*

"A fearless and harrowing meditation on the ruination and transformation of cities and of people; but amid loss and destruction, Bell finds a strain of piercing hope. This is an extraordinary book." — Emily St. John Mandel, *New York Times* bestselling author of *Station Eleven*

"Like the very best novels, Matt Bell's dark and suspenseful *Scrapper* works on so many levels that it's difficult to describe . . . People will still be reading it when all of America, not just Detroit, is crumbling under the weight of its mistakes. — Donald Ray Pollock, author of *The Devil All the Time*

"A meditative, moody work of art . . . Matt Bell is truly gifted and his latest offers more proof that he's a writer we should all be reading." — Victor LaValle, author of *The Devil in Silver*

"*Scrapper* is an offering to the grim phoenix rising out of the ashes of Industrial America — elegy, eulogy, and prophesy. Readers: listen and attend!"
— Aaron Gwyn, author of *Wynne's War* and *Dog on the Cross*

"I love this book . . . full of metaphorical possibilities . . . quite frankly beautiful. Does to Detroit what Bolaño does to Ciudad Juárez . . . Fantastic." — KTEP, *Words on a Wire*

"Splendid . . . stirrir¯ [and] can write like a dream."
—Bill Morris, autl ¯e Millions

"Bell's fiction has been described as grisly, spooky, and dreamlike. Perhaps parts of *Scrapper* are each of those things, as it takes us on a journey through trauma, destruction, and hope—hope for ourselves, for others, for those who would make us afraid.   — The Rumpus

"A tale of hard emotions in a hard environment . . . Bell poses difficult, elemental questions about right and wrong and of what constitutes morality in a place where the usual rules don't always apply. And, refreshingly, the answers his protagonist arrives at are neither easy nor expected."
                                            —*Library Journal*, Starred Review

"An existential noir that seems to merge Robbe-Grillet with the film *Prisoners*."   — *Kirkus Reviews*

"Has the feel of Cormac McCarthy's *The Road* set in present-day Motor City . . . A tale told in powerful, controlled prose."
                                            — *Publishers Weekly*

"[Bell is] a literary chameleon who refuses to be cast in a single mold . . . *Scrapper* is as much a love letter to the Detroit of old as it is a literary thriller."   —LitReactor

"Bell slowly teases [out] Kelly's failures at willed amnesia in equally beautiful and painful streaks of poetic and suggestive prose . . . Stunning, timely, and ultimately illuminating."
                                            — *Rain Taxi Review of Books*

SCRAPPER

ALSO BY MATT BELL

SCRAPPER

MATT BELL

Published by
Soho Press, Inc.
853 Broadway
New York, NY 10003

Library of Congress Cataloging-in-Publication Data

Bell, Matt, 1980–
Scrapper / Matt Bell.
ISBN 978-1-61695-765-0
eISBN 978-1-61695-522-9
1. Kidnapping victims — Fiction. 2. Criminal investigation —
Fiction. 3. Psychological fiction. I. Title.
PS3602.E64548S37 2015
813'.6 — dc23   2015009877

Interior design by Janine Agro, Soho Press, Inc.

Printed in the United States of America

10 9 8 7 6 5 4 3 2 1

Against all those who would make us afraid

And now the answer batters the sky:
with fire there is smoke, and after, ashes.
You can howl your name into the wind
and it will blow it into dust, you
can pledge your single life, the earth
will eat it all, the way you eat
an apple, meat, skin, core, seeds.

— PHILIP LEVINE, "ASHES"

And God shall say God did it.

— INSCRIPTION INSIDE ST. AGNES CHURCH,
DETROIT, MICHIGAN

.

DETROIT

SEE THE BODY OF THE plant, one hundred years of patriots' history, fifty years an American wreck. The remainder of a city within the city, a fortress of squared buildings a mile long and five blocks wide. Three million square feet of interior. A century of reinforced concrete and red brick and steel crossbeams still standing despite injury, of parking lots stretched around miles of emptiness, their lights long ago darkened, their torn and opened fences made an invitation to the gutting.

See the factory roads left open to an incurious public, see the once-famous sign stuttering in broken glass across the bridge between buildings, hung high over the dregs of opposing traffic. And in each last windowpane see a letter, together reading MO_OR CITY IN_U_TR__L PARK.

See how names were not just markers but promises. See how the first name the sign had cried had been gone even longer. How in the city the advance of history displaced what it could not destroy, erase, unfinish: an American exclusion zone. There were sights here few strangers would see again. Except in the photographs of urban explorers. Destruction porn. Except through the window of a bulldozer. Destruction.

See the unsteady structures of the plant's surface, their danger multiplying with every floor climbed above the street, every movement there a possible cascade of effect, complicating last solutions against gravity and entropy. Find the limits of bravery at the threshold of ground and underground, entrances inside the plant where if you knew where to crawl you could get beneath the piled rubble to gaze into basements, cellars, long-locked storage buried beneath factory floors, miles of tunnels for insulated electrical wire and telephone cable, copper pipes for water and steam.

Everywhere you look, everywhere see the barely imaginable past. Imagine anyway. Rewindow the walls. Patch the roof with period-appropriate tar and shingle. Whatever you make simply a confabulation, an illusion of history.

See the high discard of the room where the engines had been tested prior to installation. See the one hundred tables once arrayed here, and on every table see an engine mounted, flush with leaded gasoline and oil, running hot, each machine designed for the same task. See the engineers moving table to table in their dirty suits, grease staining their cuffs, the first generation to work under electric lights, born into the gap before the calculator, the computer, robotics. Before this room they used to test an engine by driving it until it failed. Every machine was a marvel but you could push anything until it broke.

See the room where seamstresses wove plush interiors, stitched and fitted without a sewing machine, using only human hands, human skills. A luxury made of ten thousand stitches. See the parts warehouse, four stories tall and a block long, where the company kept a spare part for every fallible inch of every model they'd made, in 1910 or 1913 or 1925, other good years. All those parts a catalog of promise. If it was broken it could be fixed. They had the parts, they had the expertise, they believed they had the will to keep their cars on the road forever.

See the newer workshops raised between existing buildings to maximize the space. As if every inch of earth were necessary to contain this industry. See the long rooms built for the first modern assembly lines, and when the war came remember how the company volunteered for the high commerce of patriotism. Then the peacetime arrival of the freeways, the newer machines the new roads demanded destined to be designed by other companies, made to devour those newest miles, carrying their drivers fast from coast to asphalt coast.

See the assembly lines at max capacity for the last time, run on this singular idea, the century's founding innovation: one man assigned one function, the fundamental principle of mass production. The promise of a car for every man and the roads to drive it on. Each man a unit of work here in the fastest-growing city in America, amid the explosion of neighborhoods, schools, theaters. Nearly two million citizens in 1950 but then fewer in every year after.

See the half-life of every man and machine and place. See

the plant closing. See the halfhearted inhabitations, the long vacancy that followed, the future lack. The slow crumble to here. Time passing, allowing failures of reinvention, squatters and thieves, until everything valuable had been carried away, leaving behind only concrete and brick and wood, the last looted structures waiting for the blow.

See the steel beams holding but the roof fallen in, wide banners of tar paper hanging between the beams, their black tarps flagging in the wind. Watch the walls for signs of life. See the word SKY written in sky-blue spray paint, in a pretty cursive long untaught. Painted names photographed but uncounted, curses everywhere, in modes both artful and artless. The new pride in slurs, their late variants. See cartoon eyes staring, an orgy of distended genitalia, cars and crowns, pitchforks and skulls. Context is king but what if the context were demolished. Every facade a surface flattened, readied for the image and the word, a conversation coming down: BAD TEMPR written in consistent font, leveled stenciling. STRUGGLE BUGGY across the fluorescent glow of a starlet's eyes, the perforation of her mouth. A pasted optometrist, a gloved hand. SLEEP written in bubbled lettering and below it the same word in a simpler script, a subtitle or a translation. GREEDY LITTLE BASTARD scrawled in white paint below a stairwell, the phrase YOUNG WILD AND FREE arced so high its writer must have had nothing left he was afraid to lose.

Read the walls, and hear on the wind the other names of the dead: Welch, Rainier, Elmore, and Marquette, all extinct. Scripps-Booth, Viking, LaSalle, extinct. Sunbeam, Humber, Singer, extinct. The ancient unremembered, the more recent dead: Imperial, Valiant, Eagle, extinct. Edsel, Merkur, Oldsmobile, Geo, every one of them extinct or nearly so.

Saturn, Mercury — they named a car after a god, but only after they killed the god.

Hear the name Packard, whispered closest to where you stand.

Now see an early dusk beginning, its reddening glare recasting the plant's brick and rust in deeper reds, brighter orange. See across the golden glare a distant plume lifting from one far corner of the plant. The plume nothing but dust, loosed from the buildings and the dirt.

See the plume lit too as it finds its upper limit. See its heights starting to collapse even as new billowing supports its base.

See the dust and the dust's cause: scrappers somewhere in the black avenues of the plant, taking their own last chance.

See history rising by their hand, the dust of a century cast into the air, mote by uncountable mote, becoming a dark tower twisting from the ruin.

See each particle a part of a whole disturbed, see the exponential increase of surface area wherever an object was broken down, the way a thing split might ignite faster than its inert whole. All the broken mess of steel and wood and brick rising, each particle alighting, each floating particle eventually coming to touch another, each touch a whisper of contact.

See how in its minute softness each contact makes a microcosm of agitation, together becoming a million tiny firestarter universes rasping, chafing, scraping smaller than sight. All these particles no longer separated by even one matching bead of distance—all these millions of spaces collapsing and reopening and collapsing again—and into every such space a lick of oxygen moves. See the impossible silence of atoms touching atoms. See the cold mathematics of their possibilities, the way air is also fuel, how every contact carries the potential for heat, wanting only a sufficiency of friction, a single arc of electrostatic discharge—the dust could get in your lungs and kill you three decades from now or it could choke you dead today or it could explode without warning—and when one pair of rubbing particles ignites, the whole cloud goes, a booming conversion of matter to energy, the rumble and the blast filling the air with black sound.

See the entire plume becoming a pillar of flame leaping into the sky, looming high over the plant. See how in its hunger the fire pulls some portion of the sky back down, the back pressure sucking the fire out of the air and into the shivering building at the base of the flame, past the trucks and chains used to tear down the steel, past the wheelbarrows meant to carry it away, back over the scrappers crying out, as in every reachable room the quickening fire finds every other bit of fuel, every wooden thing hung thick with nettings of cobwebs and more dust, dust everywhere set in motion until a second blast ignites, thrusting new heat and pressurized air against the bounds of the building, concrete and mortar and brick shattering, steel warping, every surface radiant, until the walls burst, until the imploding pressure pulls down the ceilings and collapses the floors, until the crashing structure traps within it every man who came to tear it down, to take it away, every man but the lucky last. And if there is a better motor to thank than fear then as the last man flees into the fugitive night he thinks he doesn't know its name.

PART ONE:
THE ZONE

1

WHEN KELLY SAVED THE BOY he was not yet again living any real life, just wallowing in the aftermath of terrible error. Later he would say he'd lived that year by his hands and by his back and by his shoulders and his wrists and his legs and his knees. The year of the body, he'd say, showing his opened fists, the thick white blistering of his calluses—and forget the head, never mind the heart. After the collapse began he'd barely thought, barely spoken, tried for a time to slow his thoughts to silence, or else to bury them with effort, exhaustion. He'd worked past the pains he'd known, found deeper places to lodge a throbbing, but then in the zone the incompleteness of every building became an inkblot for the subconscious. Whatever was missing would be supplied.

The farther he moved toward the center of the zone the more the neighborhoods sagged, all the wood falling off of brick, most every house uninhabited, the stores a couple thousand square feet of blank shelves, windows barred against the stealing of the nothing there. Paint scraped off concrete, concrete crumbled, turned to dust beneath the weather. Wind damage, water damage. Fire and flood. Before the zone Kelly had never known rain alone could turn a building to dust. But rain had flooded the Great Lakes, ice had sheered the cliffs of the state from off the land, shaped the dunes he'd dreamed of often after he'd left the state. The streets here were empty of traffic and in some neighborhoods the grass overran the sidewalks. He parked his truck, got out, walked the paved lanes instead. On trash days he could tell whether a house was occupied by whether or not a container appeared at the curb. There were other methods of determining inhabitation: the sound of televisions or radios, the presence of cut grass. But some men cut the grass for their neighbors to hide how they were the last ones living on their block. A way of pretending normality, despite the boarded windows, the graffiti, the other front doors never opened. Despite the absolute absence of other cars, other human voices.

Mostly it was easier. Mostly there was no question where there were people left behind. The only questions he had to ask were about opportunity, risk, metal.

Whenever Kelly entered an uninhabited house he understood he entered some life he might have lived, how the emptiness of every room pulled him inside out. A furnishing of the self. He opened the front door and the house ceased its stillness. If it had ever been inert it wasn't now. No structure was once it held a human consciousness. In the South Kelly had worked construction, had seen firsthand how a house unlived in wasn't a house. It was so easy to awaken a place. The way a doorknob awoke a memory. The way the angles of a room recalled other rooms. There were blueprints etched across his memories, and in some houses those memories activated: the bedrooms of his parents, the bedrooms of his parents' friends. An angle of light like one he'd lain in as a child, reading a book on birds. The deep dark of a basement, the other dark of an attic. How the fear of the dark hung at the lip of a basement stairs, how it hesitated at the foot of any stairs leading up, toward whatever was below or above the house, outside its public space.

With his smartphone he could check the prices of what he salvaged: the amounts offered changed day to day but he couldn't wait days to sell what he'd dug. At the salvage yards the workers weighed the truck loaded and then they weighed the truck empty, paid him a price multiplied against the difference. The salvage men photocopied his ID, took an inky thumbprint. This was a legitimate business, they said. They asked where he'd gotten the scrap and he lied. They asked again and he took a lower price per pound.

Whatever the salvage yards wouldn't take he took to other men, brokers running scrap out of a backyard or an idle warehouse. There was no trouble with space. There was space everywhere. The unofficial yards kept unofficial hours. You could show up in the middle of the day and find the place deserted, show up at midnight and find three guys playing cards, getting high, cutting scrap. They paid a fraction of the price, the price of no questions asked. Whatever was suspect they'd break until it was sellable. There were scrapyards where no one asked these brokers questions, contractors who would mix the questionable stuff with more honest trade.

Once he'd arrived to find a man cutting a copper statue with a power saw. The man shirtless, skin gleaming, working without eye protection, a stub of a cigarette clamped in his mouth. The statue's arms sawed at the elbows. The head on the ground. The saw working its way through the torso at a steep diagonal. The kerf of the cut wide like a wound from a sword. Then the smashing the hands with a sledge. Then the mutilating the head into unrecognizable shards.

Broker: a ridiculous word for such a man but everyone self-justified. Everyone wanted to be more than what they were.

The salvage men reminded him: it wasn't the function they sold but the form. It didn't matter if he broke a broken refrigerator. What mattered was getting it to the truck without straining his back. There was more steel and iron than anything else but they paid the least of anything. A hundred pounds of copper pipe paid more than double a truckload of steel. Same for copper wire, copper cable. You could ransack the rooms of a house but the best stuff was hidden behind the walls. It wasn't the metal that held the house up but you wouldn't want to live there with it gone.

Kelly could picture the city's glory days but it took a certain imagination. On the television in his barely furnished apartment he watched a blonde reporter say the collapse was still in progress but now it was down to the aftershocks. Sometimes the news interviewed one of the left behind. Once this man or woman had been an autoworker or a grocery clerk like anyone else. What mysteries they were now, the blonde reporter said, these unemployed men and women with their forlorn streets, their locked doors nested behind locked doors.

Why didn't they leave, if things were so bad.

Why didn't we understand why, if we had homes of our own.

Inside a rotting duplex, he opened a refrigerator long unplugged and pulled its bulk away from the wall, found a carton of milk dated more recently than he'd expected. A house stayed intact as long as it had inhabitants but after they left the decay began. Wires lost their hum, pipes went dry. Doors and windows could be covered or replaced with plywood but their protection would not last and then the inquiries of thieves exposed the inside of the house, then the upper floors filled with wind and rain, the changeable weather of the Midwest. Soon every carpeted room turned to molder and rot, roofs fell through, the rats and cockroaches had their way.

A howl of wind came banging through a front door, the repeated slamming of a thrown bolt against a doorframe shivered his skin. He knew it wasn't human voices that held back the fall of cities. It wasn't any number of people sharing a room, wasn't the presence of family meals. Everywhere he went he saw the quiet creep of falling down, falling in. A contest of wills, the agonies of architects against the patience of nature.

Opened to the elements the inside of a house smelled mostly like the outside. There was everywhere more emptiness than he'd imagined. The surface was void of anything valuable and so he had to go deeper. There were inferences to be drawn from the locations of outlets, junction boxes. A house changed after he saw its walls as containers. He began to understand the arcane layouts of the worlds behind walls, learned to find the bathroom before he went looking for the pipes. He opened the walls with a sledge and the older the house the more copper he found. He wrapped his gloves around the jacketing of wires and leaned back, leveraging his weight toward the snap. Or else he took a hacksaw to a piece of pipe, catching it before it fell into the wall.

He kicked through a plaster wall and after he withdrew his foot he found the remains of a squirrel nestled against the studs. Tiny skull, tiny feet, all the clamber long ago gone out of it. He cradled the bones, walked slowly toward the back of the house, the bouncing screen door he'd left open. Halfway there he caught himself in the last arc of a busted mirror. What was he doing here. What jumble of bones and the past was in his hands. What was he doing and why.

Outside another house, he found a broken window, cleared the glass to grant access to the interior. The house's first floor skewed back a couple of decades, gave off a story of wood paneling and thick carpet, avocado appliances. The furniture was mostly gone except for a sagged couch propped against the front wall of the living room, its seats facing in, and in another room he found a busted dresser, missing its drawers. He thought it was possible to underestimate how many people had lived in each room, the distance between the ideal and the necessary. Kelly had grown up in his own bedroom but his father had shared his with two brothers. His grandfather had been born in a one-room house, home to nine brothers and two parents, the ghosts of three miscarriages and a stillborn daughter. Theirs was a family of men, no women

except the ones they were born to or married. And of all the
men in this family it was only Kelly who had never married,
never bred.

He worked within the zone during the day where he could
and at night where he couldn't. In the deep dark of unlit streets
there was less chance of being disturbed but the need for light
gave away his position. He wore a headlamp strapped around
his forehead but the light meant others could see him moving.
Sometimes he thought he saw shapes swarming outside the
windows. If he heard a voice call out in the darkness, then he
paused where he was. If he heard two voices he shut off his
headlamp and let the darkness reshape his pupils. He didn't
have much imagination left but what imagination he had he
thought he could do without.

After the fire, the ringing he heard in his ears never went
fully away, but it got worse when he did too much, worked
too hard, pushed himself inhuman. Sometimes in the dark he
stood still and listened to it sing.

He didn't carry a weapon, didn't keep one in his truck. If
he bought a gun he would always know where it was and one
day he would use it. But often there was a tool in his hands,
a hammer perhaps, and even if his hands were all he had it
didn't mean they couldn't be used to defend himself, to fight
back, to hurt in turn.

At the hospice shop the newest clothes went the fastest. He
pledged anew his old loyalties to the state's teams, showed
his allegiance with t-shirts in team colors. He thought he'd

kept up while he was away but if he recognized a name on the back of a shirt maybe the player had been retired for years. The oldest shirts were three for a dollar fifty and if one fit he bought all three.

If he had to buy his soap at the hospice shop he worried it was the soap of the dead. Some weeks he could afford better but he'd traveled to the city with a new frugalness and he was determined not to chase it away. He walked the shop, wondered whose life the photo frames had contained. He wasn't ever in a hurry. He had to hustle to do enough work but it hardly took his whole week. He thought he would like reading a book inscribed with someone else's marginalia but when he got the book home he found he didn't need the voices of more ghosts. That was already what reading was.

This was his year of diminishment. Less was all there was. Even where there were people left there wasn't any of the commerce people needed to make good. He bought his cereal in the same place he bought his beer and the two choices were flakes with sugar, flakes without. There was hardly anything fresh on the shelves anywhere. At best a bowl of apples next to the cash register, a couple bananas under the cigarettes, beside the lotto tickets.

He didn't believe in luck but he believed in bananas.

A new twelve-pound sledgehammer was forty dollars, replacement handles fourteen. A pipe cutter cost twenty dollars, tinner snips thirteen. A heavy cable cutter might run one hundred ninety. He could make any purchase worth it but he had to be sure. He was never sure. The locking toolbox for the truck had cost three hundred dollars but his tools were safer there than in his apartment. His truck became his most necessary possession: an all-new chassis the better year he'd made the purchase, a multidisplacement V-8 under the hood. Live axles for maximum longevity and durability. Inboard dash navigation, maps swinging with the sweep of overhead satellites. An anxiety of attractive credit terms, secured with a down payment of wages earned and a loan guaranteed by the promise of more paychecks which had not come.

He bought a lamp, a folding table, a pair of unmatched chairs. His bedroom was small, his bathroom smaller. There were just the two rooms. There was more room than he needed. He bought dishes and utensils and a glass and a mug, took them home to the kitchenette barely hidden behind a thin wall. He had to listen to the refrigerator cycle while he tried to sleep. The apartment sat on the first floor of a converted motel, with other apartments on both sides, behind and above. During the day he had to listen to two children crisscross the floor above him for hours. As if running were so novel an activity they might never quit. At night he heard the laughter of loud men, the anger of shrill women, the frustrations of both sexes. A cheap apartment meant living in a cloud of your neighbors, their sounds and smells, the obscene evidence of their activities. He had to turn the television up at least as loud as his neighbors or he couldn't understand the shows. Often the nightly news became a lesson in lip-reading but he watched until he'd seen both the weather and the blonde reporter, smart in her pantsuits.

The floor was the only quiet surface and so sometimes he lay down upon the scratchy wear of the carpet to put one ear and then the other to the ground. Trying to hear how hearing nothing sounded.

The city was bisected by a freeway reaching from north to south, eighteen hundred miles running head to heel across the country. There weren't any mountains in this part of the state but there were mountains on this road, farther off in either direction. The road knew the ocean. It knew the greatness of the lakes. The road could take Kelly to Canada or the Deep South or the Atlantic coast. The road could take him home, to a small town two hours north, named for a tree sharing its name with a poison.

Last he'd heard everyone he knew there was still around, except his parents and the other assorted dead. The last time he visited was for his mother's funeral. All the faces in the church were so old but they were mostly the same faces he'd grown up among. The swishing movements of suit and skirt, of standing and kneeling and standing and sitting in a half-empty church. He'd seen his mother lowered into the ground but hadn't watched the ground close. The woman he'd been with had wanted to see where he grew up but he'd asked her not to come. They weren't married but they lived together, owned a house down south. There wasn't anything to be ashamed of but he didn't want to answer any questions. He didn't plan on ever going back again so better to tell his aunts and uncles he was alone.

He had some cousins there, a few lost friends. There wasn't any juice left. If he went to them it wouldn't be as their relation but as the stranger he'd become. If there was one thing he needed the zone to teach him it was how to be alone again. Unquestioned and uncharged.

When he awoke disoriented in the strobing dark of the apartment he opened the phone's map to watch the satellites locate him exactly. First a series of shrinking circles, then a blue light pulsing atop the city. The hated screen, so brightly assuring. This is where I am, he would whisper. This is what I am doing. It was so clean a fact. If the noise in his building or the ringing in his ears wouldn't let him sleep he lay on his mattress, watched documentaries on the television. There he rediscovered the life on other continents, the wilder world beyond raccoons and squirrels and whitetail deer, the ordinary menagerie of the midwestern states. On-screen, elephants mourned their dead and buried the bones, an alligator waited in a pit of drought and mud for thirst to make the meat stupid. A dung beetle pushed a ball of shit across a desert. You did what you had to do. You organized your life, moved every action into categories and compartments of time and type and task, you looked at your life and you knew who you were: this was worldview, ideology, what you had of either, who you were, who you'd been. Today he was this person, speaking these words, concerned only with this narrow sliver of experience, whatever could be had within the confines of the zone.

There had once been a magnificence to these streets and the evidence of those times was still there, in the zone, in edifices to ideas that had not endured. On many days Kelly saw the endurance of the beautiful, the way the slow degradation of acid rain and other weather could make the zone more lovely, not less. He entered churches where painted crosses faded from the walls, where wind howled some days through stolen stained glass, while on other days birds flitted between the iron braces left behind. The braces waiting for the theft. The pews remaining but the organ pipes long gone. Dust and smatter everywhere, a city's silt fallen, unswept, a manifestation, the refuse of long-ago prayers. The birds, nesting in the rafters. American gods, American temples, all the evidence anyone needed to indict the temporariness of American belief.

He walked shredded schools lacking students but not piles of serviceable desks, ran his hands along the spines of books left behind, the previous fictions of history. Stories no one wanted to steal. Bottles of printer's ink lined glassless windowsills, glowed in shafts of sunlight, colored vacant offices blue and red and black and superblue. Locker rooms lay unlocked, the locker doors removed, the opened walls spilling onto gym floors made of century-dead trees, the wax scuffed with shoes and time, tagged with layers of spray paint.

He wandered the rows of emptied houses and overgrown yards, roamed grassy blocks beneath bare-socketed streetlights. In every structure he entered he found some objects trashed and some he could sell and also some rare and better and less-valuable objects, objects abandoned by accident, chance's castaways. Soon he lifted some new bauble from nearly every site, folded a broken-spined paperback into his pocket, ripped a single pencil-marred Ave Maria from a hymnal, pocketed a child toy's heavy as lead, a bent-tined fork kicked behind a counter. He brought home some objects he planned to use and some he wanted to look at and in his apartment he chose a cupboard meant for dishes to store these more-useless thefts, an exhibit of his travels in the zone, of what relics had called out in the places he'd been, the bleak houses of the blackout city.

Kelly thought the world wasn't full of special objects, only plain ones. Nothing was assembled special, nothing and no one, but the plainest objects could be supercharged by attention, made nuclear by suggestion. He could pick up the same object in two different houses and in one sense a completely different thrumming. What he wanted was anything loved. When he couldn't remember anymore where he had taken something from, then he threw it out. Making emotion last wasn't the objects' first power but it was the power he wanted most. Anything he took from someone else's life wouldn't work forever but if he kept acquiring more maybe the feelings might remain, transferred across the overlap.

The fall sun shining on the waving grass, the hardy scrub of trees spreading across vacancies. Everywhere he took something he tried to leave something else behind. The unexpected juxtaposition of nature and ruin. Metal for memories, memories for metal. There was so much he wanted gone. There was such a sprawling untenanted city in which to dump it. And in the falling streets he discovered the great perseverance of the people who remained. Their faces shined in the light wherever he saw them, on porches or in driveways, outside liquor stores and bars. He wasn't their neighbor but he saw their beauty. They looked crazy with grief. The great glory of their sadness. The way it would last and last. He needed to eat and there wasn't any work but what was he taking from these people. Nothing, he told himself, they had not already lost.

To leave the edge of the zone for its center was to abandon the present for the future and wherever Kelly went he thought he might be the last person to see these sights. Others would come with bulldozers and excavators—or else with arson and theft—but they wouldn't see how he saw, moving carefully through these rooms and hallways, staring out these windows, marveling at the way you could see the lit skyline of the inhabited city from the endless dusk of its unlit neighborhoods. There were still some progressions in play but he saw how the zone had moved beyond time. Or at least outside of the time marked by digital clocks, smartphone calendars. Inside the zone events moved along paths solar, lunar, seasonal; new geological epochs marked by strata of waste, eras identifiable by the brand names left inside cupboards, by the industrial design of unpowered appliances. A preview of what the world would look like during its coming decline. Kelly pretended he carried the last human gaze door-to-door, window to window, exploring the first outpost of a culture pushed past repair. It could be destroyed but could it be fixed? All the better futures might not arrive. He didn't think his was the final generation, but perhaps the last might already be born.

What did this mean for him, for the good man he had tried and failed to be?

In some houses he found handwritten notes. He found one taped to the cracked plaster across from the house's front door: WE'RE LEAVING IN THE MORNING. And then the date the last inhabitants left, not so long ago. In the back of a child's closet he found a scrawl of crayon reading I'LL BE BACK FOR YOU, written to the house, to whatever the child thought a house was. Sometimes there was an animal living there still. The animal was always a cat. What did these cats eat? Where did they sleep and piss and shit? Sometimes it wasn't hard to see. The skeletons of mice. Shit in one corner of a room, the smell of piss everywhere.

The cat following Kelly from room to room, rubbing its body against his boots.

Names everywhere. On the houses. In the asphalt. Carved into trees, fences, doors.

I LOVE YOU HOUSE, one note read.

I BUILT THIS HOUSE WITH MY HANDS, said another.

GOODBYE.

I'M SORRY.

WE HAD TO LEAVE BUT THIS WAS HOME.

2

KELLY SCRIBBLED HIS FIRST NAME on a name tag, adhered it to his shirt pocket, took a seat on the unoccupied side of the circle of chairs. The group's facilitator crossed the church basement, offered her hand. She was all trunk, her middle dwarfing her limbs, had a small mole sprouted from the sensitive skin beneath her lip, a tiny flaw in a good face. She called Kelly by his name, asked if he wanted to share.

No, he said. He wanted to listen.

She nodded, patted his hand, released him. When the sharing began the others repeated the past, made it present again. The simultaneity of error and accident, of grief and loss. A red-haired woman had lost her husband in a car crash. A beautiful teenager lost her best friend in a drive-by shooting. The automobile had made the city great but look how much it took in return. The night stretched long. A house fire, a drowning, all the cancers and their medieval treatments. Whenever there were suicides no one ever mentioned the methods. There was a parade of misery described but much of it sounded familiar, stories whose ends could be known by their beginnings.

Kelly's face twisted and he didn't know how to make it stop. How long had the others been coming. How many times had they come together to share their stories, in these words. There was change pushing forth from their faces but he could see how deep the past had carved them. He didn't know how to escape the constraints of the past either but maybe he'd come to the group to find out.

If Kelly had shared he would have said that he was afraid, that what he wanted was a way to end his fear.

For a long time, he might have said, he had at least succeeded in feeling it less.

Love meant letting his vigilance down but his vigilance had served him better. He had slipped only once.

As the others talked Kelly remembered the hardness of his father. How big the man's face had been, all jowls and grinding jaws, the father chewing side to side like a ruminant. Those square teeth against pot roast, carrots, root vegetables. Biscuits from a can. The way the man's joints popped when he walked, how he cracked his knuckles at the table and during the news and after, his father's limbering of his body for food, information, fucking. The way he shook his shoulders loose when he stood from the table, when he exited the bedroom pale and spindle legged and splendid in his underwear. His father the wrestling coach, Kelly his best student, a state champion like his father before him. In those boyish days Kelly had loved the father with an intensity never again felt, loved the way the man strode the earth grimed with work, his bones shining through his skin as he sat silent before the glowing television, his voice rarely eloquent except in the darkest hour of night, when sometimes he came into Kelly's room, as some stranger Kelly would have to pretend was not still there when they awoke.

Wrestling in high school had led to wrestling in college but he hadn't lasted. With others it was a knee or a shoulder but his injury had been some failure of will, an inability to show up. A deep lethargy had come over him once out of his father's home, out from under his father's coaching. He'd started sleeping long and late, ten or twelve hours a night. In classes he'd dozed and dreamed and at practice he'd refused to work his hardest, turning in the slowest laps, the laziest reps and calisthenics, shying away from the contact of position drills, mock rounds.

Takedown, reversal, escape, takedown, breakdown, fall: a basic plot that could be complicated by a clever strategy, some technical achievement. He stopped shooting on the legs, stopped working toward the pin. A flinching from the fight. Three rounds passed, three minutes then two minutes then two more. During matches he got cited for stalling, a refusal to engage. If he started on top the other boy would explode unchecked to his feet. Kelly tried to keep his distance but it was after he was taken down his real talents emerged. There were only a few ways to escape: the stand-up, the switch, the sit-out, the roll. He didn't engage but he didn't give up either. He could be taken down and turned on his back but he was hard to pin, grew more stubborn the closer he got to defeat. Maybe he wouldn't try to win but he couldn't stomach losing.

Weigh-in days you could check your weight in the morning

with a banana in your hand and if you were underweight you could eat the banana. In the mirror there were always the folds of your former self, the hanging skin around the waist, self as shame refusing to fall away. You ate or didn't eat the banana. You ran the miles. You carried the carcass of before. You climbed the scale naked and nervous and old as you had ever been and you were so young and you wondered if today was the day you measured light enough for battle.

He remembered the bodies of the other boys, lean and carved, organized by weight class. Veins cording forearms and calves, throbbing out of a neck the size of a thigh. Fingers cracked and broken and taped, eyes screwed and bulged out of a drawn face, all bones and bravery. He could go days without food, without any more liquid than it took to rinse his mouth. All your own meat could be made of was food and if you didn't eat any food there'd be less meat.

Every morning he lifted and ran and every afternoon he threw his body at the body of another boy, practiced takedowns and reversals and arm bars, the half nelson, the quarter nelson. There were illegal moves no one ever taught but the team learned them anyway, taught each other, passed them down. Armlocks, leglocks, spinal locks. Small-joint manipulation. Choke holds, other methods for smothering. Slamming or spiking. No punching, no kicking, no gouging of the eyes. No fishhooking the mouth or nose. No squeezing the genitals. These were the ways to hurt a man, to bend his will faster than the rules would allow. You couldn't use them in a match but after you had the knowledge weren't you waiting for your chance.

His coach yelled but Kelly's failure wasn't a matter of

motivation. Kelly skipped a practice, failed a weigh-in, missed the bus for a meet. There were better weeks where he found his enthusiasm and the coach said he thought maybe Kelly was shaking off a freshman slump but before the season ended Kelly packed his dorm room and left campus. There wasn't anyone to tell he was leaving. He appreciated the coach giving him a chance but he didn't owe the man a call. They weren't close, not like the coach was close to the other guys.

He hadn't made the kind of friends he wanted to make. He knew he wasn't stupid but the classes had bored him too. Their steady drip of fact, fact, fact. He didn't call his parents but before he left his father called him, said the coach had called first.

You can always come home, his father said.

Back home Kelly's grandfather had worked for the copper mines in the state's Upper Peninsula, his father in the auto factories near the town named like poison. The mines were long exhausted, the mine towns exhausted too. The factories weren't hiring or they were paying half wages and no benefits or they were closed. If there wouldn't be work, what else was there to go home to? Nothing Kelly wanted again.

Gas was cheap and a dollar could buy Kelly twenty miles in his ancient red Firebird, the car all he had to show for a year spent in fast food, his wrestler's body hungry over the fryers. How far he escaped depended on how he drove but he wasn't so careful in those days, liked to depress the pedal past prudence. He picked a southern city, rented an apartment, slowly bought used furniture, dishes, appliances. Then a progression of years, compressed into a list of occupations: there was work in kitchens, work in lumberyards, work painting the sides of houses, and then building houses too, framework and roofing and drywall, wallpaper and paint. There were girls but for a long time nothing steady. All he had left were isolated incidents, recurring images preserved by their rarity: the opening clasp of a front-closure bra, the first time a hand slid down the front of his undone jeans without his asking, the way community-college legs crossed in the low cramp of the Firebird's passenger seat.

He didn't remember anyone's name from those years. Not the names of the girls, not the names of the boys he had wrestled with, not the names of the men he had worked beside.

As a boy he'd thought to know the name of a thing was to love it. But his father had known his name. So had his mother who had done nothing, said nothing.

There was a painter with the construction outfit with hands too big for his body and after a shared brawl in a dive bar parking lot it was this man who first took Kelly to the gym, said he saw a nervous energy Kelly needed somewhere to put. Kelly lowered his bruised face and said yes, lifted his busted hands. He'd missed the combat part of wrestling, the working out of aggressions in the mat room. Together Kelly and the painter lifted weights, hit the speed bag and the heavy bag until the painter said Kelly was ready to spar.

The painter was right: there was something Kelly had been looking for and here in the gym he was finding it, better than wrestling. More his own. The absence of his father, his father's coaching. The complete absence of *team*. When sparring Kelly didn't have the right kind of quickness and he wasn't strong enough but he was plenty angry if provoked right. He'd move his feet wrong, sluggish, hold his hands too wide, but after the first few punches got through he'd discover his anger, find his gait. He wore himself out quick and never won anything but he made a lot of faces uglier, colored some ribs black and blue. He told the painter he saw better with blood in his eyes, with one eye bruised shut. He didn't smile when he was joking. He didn't know how to look friendly enough with his teeth bared.

What he remembered most was how much he had wanted the hitting, the being hit. Direct damage replacing submission, fists in place of locks and holds. He craved the space right before a punch landed in either direction, how there was a second where you could put a thought in harm's way, let it get pulverized within a crater of flesh. He started to cut all ties with home, as easy as refusing to call. By the time he came back north, many years later, he had all the agency he'd ever thought to wish for. Even if his parents had lived forever he would have found a way to orphan himself.

He went to the church on the wrong days too, to watch other people pray. The kneeling and rocking, the low murmur of their speaking in tongues, mimicking the voices of angels. The habits of his parents, his parents' friends, the parents of his friends. The prayers of thanks, the prayers of protection from suffering, the prayers of thanks for how suffering made them strong. He'd carried a rosary in his pocket long after he stopped believing but one day he'd left it behind, abruptly filled with ridiculous mistrust of its possession. He wasn't about to start speaking in tongues again but he still liked the way those beads looked between other people's hands.

When he didn't understand what he saw he took a picture with his phone: a sign he hadn't seen before, the absolute shadows of dusk on a street lacking streetlights, a high cast of graffiti, a flyer bearing the insignia of the city watch, the orange-clad volunteers he occasionally saw in the zone. Or else inside the houses, some configuration of wiring he wasn't familiar with: knob and tube, the Carter system, the California three-way. He took pictures of his queries and sometimes he discovered their answers but other times he hit some wrong button and reversed the camera to accidentally take a picture of his own face, this man covered in dust and sweat and always sporting the same grime-stained expression. There was a record of his year in the city accumulating in the camera roll but who was he supposed to show the pictures. There was an icon on the screen meaning *share* but it wanted to know who with.

The city was famous for its music and when Kelly knew he wouldn't sleep he went looking for the sound he remembered. On the best nights the music pounded heavy from the PA, its rolling torpor loud enough to make talent an irrelevant measure. He set himself apart, moved his feet and his arms in his own approximation of the rhythm. He wasn't without feelings but he was aware of their constrained range, his distance from their centers.

The band quit the stage, the drinkers hung on to the rail. The door to the parking lot opened, admitted a woman on her own, arrived late enough to skip the cover. There was an open seat beside Kelly but there was a longer run of seating on the opposite end of the rail, around the curve, past the uninhabited waitress station.

Kelly watched the girl make the turn, sensed something surprising drag at his gaze.

When he thought about this moment afterward, he could see her limp more clearly, but this wasn't memory, just familiarity's revision.

He would call her *girl* from the start but even then he knew she was the same age as him, maybe older. From across the rail he watched her hands move, her bare fingers lighting cigarettes, tearing the labels away from consecutive bottles of beer, her painted nails scratching at the brown glass. He raised a hand to the bartender, sent another beer around the bar. The girl with the limp didn't acknowledge the drink but he watched her smile to receive it.

There was a kind of bravery in his heart but it didn't prevent him from knowing what he was. He wasn't afraid of self-deception except in others.

When she left the bar she left on foot, which meant she lived in the neighborhood. There were others who lived here too but not in every house. She was a block ahead and now he saw her limp entire, the way one foot dragged and turned, the extra sway it added to her step. She slowed, turned the corner away from these houses and toward the rare apartments beyond. Even before she reached the stairs leading up to the barred gate of her building he knew she knew he was behind her. He tried to signal his innocence but what did innocence look like. He could smell the city and he could smell himself, a shared pungency. He wiped at his face and ran his fingers through his hair and on his hands he smelled his cigarettes mixing with stolen steel, copper's tang, the other alloys and elements each inert until touched. Even every handful of coins smelled like its owner and on his hands he could smell all the old metal of the city, the dead sweat of its lost citizens mingled with his own living scent.

The girl with the limp turned upon the stairs and he saw her face clearly for the first time. He hadn't realized he'd gotten so close. There were words he wanted to say. Who she looked like. Why he had bought her a drink. Why he had followed her home.

He said, I'm sorry I followed you.

He said, I thought you were someone else.

He had, back in the bar. And there was no mistaking the resemblance now.

He said, I think I knew you.

But what he'd meant to say was *I thought*.

She put her key in the door, turned the key. Even from his distance he could hear the clunk of the bolt. She pushed the door inward an invisible inch. When she turned back he could see the damage, had learned to recognize it in others. The way what happened to you either made you defensive or reckless and how now it was the reckless who were his people. When she entered the white light of the hallway beyond the door he knew she would invite him in without additional word or gesture, by leaving the door open wide to the street, by waiting for him to leave it yawning or else to close it, to close the door behind him as he entered.

THE CITY CLOSED ANOTHER DOZEN schools and after the students were gone the scrappers came. The schools left the security systems intact—cameras, passive infrared monitors—but eventually someone cut the power, hauled away the transformer box. The battery backup kept the security live for eight hours but turning the power back on would take days of work, twenty thousand dollars the city didn't have. When the security died the most aggressive scrappers came first, headed straight for the copper: The concrete in every bathroom shattered with hammers, the wire mesh inside bent with pry bars or else yanked free by grabbing hold and leaning back, letting body weight pull the mesh free of its fastenings. Then turning a pipe cutter around whatever they could see. Then down to the basement for the boiler, its own set of copper piping. Dismantling the plumbing could set off the sprinkler system. Then water cascading on chalkboards, bookshelves, hardwood floors, destroying whatever the scrappers left.

The other scrappers didn't wait for night. The scrapyards closed at five and so you took the five o'clock price if you didn't have somewhere to stash what you took. Or else the scrapping started at three or four or five in the morning, so it could be done by the time the scrapyards opened again at eight.

Kelly refused to be the first thief. He worked other sites during the day, dropped his scrap, hit the bars. By midnight he was back in the truck, driving a loop of closed schools, looking for broken glass, a pryable door. The city boarded windows, put up chain-link fences. But boards didn't stop anyone. But scrappers would take the fences too, cut the posts off at the dirt.

Inside an elementary school Kelly dragged a makeshift sled of locker doors down the front stairs, busting the concrete with the bounce of the weight. Outside the night air was cool, the sound of the season's last crickets louder than anything else, the school surrounded by pasture, grass overtaking the long absence of nearby houses. Kelly had parked his truck within the school's courtyard, the most convenient cover, but if anyone else came while he was inside, they might take the scrap out of the truck instead of heading in. They might take the truck.

The men came for him in the darkest hour of night. A gloom of moonlight fell through the tall windows of the second-floor gymnasium, where Kelly piled coils of insulated wire pulled from the circuit breaker, the conduits within. He thought he'd been listening but by the time he heard their footsteps coming they were in the vast room with him, rushing out of the shadowed hallways. He turned his headlamp fast, caught white eyes and white teeth in its light as the first shape struck him, knocked him to the ground. Fists bruised his face and forearms and when he was almost stilled the man's hungry hands pushed into Kelly's pockets, looking for his wallet, keys, phone. Kelly brought up a knee, cracked some breathing room from the man's ribs, rolled him over and off.

The lamp slipped from Kelly's forehead, its beam falling uselessly diffuse across the gym floor. Before he had his feet the other was coming fast and Kelly reached out blindly for the man's head, catching the hood of his sweatshirt. He spun, dropped to his knees, turned the fabric around the man's throat, bunched and twisted, and the man cried out, kicked, and tried to pull out of his shirt. Kelly lifted the man to his feet, tightening his grip, reeling him in. Robbers in the night. He wouldn't have to hurt them much more. These weren't the actions of brave men. Kelly was a thief too but he told himself he only stole what no one wanted. What he could tell himself hurt no one. A hierarchy of opportunity and morality.

The first man stood too, a slimness of air between him and Kelly and the second man. The darkness massed in the high room, everything sure reduced to touch and smell and sound, to echo, to the fear expanding inside everything you couldn't sense.

I'll let him go, said Kelly. But if you come back at me I don't know what I'll do.

Neither man spoke but the man caught in Kelly's arms stopped his struggling. Kelly released the man, watched him flee in the same direction as the other. He crouched into the silence of the room, found his tools. First the hammer, then the headlamp. He moved the beam of light across the gymnasium but the men with white eyes and white teeth stayed gone. He couldn't catch his breath and bruises lifted from his skin but otherwise he could pretend the men had never existed. Once he had been stronger than he was but had he ever heard his heart thudding so loudly. He shut off the lamp, sat down on the floor among the wiring he'd pulled from the wall. He waited, listened. He moved to the windows, watched the courtyard, saw his truck untouched. Still no sound from below but there were exits without doors, windows without glass. You could walk through the broken world like a wraith. As Kelly waited the night spoke to him, crickets again, wind and far-off traffic and what he swore were voices, speaking somewhere at the limits of sense. At such great distances it was impossible to understand the words the voices said, what they intended, whether these were the voices of bad men, whether the invisible evil all men carried was something they were born into or something they chose.

THE GIRL WITH THE LIMP wanted to see a hockey game but Kelly didn't think he had the cash. He asked her when her birthday was, calculated the distance. He wasn't confident making the promise but maybe the question was enough to suggest his hopeful thinking. There was the arena by the river where the hockey team played and all around there were banners above the street proclaiming the team's championships, redubbing the city Hockeytown, and on game day he offered to take her to a bar nearby.

It wasn't what she wanted but close enough would work to start. When he picked her up outside her apartment she wore a red-and-white jersey over skintight jeans and in the car he admired the way the jersey's shapelessness draped her form, worked by suggestion. You couldn't tell she limped when she was sitting down, standing still. There wasn't anything wrong with the shape of her muscles, only their function.

At the bar, she said what was wrong with her was going to get worse and in its progression she had lost her fear of everything else. Her limp didn't keep her from getting places, didn't affect the quality of her walk, just its character. She told him she couldn't hurry anywhere and he didn't argue. He liked where they were starting and what it required. There were other places they might end up but he thought it might take something dramatic to get him there.

She worked as an emergency dispatcher but he hadn't known the first night, hadn't asked, had only learned her name beyond the point of further questions. *Jackie.* When she revealed her profession she said she'd just wanted a job, hadn't meant to get so close to the unfolding tragedy. She laughed before he knew he was supposed to. It was a cynical view, and sure, she said, she never saw the endings of things. All she had was the prologue, the in medias res, the confusion amid the disaster.

Panic sets in, she said. People lose their heads. It's my job not to lose mine.

When she laughed he could see more of her teeth than when she didn't. Her teeth weren't perfect but what did it matter. Her name was Jackie but her name wasn't what he thought when he saw her. He didn't tell her what he called her in his head.

On the big screen the game unfolded and the crowd in the bar erupted whenever there was a goal scored or a fight started. Between highlights she told him about her week and this week was the week a teenager burbled into the telephone for three minutes after his grandmother shot him in the chest.

This was the week a mother miscarried in the checkout line, squatting over the linoleum, crying and screaming and surrounded by strangers, all bonded by the intimacy of her disaster.

This was the week a toddler drank drain cleaner and this

was the week Jackie didn't know if she'd ever know if the toddler was alive or dead.

Despite her week she smiled more than he did and he didn't know why. She touched his arm across the table and she said if she was sure a caller was passing then she never hung up, not before the paramedics arrived. She didn't want anyone to be alone when they died. It mattered to her even after it couldn't matter to them. He bought her a beer and himself a beer he couldn't afford. Even after the game went bad for the home team he thought his face might hurt from happiness in the morning. Joy's spreading warmth, starting low and swelling fast. How long had it been since he'd lived this close to its hum.

They met for coffee, drinks, lunch, made the expected small talk. She told him more about her work, her week, about new car crashes, heart attacks, domestic violence. She asked him about his days too but he didn't know what he wanted to tell her. The work was a series of repetitive motions. There were surprises but all of a kind. Before he met her, he had been training himself to feel less about everything and now he gave her the unadorned actions, without explanation or inflection, what sights he saw in the zone's abandoned places: A busted flip-flop found in an alley, its imagined implications like at the scene of a crime. A bird he couldn't save, trapped in a crumbling chimney. A house whose roof had fallen in, seedlings growing where the living room turned to moss. Because after you broke the shell of the house who knew what might come next.

He said, I never imagined how hard we worked to keep the world out, to stop its taking back the places we'd claimed.

There were streets with every business barred and nearly every house vacated and still there could be a shamble of people shuffling the sidewalks. He required an enormous vocabulary for describing degrees of distance, a vocabulary he didn't possess. He called a lot of parts of the zone *empty* or *abandoned* or *derelict* but those words never meant there was no one there.

He said, I saw a child hollering in a front yard yesterday, in a block I thought was vacant. A boy, eleven or twelve. The child alone, shirtless, his skin glistened with sweat, sunshine. It was fall but the year had a few warm days left.

He told her this but what he told her wasn't a story. It was something he'd seen, not something he'd done. He was merely a spectator, didn't want to paint the image tainted by his action or inaction, didn't want the responsibility of cause and effect.

There's this creeping kind of fatigue, he said. If he thought harder about what he heard and saw from his apartment he didn't think he could live there. The vast turnover of the people with loud voices, louder problems, the small miseries and the daily cruelties. Better to focus on external anxieties, on crises more far-flung, the news. On what he read in books or saw in documentaries. It was easier if he could pretend the tragedy was happening somewhere else.

She touched his hand until he calmed. She said, You think the world is a bad place but you want to be a good man in it.

Yes, he said. The fatigue, the exhaustion, his own mistakes:

he'd seen bad things happen in the zone but so far he'd kept his distance, worked to forget what he'd seen. What he was most afraid of was the time when he would be the only one who could help, when there was a choice between letting harm continue and getting involved.

He liked her but it was simpler to talk about the hockey team, the news on television. It was easy to get her to switch topics: she liked him but she loved hockey, and this was the week her team was winning. She filled their table talk with Russian names and American rules and he nodded along and when without warning she asked if he was divorced he was able to say no and let the subject drop.

After the confrontation in the gymnasium he decided he didn't have to work in the night, didn't have to live in the darkness. He could live in the distance instead: the distance between inhabited houses, the distance between open schools and working hospitals and still-thriving businesses. The distance between a family sleeping softly on a Saturday morning and the wind clanking a twisted metal door against a doorframe it no longer fit. A single lot could be enough. A single lot bought plenty of looking the other way.

He worked harder in the day so he could spend his evenings with her, and at the table even sitting still his muscles ached. She was the one with the limp but by the time they went to bed he wasn't standing straight either. One day he noticed her fingernails were a different color every time he saw her. She wore so many shades of lipstick. When he woke up the next morning he saw in the mirror where she'd marked him, the drag of a lip across his stomach, his hip bone. Little she did outlasted his shower but for a moment he remembered. With her, he was getting his color back, began to dress a rack better, again paid a whole price for a whole shirt. He'd kept himself up before but he'd never liked maintenance for its own sake. Now there was a reason.

They didn't go many places he wouldn't have gone on his own but he was louder in the places they went. He had kept his own company so long their conversations renewed the ringing in his ears. She called him the quiet type. He nodded and she laughed. It was so easy, this beginning. He hoped it lasted a long time. He struggled with the absurdity of middles, and endings happened so fast or violent there wasn't anything to do but let loose and wait for the impact. He had the kind of blank face women liked least to fight with, his features passive even when he was angriest. Almost every woman he'd ever dated had one day learned to hate it.

They both failed at darts and pool but they celebrated the arcade machines left in their kinds of bars, the residue of an earlier age. With her by his side he got better at moving the frog across the street than when he was a kid but he got worse again as he drank. Then the digital splat and splatter. She couldn't pilot a spaceship for anything but loved any game with a trackball, analog action making digital moves, the imprecision of desire. Once they played a bowling game inside a bowling alley and he grew irritated when she liked it better than the real thing but she said she preferred wearing her own shoes. She couldn't wear high heels but he said heels weren't everything. In another game she spun the ball as hard as she could, then lifted her hand, letting fate take over for control. It didn't save her life but he could buy her three more for a quarter.

He obsessed over certain parts of her shape, the ways of her speech. The swoop of her clavicle, the word *clavicle*. He could catch a sound or an idea and good luck getting rid of it. The titles and designations, the taxonomies of compound words. The exactness of language he desired, the way the right word might be used to name an object. The girl with the limp: it wasn't like she hadn't told him her name. He'd learned it the first night, never forgot it, could reproduce it immediately if asked. *Jackie.* He thought often of the sound of her voice but he didn't hear her voice saying her name. Her name wasn't who she was. When he thought of her he saw first her shape, her way of movement, her facial expressions. His affection wasn't for the name but for the shape, wasn't for the name but for the action it contained.

The girl with the limp reminded him. She had slightly darker hair, a similar arrangement of curves. Her personality was different but he learned to adjust. He no longer thought the wrong name when he awoke and found her beside him, turned away. He wasn't confused anymore: this was Jackie and no one else. Sometimes she woke to find him staring. Sometimes he woke up and found her on top of him. This was another way she was different. They ate and they talked and they watched the violence upon the ice, they fucked and they stayed hungry. He watched her take pills for the nerve damage, another prescription for depression. She wasn't sup-posed to drink on either but they stayed thirsty too. It would be winter soon and he wondered what would last until spring came. After the first month her resemblance to the past waned. Or else her body had come to supplant the memory of the other body, his southern woman. An intercession of the physical: he'd had this happen before, with other pairs of women. He started seeing someone new because her outline reminded him of someone else but one day he couldn't remember how the first shape had felt.

She didn't shave her legs as often as other women he'd dated. They were harder to reach in her condition or else she always wore pants or else she was comfortable with him, with herself. In bed she commented on his suntan, on the contrast between the darkness of his public skin and the paleness of everything else. He said his tan persisted all winter. You could work hard enough in January to not need a coat and some years he had. Her skin was a paleness everywhere, a luminosity in the dark. He could walk back into the blacked-out bedroom and know exactly where in the bed she was sleeping.

Her car was low and bright yellow and growled when she punched the gas, she had nerves but she wasn't nervous. She wasn't supposed to drive in case she had an attack but she said the doctors weren't going to take anything from her. At night she would drive them twenty or thirty miles above the speed limit on the darkest stretches of freeway and on the right nights they might see no one else. She took risks because she wasn't going to live forever, because, she said, there was a finite length of time she could be punished for her mistakes, and Kelly knew this already, understood this was how they had met, why she had invited him in their first night. She kept another cane in the backseat of her car but worse than the canes, she said, were the forearm crutches. Psychological torture, she said, and when you got prescribed a forearm crutch you knew you were never going to get better. He said he didn't know there were prescriptions for objects but he could see how he should have.

I've been healthy all my life, he said. It wasn't ever my body I've had trouble with.

With his southern woman he hadn't used anything. With her he had let down this guard, then that one, some at her request, some out of the creeping apathy of the familiar. It had been a mistake, his walls built for a reason. Now he was using protection again and said the condoms caused him trouble. He got nervous about the delay ripping the packages, snapped the latex against the skin during removal. All the little indignities collected. The reservoir nippled at the end of his cock made him feel ridiculous. If he couldn't stop thinking, then he had trouble staying hard but he pretended his lack was something he could hide with enthusiasm. The girl with the limp wasn't on the pill but she told him she couldn't get pregnant. Something about ovarian cysts, surgical scarring. He didn't ask questions. He let her know he was willing to listen but more often they kept their pasts behind them.

When she said *Kelly* during sex or after waking it was like a mystery unfolding. He had never loved his name except in the way a woman said it, except when she said it, when she said it like the woman before had. Their sex was slow and quiet and he did most of the work so the exertion wouldn't cause her an attack. It wasn't what he wanted to think about but he had to keep her safe. When her orgasms came they were soft and sudden: a movement of her mouth, a quick clenching, then the shuddery squeeze and release, the subtlest of hiccups.

Afterward they laughed and talked and smoked. Survivors of the day, sharing the inexplicable unspeakable elation that everything wrong in their lives had not brought them to ruin. But then she said that if she did get pregnant she would have to have an abortion because the pregnancy could worsen her condition.

He said there wasn't anything to worry about. He wasn't getting anyone pregnant, ever.

I had a vasectomy years ago, he said, speaking softly. He waited, listened to her breathing until he wasn't sure if she was awake.

I never wanted kids, he whispered. I'm glad you can't have children.

He'd thought she might be sleeping but now he saw her mouth contorting in the dark. She turned over, pulled the sheet across her bare back. He said, There was a woman I loved. The woman had a son. We lost our house and then I lost them.

IN THE CHURCH BASEMENT THEY circled the chairs, found a volunteer to begin. One by one they shared what had been lost and when a speaker completed her story the others clapped, hugged her, thanked her for sharing. Never a critique, always an acceptance. All those quavering voices, their narratives of death. The living came to meeting after meeting until they knew how to structure the story. These were the basic redemption tales, stories of education through suffering: All they had to do was learn to love someone through their hurt. To love them as much as when it had been easy. Or else learn to let someone go because of how bravely they'd borne their dying, their death. Or else they hadn't come over to forgiveness, harbored some old pettiness or even well-deserved hate, because who hurt us like the people who were supposed to love us?

Kelly liked the people who couldn't name their grief the best. If your betrothed died you were not a widower. There was no word in the language for a man who had lost his child before he ever got the chance to say the word *father*. It was impossible to offer your story by your title, to transfer it easily and without explanation, in the way *husband* told a tale, in the way *father* did.

If he told a story, this might have been one story he told. It wasn't exactly the truth but for him the absence of the

southern woman and her son had become a kind of death, a
going away of love never to be undone, unfelt, forgiven.

Or else he might have told an earlier story, might have spoken of his father, about how he could have chosen to sit beside
his mother at the moment of his father's death, witnessed the
spittle and the gurgle and the waste. What revenge would it
have been to see the bones shining beneath the skin, to see
all the crawling blue scrawl between? His father would have
been enfeebled, weak of speech, unable to breathe. A tonnage
of tubes pumping life back into a black balloon. A sack of air
and blood, some deathly monster. Not the shape of myth he
remembered best, the man taller and stronger and smarter than
himself, always and forever the hale creature of his youth.

There was a man who cried at the end of every story and
there was a man who never cried and Kelly thought he knew
where his own sympathies lay. Outside in the dark the three
men smoked and the man who never cried said the suffering
of the individual had been eclipsed by the suffering of the
masses. Earthquakes in Haiti, tsunamis and nuclear devasta-
tion in Japan. Genocides in Africa, riots in the streets in Lon-
don, Athens, Los Angeles. It had happened here in the city,
the city burning three times. There was what we had made
with our wars in Afghanistan and Iraq, in places we probably
didn't know our country's forces were fighting, and *What is
Syria* was at least as good a question as *Where*. The longer the
man spoke the more the qualities of pronouns got nebulous.
Who was *we* and who was *they*. He said there were diseases
in Asia making our vaccines look like the toys of children,
unlucky Americans returning from foreign vacations with

their flesh falling off their faces, crying out their disbelief for the nightly news.

The man who never cried said, It could be any one of us before the cameras, insane with the odds. While in vacation-land there's a thousand natives sick, unrecorded, unbroadcast.

Here we are, the man said. And am I the same as my complaint or am I worse for knowing better.

The other man was at it again. Still crying he tried to comfort the man who never cried but the second man nearly shoved him from the church steps.

All I'm saying, the man who never cried said, is there are whole cities falling into the ocean, whole species going extinct beneath the hottest sun in ten thousand years. We're here wailing about a single human life.

He said, I loved my wife but she's gone.

He said, I loved my wife but is she the equivalent of a thousand starving children I can't see well enough to mourn.

My wife, he said, is statistically insignificant no matter how you're counting.

The girl with the limp had a bad day and the cane came out from the side of the bed, its handle curled beneath her clenched hand. The muscles in her bad leg knotted and Kelly rubbed their tight cords, made amateur improvements. This was a different way of touching her body, her sickness more private than their sex. She had a bottle of muscle relaxers, a physical therapist she could call. He cooked the food she needed to take the pills, refused her the drink she requested next, poured them both water instead. And when was the last time they drank water.

How bad is it, he asked, and she lied to him: I'm fine, she said, I told you I'm fine. She could barely talk through the pain and as the pills took effect her voice thickened. She gestured aimlessly with the remote, hit its buttons with a senseless violence, found her hockey game and settled onto the couch. She knew the names of all the players, complained when Kelly forgot what she'd taught him. He wasn't good with names, he said, and she laughed because she knew, because it was one of the first things she knew about him.

When he lost track of the game he watched her watching instead. There was something local to know about octopus, a play-off legend she couldn't explain. Tradition, she said. Its origins were in the past and she didn't care about history, only victory. She couldn't be an athlete anymore but she cheered anyone who was. He had been one himself but he didn't tell her the details. Boxing, he said. Wrestling, he said. More history. After the game ended they watched the news and at the bottom of the screen the scrolling ticker announced again the results of a televised singing competition, the flavor of a new color of soda, the failure of a bill promoting equal pay for equal work. The long emergency was visible anywhere the ticker ran. The ticker had come to life on the country's worst day and it had never gone away: How you couldn't always guard against what scared you most. How the urgency of your watchfulness dulled with time. How knowing this only made the remaining fear worse.

She pressed her body against Kelly's, slurred through the pills until she slept with her feet in his lap, her bad leg twitching against the couch, scraping sweatpants over rough fabric. A series of the smallest gestures followed: one man, one woman, sleeping together on a couch in a rented apartment. When Kelly awoke the nightly news was flooding the screen with the day's events, the political pronouncements and product releases. The president appeared again in his favorite hallway, a West Wing locale saved for announcing the deaths of enemies of the state, the upheld constitutionality of his laws. He claimed to have ended wars from this arrangement of white columns and gold light and red carpet, spoke his prepared speeches with his preacher's cadence, allowed his hands the few acceptable motions of the American president: the fist-with-pointing-thumb, the chopping hand, the open clutch. Kelly thought the president was speaking directly to him, another of the president's gifts. His undeniable charisma. Always his own people were beyond reproach, always the president had to believe in our exceptionalism.

In another story an iceberg sloughed off an ice shelf and fell into the sea. Competing viewpoints were offered but all Kelly believed in was human agency. As a child he had tried to imagine the state as it might have been before it was settled, still forested everywhere, the old growth dense and dark and endless with mystery and megafauna and tribal law. Later he'd watched a documentary that claimed the indigenous peoples decimated the trees so thoroughly they removed enough carbon dioxide from the atmosphere to cause an ice age. There was no end to the great harm men could do to the world, the unwitting cost of dominion. So far, every time the doomsday clock went off it got reset, but who knew how long such luck would hold. Sometimes when Kelly watched the president speak he thought the man could hear the dread clock ticking.

ON SATURDAY AFTERNOON THE CRUISERS parked their cars in rows, idled engines in a show of chrome, combustion, exhaust. The girl with the limp knew the makes and models and approximate years, had the arcana of automobiles down. There was talk of other men but she said her interests were hers, didn't rely on outside influences. Kelly poked his head under raised hoods, searched out the parts he could name. He had never changed his own oil, didn't necessarily know what the bottom of his truck looked like. He knew the word *carburetor* but that was another knowledge passing from the earth. There were questions he might have asked if he didn't hate to open up his ignorance to others.

Everything mechanical sounded better in her voice. The way she said *1955 Chevy, 1964 Dodge*. A throaty appreciation, an audible desire.

They surveyed the majesty of hood ornaments, the leaping jaguar, the Pentastar, the impala, the three-pointed star, the Spirit of Ecstasy, the cormorant. A Greek goddess, the archer, the Plymouth ship, the greyhound. An array of rockets evoking a future destined never to come, the face of a chief forced to roam taken lands at new speeds, a golden-winged Cadillac beauty the reminder of a past no one believed. In others cars they saw well-maintained seats, leather made of real animals,

preserved to perfection fifty years after the skinned beasts
were dust. They peered through windows, examined dashes
crowded with dials and meters, buttons and knobs, analog
extravagance. They saw a record player in a Dodge Polara
and he asked when the car had been built. She didn't know
but she touched his arm, the gesture better than any answer.
Before 1930 there were no radios in automobiles, she said, and
so what did people listen to when they drove? The sounds of
the road, the engine, each other.

She pointed and said, A 1947 Packard Clipper, a car red like
all these cars were red. He walked around the vehicle, kneeled
before its skinny grille, considered its endangered curves. He
no longer thought about the fire at the plant every day. You
couldn't escape the past but he hoped you could choose what
to restore, what to keep gleaming. This was the progress Kelly
had seen, not the replacing of the old city with the new but the
building of smarter exits and bypasses.

It wasn't the cost of the object history wanted preserved,
only the object. And this was the week a scrapper died inside
a closed hospital, cutting steel beams, buried beneath a collapsing roof. This was the week a scrapper was shot by a private security guard inside a tenantless apartment building.
This was the week a scrapper dropped an acetylene torch
from atop a ladder, cutting the hose between the tank and the
torch, igniting the insulation falling out of the ceiling. This
was the week a scrapper climbed a power pole to cut through
the dead wire and found the wire fully charged. When the
fire trucks arrived the men had to wait, hoses in hand, until
the utility company could turn off the power. By then the

scrapper was fused to the pole and the firemen had to cut down the top half to take him away.

This life Kelly was living. How long did he expect it to last.

What are you thinking, the girl asked.

He looked up, shook his head, thought her name, said it aloud: *Jackie*. Sometimes it was so easy to say it.

Later they lay beside each other in her bed, hands touching, legs intertwined, and into the silent dark she said she didn't like to talk about her past either but she couldn't put off the future forever. She asked if he knew what he was getting into. Her limp wouldn't be the last thing. Already there were attacks where she struggled to breathe, where her vision blurred and she lost sensation in her fingers and toes. Involuntary systems got confused, voluntary ones unresponsive. Once she'd shit herself at work. She was older than he was and she wasn't going to live forever.

He shushed her, said it didn't matter. He said, Okay. He said, Tell me everything. Tell me what will happen and I'll tell you if I can handle it.

She said physical activity could make it worse. She had to be careful not to overheat herself or else it would cause an attack. No matter what she did there would be attacks and there would be relapses and after every attack she would be worse than she was before. There was no going back. The disease was progressive, untreatable, incurable. The doctors believed they knew how to slow it down but a delay was the best they could hope for.

Some patients smoked pot. Some self-infected themselves

with hookworm to train their immune systems to fight. It was all guesswork. She took her pills and lived her life.

He nodded, slid closer, made a move.

No, she said. First tell me how much of this you want.

We're together, he said. And not because of this. If we come to an end this won't be why.

3

THE MORNING OF THE FIRST snow, Kelly drove an unexplored length of the zone, coasting the truck slowly from driveway to driveway, assessing doors left open, windows missing, porches collapsed by the removal of their metal supports. Some of the houses had been scrapped already but he knew he would find one more recently closed, with boards in the windows and an intact door. A space empty but not yet shredded. The zone sprawled beneath the falling snow, cast its imperfection wider than he could accept, but eventually he chose a house—two floors, blue paint on the siding, gray boards over the windows, a yellow door, surrounded on both sides by vacant lots, with only a burnt shell standing watch across the street—then went to the door and knocked, yelled greetings loaded with question marks.

He waited, yelled again.

He raised his hood, returned to the truck for a pry bar. He moved out of the front yard and along the side of the house, the brown grass crunching beneath the snow. Beside the blue house was a metal gate in a chain-link fence but the gate wasn't latched. At the first window he pulled back the covering board, found the glass gone. He peeked in, searched for furniture, a television or a radio. Instead stained carpet, signs of water damage, a kitchen with no dirty dishes but an intact gas range, a sink and faucet he could wrench from the countertops.

He lifted himself through the window. Leading away from the kitchen was a staircase to the second floor and also a basement door, closed and latched with a padlock. He'd cut the lock later, after the other work was done. Upstairs the bedrooms were small, sloped to fit beneath the peaked roof, but there was enough room to swing a sledge. Back downstairs he opened the front door — the door not even locked, but he hadn't thought to check before climbing in the window — then crossed the snowy yard to the truck for the rest of his tools. Already his first footprints were buried beneath the accumulation and afterward he wouldn't be able to convince himself there had been others, no matter how insistently he was asked.

In the master bedroom he flicked the light switch to check the power, then aimed above the outlets and swung. He took what other scrappers might have left behind. With a screwdriver he removed each metal junction box from the bedroom, then in the bathroom he cut free the old copper plumbing from under the sink and inside the walls. He smoked and watched the snowfall through a bedroom window, the world hushed wet under its weight. In the South he'd forgotten the feeling of a house in winter, the unexpected nostalgia of watching the world disappear under snowfall. He put his forehead to the cool glass, watched the stillness fill the pane.

Downstairs he dismantled the kitchen, disconnected the

stove from the wall, cut the steel sink from the counter. He worked quietly in what he thought was the wintry hush of the house but later he would be told about the amateur soundproofing in the basement, about the mattresses nailed to the walls, about the eggshell foam pressed between the basement rafters.

The soundproofing meant the boy screaming in the basement wasn't screaming for Kelly but for anyone. There would be talk of providence but what was providence but a fancy word for luck? If the upstairs of the blue house had been plumbed with PVC Kelly might not have gone down into the basement. But then copper in the bathroom, but then the copper price.

It wasn't until he cut the padlock's loop and opened the basement door that he heard the boy's voice, the boy's hoarse cry for help rising out of the dark.

As soon as Kelly heard the boy's voice the moment split, and in the aftermath of that cry Kelly thought he lived both possibilities in simultaneous sequence: there was an empty basement or else there was a basement with a boy in a bed and it seemed to Kelly he had gone into both rooms. Kelly thought if he had fled and left the boy there and disappeared into the night he might never have had to think about it again, couldn't be held responsible for everything that followed. Instead he had acted and now there would be no knowing where this action would stop.

Kelly climbed downward, descending the shaft of light falling through the basement door. His clothes clung to the nervous

damp of his skin as he stepped off the stairs toward the bed at
the back of the low room, toward the boy restrained there, all
skin and skinny bones, naked beneath a pile of blankets and
howling in the black basement air.

One by one each element of the scene came into focus, the
room's angles resolving out of the darkness, each shape alien
in the moment, the experience too unexpected for sense:
the humidity under the earth, the musky heat of trapped
breath and sweat, piss in a bucket; the smell of burrow
or warren, then the filth of the mattress as Kelly slid to his
knees beside the bed, his headlamp unable to light the whole
scene; the boy atop the stained and stinking sheets, confus-
ing in his nudity, half hidden by the pile of covers, a nest of
slick sleeping bags and rougher fabrics partially kicked off
the bed, and beside the pile of blankets a folding metal chair.

The boy's screaming stopped as soon as Kelly lit his features but Kelly knew the boy couldn't see him through the
glare. He shut off the headlamp, removed the glow between
them, let their eyes readjust to the dimmer light. He leaned
closer, close enough to hear the boy's rasping breath, to smell
his captivity, to touch the boy's hand. To try to bring the boy
out of abstraction into the sensible world.

Kelly's body was moving as if disconnected from thought
but if he could retouch the connections he would begin to
speak. He tried to say his name, pointed to himself, failed
to speak the word. He shook his head, reached down for the
boy. The boy flinched from Kelly's touch but Kelly took him
in his arms anyway, gathered him against his chest and lifted
quick—and then the boy crying out in pain as Kelly jerked

him against the metal cuffs shackling the boy's feet to the bed, hidden beneath the bunched blankets.

The sound of the boy's voice, naming his hurt into the black air: this was not the incomprehensible idea of a boy abducted but the presence of such a boy, real enough. And how had Kelly come to hold him, to smell the boy's sweat, then the sudden stink of his own, their thickening musk of fear? Because what if he had not left the South. If he had been able to find work instead of resorting to scrapping. If there had not been the fire in the plant so that afterward he worked alone. If he had not met the girl with the limp. If she had not been working today. If she hadn't had another attack the night before, keeping him from drinking so much he couldn't scrap. Providence or luck, it didn't matter. He told himself he believed only in the grimness of the world, the great loneliness of the vacuum without end to come. You could be good but what did it buy you. You could be good and it meant more precisely because it bought you nothing.

Kelly cursed, lowered the boy back on the bed, felt the boy's heat linger on his chest like a stain. He touched the place where the boy had been, felt the thump of his heart pounding beneath the same skin, listened to their bodies huffing in the dark as he relit the narrow beam of the headlamp, its light scattering the boy's features into nonsense.

I have to go back upstairs, Kelly said. I'll be right back.

No, the boy whispered, his voice swallowed by the muted room. Please.

Kelly quickly removed his coat and wrapped it around the boy to cover the boy's nakedness, then moved toward the stairs as fast as he could, trying to outdistance the increasing volume of the boy's cries. But there was no way of freeing the boy without his saw, no way of getting the saw without leaving the boy. The basement door opened into the kitchen and in every direction Kelly saw the destruction he'd brought, the walls gutted, the counters opened, the stove dragged free from the wall, waiting for the handcart. The day was ending fast, the light fading as Kelly moved across the dirty tile, looking for his backpack, the hacksaw inside.

Outside the opened window the wet whisper of snow fell, quieting the world beyond the house's walls while inside the air was charged and waiting. When Kelly turned back to the basement he saw the door was closed, the boy and the boy's sound trapped again. It was a habit to close a door when he left a room but this time it was a cruelty too. Back downstairs Kelly found the boy sitting with his bare knees curled into his naked chest, all of his body cloaked under Kelly's coat. Kelly raised the saw so the boy could see what it was, what Kelly intended. I'm here to help you, Kelly said, or thought he did, the boy was nodding, or Kelly thought the boy was, but after he switched the headlamp on again he couldn't see the whole boy anymore, only the boy in parts. The boy's terrified face. The boy's clammy chest. The boy's clenched hands and curled toes. He ran the beam along the boy's dirty bony legs, inspected the cuffs, the bruised skin below.

Kelly put a hand on the boy's ankle and they both recoiled at the surprise. Hold still, Kelly said. He lifted the chain in one hand and the saw in the other and as he cut he had to turn his face away from the boy's rising voice, speaking again its awesome need.

The boy was heavier than Kelly expected, a dead weight of dangling limbs. He asked the boy to hold on and the boy said nothing, did less. When Kelly looked down at the boy he saw the boy wasn't looking at anything. Out of the low room, up the stairs, into the dirty kitchen. All the noise the boy had made in the basement was gone, replaced by something more ragged, a threatened hissing. The front door was close to the truck but the back door was closer to where they stood and more than anything else Kelly wanted out of the blue house, out into the fresh snow and the safety of the truck, its almost escape.

Other scenarios emerged. Other uses for the basement, what might happen to Kelly if they were caught here. What might happen to the boy for trying to escape if he were caught too. Outside the wind was louder than Kelly had expected and the thick wet snow would bury his newest footprints but there wouldn't be any hiding what he'd done. Kelly carried the boy around the house to the truck, adjusted the boy's weight across his shoulder so he could dig in his pocket for the keys. The boy was shoeless and Kelly couldn't put him down. The boy was limp and shoeless in his arms but Kelly thought if he put the boy down the boy might run.

At the truck Kelly lowered the boy into the passenger seat, then stripped off his own flannel shirt. Kelly's arms were bare to the falling snow but he wasn't cold as he helped the boy stick his arms into the shirt, its fabric long enough to cover most of the boy's nakedness. He bundled the boy back into the coat too but the truck was freezing and the boy's legs were bare and Kelly wasn't sure the boy's shivering would stop no matter how warm he made the cab.

Kelly walked around to the driver's side, opened the door. Without climbing inside he reached under the steering wheel, put the keys in the ignition, started the engine. He punched the rear defrost, cranked the heat, hesitated.

I have to go, he said. I have to go back into the house but I will be back for you.

The boy didn't speak, didn't look in his direction. It wasn't permission. He didn't know if the boy understood. This was shock, trauma. The boy needed to go to a hospital, he needed Kelly to call the police, an ambulance. He needed Kelly to act, to keep rescuing him a little longer.

However many minutes it took—moving back into the kitchen to gather his tools into his backpack, then down into the basement for the hacksaw he'd left behind—each minute was its own crime. In the basement Kelly knew the bed was unoccupied but when he entered the low room there appeared a vision of the boy still chained to the bed, an after-image burning before him. He knew he'd saved the boy but when he made it back to the truck the doors were locked, the boy gone. A new panic fluttered in Kelly's chest—but then he looked again, saw the boy hidden in the dark of the snow-covered cab, crouched down in the space near the floorboards beneath the passenger seat—a space which, Kelly remembered, as a kid he had called the pit.

The boy wouldn't come out of the pit, wouldn't unlock

the doors or turn his terrified face toward Kelly. Kelly waited until he was sure the boy was looking away, then pulled his undershirt sleeve over his bare elbow and shattered the truck's driver-side window. And before he drove the boy to the hospital he had to clear the safety glass from the boy's seat, from the thick scrub of the boy's hair.

As Kelly pulled into the hospital parking lot his cell phone rang and without looking he knew it was her. He wanted to answer but there wasn't time. There weren't the right words yet for what he needed to tell her, what he wanted to ask. He parked the truck under the EMERGENCY sign, stepped outside into the unplowed parking lot, the snow turned heavier than at the blue house. He walked around the truck, opened the passenger door, lifted the boy's limpness into his arms, said his own name to the boy for the first time. The snow fell on Kelly's face and on the boy's face and neither said anything else as Kelly carried the boy across the parking lot. The boy didn't look at Kelly and Kelly thought he had to stop looking at the boy, had to watch where he was going instead of taking in every feature, every eyelash and pimple and steaming exhale, had to concentrate on making his body move. A few more steps, he said to the boy. A few more steps and they would be inside, passing through the bright and sterile and inextinguishable light of the hospital, toward the company of others, where they would be safer than they were now, alone.

GUANTÁNAMO

THE RAPPER HAD THREE NAMES: his father had named him first, then he had given himself a rap name, and then later still he gave himself a Muslim name. The freedom of life under an alias, then the charge of a truer name, the strived-for self, after the alias had become a product, commodified, shrink-wrapped, labeled with parental-advisory stickers. His publicist asked reporters to call him by his Muslim name but the reporters put his rap name in parentheses, didn't care if this wasn't who he was anymore, preferred its controlled danger.

Now the rapper could move freely again, work within his new title. The rapper had given up one name to become a new person and in the press briefing his first day at Guantánamo he listened as the base commander offered his own names for the new world he wanted the rapper and the documentary crew he'd accompanied to see: These were not prisoners, the commander said, but detainees. This was a detention facility, not a prison. The detainees had not been captured, only rendered, turned over, extradited. This was not a court. The

soldiers did not work in a courthouse. This was a military tri-
bunal, meeting in the Expeditionary Legal Complex.

Language replaced what could no longer be borne, *terror-
ist* became *enemy combatant* became *unprivileged belligerent*,
each phrase meaning less than the one before. The official
view of the legal complex could only be photographed from
one particular location, a three-foot square spray-painted
onto a walkway, requiring a certain kind of tunnel vision.
They were permitted to capture only what lay between two
green lightposts, the legal complex barely visible over a
series of fences, silver chain link, green sniper netting, coils
of razor wire, a red anticar barricade. The barest aperture
through which to glimpse a secret. There could be no photos of detainees' faces, no photos of large stretches of the
coastline, no images of unoccupied guard towers, a rule that
admitted there were unoccupied guard towers. Whether
they followed the rules or not, every photo would be either
approved or deleted at the end of every day and there would
be no appeals.

The commander: buzz cut, pressed uniform, stern face.
Everything about him so expected it was hard to fix his features in memory. The commander didn't say but the rapper
knew whatever he asked the detainee could be used against
the detainee. The rapper had come to help him but not in the
military courts, only at home, in the public eye. The slow
progress of art: the crisis was happening now but the solu-
tion waited in the future. The detainee's release hearings were
under way again. He was uncharged and never convicted of
anything but he had not been sent home and this was what the

rapper had come to make happen. But even if art could move the masses — and this the rapper no longer knew, although he had staked his life on the question — it would not move them soon. The director said they'd have to hit the festival circuit before any general release, could maybe seek a streaming deal to speed up the process. Six months, a year.

The photographs:

Approved: The personal items given to each detainee. Orange jumpsuit. White underclothing. Blue flip-flops. Blue laceless shoes. Olive-green jumpsuit. A bottle for water. A copy of the Koran. Comfort items, prayer rugs, sudoku. A clear plastic container to store these possessions.

Approved: The spoon, the spork, the plastic knife. Yellow cake. Onion and garlic. Soft fruit. Bread. Tiny packets of salt and pepper and ketchup and honey, all the tiny condiments of the tiny life.

Approved: A single shelf of the detainee library. An array of foreign-language newspapers. *USA Today*. Teen paranormal romance translated into Arabic. Materials for a living-skills course on home budgeting and résumé writing.

Approved: A plush recliner in a room meant for a single detainee's television privileges, to be enjoyed in leg chains, also pictured.

Approved: A photo of the commander standing in the hallway of one of the detainee camps. Photographed from the rear to hide his face. The walls and floor of the camp gleaming. The clean silence of a photograph.

Approved: A painted arrow stenciled onto the concrete,

pointed toward Mecca. So detainees knew which direction to send their prayers.

Approved: Cans of nutritional supplement, a single stretch of feeding tube. Supplies stockpiled against a growing hunger strike.

Approved: A hospital bed inside a chain-link fence. The detainee medical clinic.

Approved: A sign reading DETAINEES IN VICINITY—MAINTAIN SILENCE.

Approved: A sign bearing the slogan SAFE HUMANE LEGAL TRANSPARENT.

Approved: A sign reading NO PHOTOGRAPHY.

Deleted: A white board in the commander's office with a handwritten note: TOP STORY THIS WEEK—RULES INCONVENIENCE REPORTERS.

Deleted: A photo of a water tower, though the water tower could be seen online, on publicly available maps.

Deleted: A photo of a communications antenna, despite the same.

Deleted: A length of film where a detainee's face accidentally showed in a window.

Deleted: A length of film where a migrant kitchen worker stopped facing away, turned toward the camera.

Deleted:

Deleted:

Deleted:

Deleted: They couldn't remember everything. This was the point. They had outsourced their memory to film and photograph and their memory was being deleted.

Deleted: The face of Adnan Fahim.

Adnan Fahim. This was the man the rapper had come to see. Detained in Yemen in 2002 on suspicion of giving material support to terrorists. Twenty-one years old at the time. Active for less than three months from first contact to capture. Held and interrogated overseas in a top-secret black site for four years, then transferred here, interrogated again, during the years referred to as Bad Old Gitmo. Torture between 2002 and 2008 meant everything they'd made him say wasn't admissible in court but so far no release was forthcoming, only more hearings, more imprisonment. They hadn't questioned him in five years. All previous evidence was tainted but reports suggested the government had once expected him to be charged in 2006 under a retrospective law changing the definition of *material support*. By then he had already been designated an *enemy combatant*, before there was an official definition — but then the definition turned out to be if the president said you were an enemy combatant then that was what you were.

The rapper was allowed into the windowless cell first, directed to take his seat across from the door. The commander said the detainee would be brought shortly but there could be delays. They would let the rapper get tired, let him lose his nerve. There were no clocks inside the room, no cell phones or watches allowed. A nervous boredom accumulated. He smelled the sour stink of his body, already sweating in the humidity and the tight box of the cell. He had been instructed not to touch the detainee — always *the detainee*, never *Adnan Fahim* — and also not to ask him for any information possibly deemed classified. There would be no one else in the cell with them but a guard would be posted outside, with the commander listening on a monitor nearby. If at any moment his line of questioning veered from his instructions, then the interview would be terminated.

The door opened. Adnan Fahim entered alone, his slim frame draped by an olive-green jumpsuit, a body belt of chains hanging from his wrists to his ankles. Adnan was one hundred days into a campwide hunger strike but he wasn't allowed to starve himself and so the man before the rapper didn't match the mental image of a hunger-strike victim. The rapper had seen a file photo of Adnan but the photo was from years earlier and the Adnan chained to the chair was older, his face more tired, more worn. Only the sharp expression in Adnan's eyes had not changed. This was a man the rapper believed he could talk to, who would make a compelling testimonial against the persistence of the camp, help reignite the rage necessary to close it.

Their conversation was allotted ninety minutes but it did not last ninety minutes. The rapper believed Adnan had made only a small mistake, despite the events that followed. A paperboy. His crimes were indirect, passive. The rapper expected his help to be welcomed but soon it was clear this wasn't the case. The rapper thought he was angry for his own reasons but when confronted with Adnan's anger his reasons withdrew, childish and petulant.

The two men took turns talking but the conversation was frustrating from the start.

The rapper said, I've come to ask for your cooperation. I

want to make a movie about you, to bring attention to the problem of your detainment, your treatment. How you are cleared for release but haven't been released. The government hasn't said yes but they will. They wouldn't have brought me here otherwise.

Unless, Adnan said, they brought you here so I could discourage you.

Already Adnan looked disappointed. The rapper continued, speaking faster: I want your name to be on the lips of outraged citizens, calling for your release. I want the president to hear them calling your name.

The president of the United States already knows my name. I know this. He thinks of me while he lies in bed at night. About what he ordered done to me.

It isn't the same president now, the rapper said. The president who had you tortured isn't president anymore.

There is only one president, Adnan said. You vote or don't vote, it makes no difference. There is just one president.

You're wrong. Every president is problematic but this president is different.

Adnan leaned back in his chair, lifted his chained hands in an apology, one he couldn't have meant. Their time was short. This wasn't what the rapper had come to speak to him about. He needed permission, access. It would be impossible to speak to Adnan again as long as he was in the detention camp but they couldn't silence him forever.

They can, Adnan said. They have.

Adnan said he didn't want to die but his hunger strike was already one hundred days old. Every day the guards came, strapped him into a restraint chair, used it to prevent him from forcing himself to vomit. Fifteen hundred calories in two blue-and-white cans. They'd tortured him ten years ago and they were torturing him again, this time with nasal tubes and lubricant and nutritious slime. Adnan gestured again, invited a survey of his body. The chains on his hands and feet, the anonymous clothes. The scarring and irritation of his nasal passages, his throat. How he was losing his voice because he was so rarely allowed to speak freely.

Adnan asked, How old are you?

Thirty-three, the rapper said.

Thirty-three. I'm thirty-three too.

I know. Your age was one of the reasons—

You want to think we are the same.

Yes.

We are not.

I know.

Thirty-three. Your country at war a third of your life.

Yes.

And I have been imprisoned a third of mine.

Yes.

In your country, if I had shot a man in my youth, could my crime be almost an accident, an inevitability, an unavoidable outcome of a system?

Some people would say so. Some people would say all those things.

A crime, yes, but the crime of having been younger, less educated, less patient. There would be those who would protest my harsh treatment.

Yes. A killer but a killer at a disadvantage.

Material support. That's my crime.

The rapper wanted to speak but couldn't. He had come to see a wronged man speak in his own defense but what was he getting instead? His sympathy unfairly played against him.

Adnan continued: Material support. I moved money. I was poor and my father was dead and I was twenty-one years old and I was angry at the country the old men said killed my father and the old men said *Vengeance* and they said *Your anger is righteous* and they said *God is on our side* and they said *The feelings you carry are true feelings* and they said *You do not have to hurt anyone* and they said *We only need you to help us move money*.

The rapper whispered, Don't say this. They can hear you and they will never let you go.

Already they will never let me go, Adnan said, so what does it matter if I speak the truth? I was young and ignorant and I wanted to do something to end my fear. I was afraid because I was angry and I wanted to end my anger too. I am still angry but the guards now are not the guards of my youth. They no longer strike me. They no longer beat me awake. They do not know the short shackle or the waterboard. They let me wear my clothes, let me see the sun, let me read my books and pray my prayers. They do not let me starve myself but they believe this a kindness. The men who tortured me are long gone, gone home to America or back to Iraq or Afghanistan, and I do not resist those who have taken their place. Every soldier is not the same soldier. The men I hate I will never see again but I wait for their names to be spoken. In their absence I will hate no one else.

The conversation was allotted ninety minutes but it did not last ninety minutes. The rapper walked around the table to knock on the door and signal the guard, then returned to his own seat. Before the detainee was taken from the room he tried again to speak to the rapper but now the rapper wouldn't listen, couldn't meet his gaze. Their conversation did not end with goodbye, and later the rapper would find he did not believe the conversation had ended.

Once back in the States the director explained her new intent: a white room, a restraint chair, the standard operating procedure for force-feeding hunger strikers. She did not speak in the vernacular of the military. She never said *detainee*, only *prisoner*, only *victim*. She did not say *detention center*, only *prison*, only *torture, violation of free will, civil rights*.

The rapper did not need the argument. The rapper had already volunteered.

The rapper arrived in the white room, dressed in the orange jumpsuit the crew provided, allowed them to chain his hands and feet. The surprising weight of the cuffs. The rapper shoeless, hatless. He sat down in the restraint chair, wondered briefly where the crew had acquired the equipment. They strapped the restraints around his hands and feet, the chair cold against his sweating skin, then fastened another strap across his forehead, holding his skull angled backward. Then the nurses hired to play nurses, then their teal scrubs and purple latex gloves, the measuring of the feeding tube, ear to xiphoid process. The rapper had been instructed to stare straight ahead into the camera but he couldn't resist a glance to the side, to watch the purple gloves coating the end of the feeding tube in lubricant. Once he saw he couldn't unsee. Then the purple glove across the forehead, the thumb opening his nostrils. The tube slipped in, pushed past. The rapper squirming in the chair, another set of gloved hands gripping his head to hold him steady. He heard himself groan, heard himself grinding his teeth. He tried to keep his mouth closed but the tube was bypassing the mouth altogether. There were tears in his eyes and who wouldn't cry at this, how could anyone not. Another inch of tubing, his head thrashing side to side, and the purple gloves kept working. Inch after burning inch. How to know how many inches had gone in? His eyes were closed and he couldn't open them to check. The unbearable burning increasing. The tube wasn't anywhere near his brain but his brain was what burned. Arching his back didn't provide any reprieve but when he wouldn't stop bucking a third nurse came to hold him down, this one's hands ungloved. One of the rapper's arms pulled free of the restraint strap and the ungloved nurse pinned his freed hand to the armrest, applied strength against frightened force.

Stop, the rapper begged.

I can't, he said.

The tube snaking back out of his nostrils. His body relaxing, a deep breath gathering, but when he opened his eyes the purple gloves were dipping the tube back into the lubricant.

Please, please don't.

When the rapper started screaming a nurse slid his arm around the rapper's neck, applying pressure to put his head against the headrest, placed another ungloved hand across his forehead. The bluing tattoos on the nurse's arms reading like faded threats. The muted sounds of the nurse's attention. How the nurses never spoke. How they instructed only with their hands.

Please, the rapper said. Stop. Stop it. Please stop.

The flatness of the imperative, spoken in the weak voice of a prisoner.

This is me, he said. This is me.

This is me, he said. I can't do this.

This is me.

The three men released him, their hands returning to comfort, to assure the end of the demonstration. The rapper cried as they rubbed his shoulders, as they gently touched his head and face. Less than three minutes from beginning to end. The feeding tube never fully inserted. The nutrients hanging untouched from an IV stand, like oatmeal in a plastic bag. The rapper moaning with his face in his hands.

When he watched the finished video he knew exactly when they would fade to white, at the worst moment of his disgust with himself, his failure to suffer once what Adnan Fahim was suffering twice a day. The unfreed man, left behind after all the men who had brought him to his prison were sent home, at the end of the bad days. As if the bad days of a prison ended when the guards decided they did.

See the rapper in his street clothes, face-to-face with the rapper in the orange jumpsuit trapped on the screen, the rapper watching himself on the director's laptop, in the director's hotel room. Watching it again, his failure to commit. The fade to white reversing, the rapper's face returning to the screen, himself sitting in the restraint chair, unmolested again, alone inside the frame. Tears in his eyes but the words read off cue cards. The rapper on the screen saying the words scripted before the demonstration began, the way the rapper had always known he would be expected to end his statement.

Peace, the rapper heard himself say. His eyes bloodshot, his lip shaking.

Peace, he said again.

Peace and good morning.

PART TWO:
THE CASE

4

AT THE PRECINCT, IT WAS always the same detective who questioned Kelly, a baby-faced man with a hard belly busting over his belt. The heavy detective came in and out of the blank square of the interview room and each time he entered he questioned Kelly and each time Kelly promised to tell him everything he could. At first Kelly thought he remembered almost nothing, that finding the boy had overwhelmed every other possible interest, but with every new question he remembered a little more, and so how to trust what he wanted to say, if he knew it could change?

What do you remember, the heavy detective asked again. What do you remember now?

The boy, he started to say, before the detective interrupted: *Daniel,* the heavy detective said, and Kelly blinked, said, Who?

The boy, the detective said. The boy's name.

Daniel. Kelly knew he wasn't a reliable eyewitness because when he was confused he believed everything he was told. He remembered more about going into the basement than he had when he walked into the hospital. Or else he thought he did. He could see the shape of the low room, its walls that before had disappeared into the dark. He had not recognized the mattresses nailed to those walls but as the heavy detective described them he saw the sagging outline of each one, the rolled towels and eggshell foam duct-taped to fill the creases between.

The detective searched his notes, shook his head. He was testing Kelly's recall but Kelly recalled mostly only what the detective had told him first. The detective said the boy hadn't seen much either, only a mask over the kidnapper's face, only the hood of a red slicker worn against the weather.

The detective asked, Why didn't you call the police?

I didn't think, Kelly said. But whoever put the boy in the basement must have meant to come back for him. I wanted to be gone when he did.

He asked the detective if they knew who took the boy. *The man in the red slicker.* Who was he? The detective didn't know, wasn't afraid to admit it, at least here in this closed room. The boy's parents had reported him missing but not until he'd been gone a day. Investigation revealed it was just a miscommunication—each parent had thought he was with the other—and bad parenting wasn't necessarily an indicator of foul play.

The heavy detective said, There's a reward, you know. Did you know about the reward?

Kelly hadn't but he said, I saw *something*, and the detective nodded, made an appreciative noise. It was best when they could agree. What Kelly remembered most wasn't any particular detail but how the experience had split, how there was a basement with a boy and a basement without. How somehow he had gone into both basements and perhaps two people had come out, with slightly different ideas about what they had seen.

He'd felt this way before, when he was a boy himself.

The boy, the reward, Kelly wasn't sure what he knew and didn't know. The boy's face wasn't the same as in his last yearbook photo, the one the news had shown, broadcast beside some stranger's cell-phone picture of Kelly cradling the boy in his arms, carrying him into the emergency room, the boy's face blank, the chainless cuffs clasped around the boy's ankles, the boy's skinny bones swinging limp from Kelly's grip.

The expression on Kelly's face hadn't been one he recognized. The blonde reporter had called it bravery but Kelly didn't think this was the word.

When there was nothing else to say the heavy detective put his card on the table. Probably they would have more questions but Kelly wasn't a suspect. The detective said this several times and each time no qualifications followed, no *yet*, no *at this time*. Kelly knew he wasn't guilty but it was good to hear the detective say the words. Surely the detective must have said his name before this but here it was on his card, seemingly for the first time: SANCHEZ.

The heavy detective taped the interview, would file the recording for future use. Other officers wanted to collect other evidence and Kelly let them take whatever they wanted. In the parking lot they photographed his truck, measured the tread of his tires, and in the precinct house they did the same with his shoes before attempting to take his fingerprints without success. Fifteen years of manual labor had worn away the ridges on his fingertips and perhaps for years he hadn't left a proper fingerprint on anything he touched. He'd committed crimes but he'd left less of a stain than he'd thought. He pulled his hood over his hair, shivered in the precinct lobby, waited for the police to release him into the remainder of the night. Perhaps he was freer to act than ever before. But even without fingerprints there were other ways to leave a mark.

THE EVENING NEWS BROADCAST HIS face, showed his picture every night for a week. To pass the boredom of workless afternoons he visited his regular bars but now everyone there knew his name. He hated beards but started growing one anyway, layered hooded sweatshirts beneath every jacket. He couldn't go back to scrapping but with the promise of the reward he rented a new apartment in a better neighborhood, farther from the places where he'd worked.

The phone rang. Once Christian women knew his name they found him too, dropping off casseroles and staying for prayers. More reward. The first woman sheepish when he opened the door, then bold once in his kitchen, opening cabinets and shaking her head at the paltry plates, glasses, silverware. He lived alone but the next day the first woman returned with others, women who brought him food for a family, then circled his table in their Sunday dresses, and when he wouldn't take their offered hands they closed their circle around him, centered him in their words.

His kitchen table only had two chairs but the women said they didn't mind standing. He opened their packages of paper plates, plastic silverware, fed their food back to them: rigatoni for days, a deli platter feeding a dozen. The Christian women said saving Daniel was his penance for the scrap he'd stolen.

He listened but he didn't agree. He didn't believe in the god they did, didn't see the benevolence in the universe. Instead the past repeated, with every action representative of a type, every thought representative of a common idea. The Christian women patted his hand, held his in theirs. They said their prayers as if unafflicted with doubt but he thought doubt and fear were the only places he'd found to put his faith.

The girl with the limp came over to help but what remained was more than any two people needed. She wasn't supposed to eat food this rich, started to complain. He put on weight too, found the ten pounds of beer weight held back by the swing of the sledge. When he opened his new refrigerator he already thought he could smell some excess turning. The way sealed plastic filled with moisture. The yellow sour of thickening milk, a waste of greening ham.

The phone rang. The husband of one of the women called Kelly to offer him a job. The husband worked in demolition, owned a small outfit working the zone, removing the wreckage of industry, tearing down other buildings on government contracts. The husband said Kelly would have to start at the bottom but it was fair money and at least it was honest work.

It's work you're used to, the husband said. Though we might do things a bit different. More professional.

What to call the tone in the husband's voice. In the word *probationary*. In the words *trial basis*. Kelly listened, waited for his chance to speak. He said, How did you get this number?

The husband's voice changed, expanded its reproach. The offer was a favor to his wife. Did Kelly want the job or not?

He did want the job, knew it could last. He had his own

truck, he said, his own tools. He had the reward money but it was better if he didn't have to touch it.

He said *Thank you* but not before the husband hung up the phone.

The phone rang. The heavy detective again, working through the same questions, searching for new angles of entry. There were no suspects. No family enemies, no finger-prints in the basement. The detective said undercover cops had watched the house but no one had returned after the boy had been removed.

He said whoever took the boy might have seen Kelly's truck, seen Kelly's face. He had to assume the kidnapper had seen the news, would remember Kelly's name.

Be careful, the detective said. Don't make a big deal of where you live. Be as cautious as you can, but if you see any-one suspicious following you, you know my number. Prob-ably there isn't anything to worry about. Probably a person who kidnaps little boys is a sex criminal. He wouldn't come after a grown man.

Kelly tried to use the word *rape*, the word *molested*. Was this what had happened to the boy?

There's a lot of confusion there, the detective said. When we asked Daniel what the man did to him, the boy insisted the man who took him had *watched*. That's it.

The man had worn gloves and a mask and a red hooded slicker and he had cuffed the boy to a bed in a basement and then he watched him. The detective said this as if it were hardly anything at all.

The detective said there were court psychiatrists, social

workers, a process they had to go through to question the boy. The detective joked he could call Kelly whenever he wanted. No rules against talking to you, he said, then laughed, a sort of nervous grunting.

The detective said, Once in a while a kidnapper gets nervous, brings in the victim himself. Even if he's done everything right, even if he might never be caught. The kidnapper gets nervous or scared or he becomes concerned for the victim, having come to care for him. Maybe he decides to get out before something worse happens.

Kelly could deny the insinuation but he didn't have to. He knew who he was, what he'd done. The detective said the house belonged to the bank but the bank wouldn't press charges. Kelly was a thief but he was a hero too. Fighting over copper at three dollars a pound wouldn't buy the bank anything it wanted.

THE BLONDE REPORTER CALLED AND Kelly made her repeat her name until he believed it. Would he see the boy again? She wanted a story of the two of them reunited, the saver and the saved. The *salvor*, Kelly said—drunk again, slurring into the receiver, and where had this word come from?— and she said, What? He wasn't sure this was a good idea, hung up. Later she called again, put a number on the table. He could take it or leave it, she said. They weren't in the business of negotiating for human interest.

When the reporter appeared the next morning she wore knee-high boots under a pressed tan skirt, had so much blonde hair he couldn't believe it was all hers. She lingered in Kelly's doorway, considered his living room, the clothes he'd picked out to wear.

Do you have a suit, she asked, or at least a tie?

He'd meant to buy one but there hadn't been time. There was his new job, the girl with the limp. She had wanted to come along to support him and he'd told her he didn't know what he needed support for but now he did. The parents would be waiting with his reward, ready to pay him for the boy's return. They had lost something precious and he worried he'd returned them something quieter, skinnier upon its bones. On the television, the reporter had said only three days had passed between the boy's abduction and his rescue, barely any time at all. The boy was physically unharmed, except for where Kelly had bruised him, when he'd pulled the boy's ankles against the cuffs.

A miracle, the reporter had said, almost as if nothing had happened. But even in a local story you had to listen for what no one was saying.

At the hospice shop the cameraman stayed in the car while the blonde reporter led Kelly between the crowded racks. She was good at colors and sizes and she said she knew what would look right on-screen. She made him try on the suit, then came into the dressing room. He saw she wore a wedding ring when she reached up to straighten his tie. She saw him looking, said she wasn't married, said the station made her wear the ring to boost her credibility.

It's cubic zirconia, she said. This close to worthless.

I'm so young, she said. And no one wants the young telling them anything.

The shoes she picked pinched his toes but he didn't complain. They were close enough and they were cheap and they matched the suit. After she approved she reached up again, fixed his hair with a licked finger. Every time she moved he could smell her. He didn't know the names of perfumes but he'd smelled this one before. The confines of the dressing room were tight and their bodies kept touching at new angles. They were all brushes but they started to add up. He knew better than to expect more. Yesterday she'd said he was a hero but this was only the story the news at five had wanted to tell.

It was the presence of the reward that confused him, a number large enough he assumed the boy's family would live outside the city, farther north in the surrounding suburbs. Instead the reporter exited the freeway early, staying within the city limits, within the zone. Now the vague terrain of lonely blocks, the way the old and hopeful names for neighborhoods no longer described what you found. Trees grown close around houses, fallen leaves over trashed yards, tall brown grass sticking through the early snow. The blackened frame of a house, all the doors and windows stolen, all its insides gutted, dragged outside and left in the yard.

A spray-painted sign over a burnt storefront: PET STORE ANY VARMIT YOU WANT FREE.

Now the house of the boy's family, as old as the other houses on the block, built of the same architecture but otherwise seemingly from another era. The brick powerwashed and graffiti-free, the porch a new bit of construction and nicely stained, the siding painted a cheerful green. Last week's snow covered the earth but Kelly could see flowerbeds in front of the house and trellises built along the sides, ornamentation readied for spring growth, summer bloom, the future.

This was the kind of home he desired, maybe the kind of life.

The boy's father answered the door, shook their hands, invited them in. Kelly hadn't thought to guess the boy was adopted until he saw the father, the bearded man around the same height as Kelly but heavier, dressed in dark jeans and a short-sleeved checked dress shirt. In the boy's house

Kelly found himself more aware of his movements, knew he was being watched by the father, the cameraman, the blonde reporter. He wiped his forehead with his sleeve, tried to smile. The walls were decorated with pictures of the boy, all the official documents of a child, starting when the boy was a toddler and ending at whatever age he was now, ten or eleven or twelve. In the photos from later years another boy appeared in the pictures, after which Kelly assumed the children had taken on new titles: the boy, the brother, the boy's brother.

The mother came out of the kitchen to meet him, her long dark hair restrained in a single braid, faded freckles on her face and arms and hands, everywhere else pale skin escaped the bright fabric of her dress.

Thank you for bringing Daniel back, she said. Thank you for finding him for us.

As if Kelly had done something purposeful, something tried. She called the boy's name up the stairs and the boy appeared, dressed in his own gray suit. Kelly knew the boy's name but there were so many Daniels in the world, so many Dans and Dannys. *The boy?* There had been a boy before. There was this boy now. It was only generic in the mouths of others.

The father talked to the blonde reporter, explaining their move back to the city, the price they'd paid for the house, the sorry shape it'd been in. Kelly flushed when the father spoke of the house being ransacked, how the hardwood floors and the winding staircase and the brick walls had held but how scrappers had come in and taken the wiring, the plumbing.

They did us a favor, the father said. We would have had to

tear it all out to put in a modern system. Now the house has grounded plugs, new pipes, central air.

All new appliances, as of last winter, the mother said, joining in. The walls were already gutted so we took down the plaster to put in drywall, painted the rooms brighter colors.

In the summer we mow the neighbors' lawns, the father said. To keep up appearances. To make it easier to hope other people might move here too.

The mother and *the father*: their titles made them sound older than they were but they were the same age as Kelly or else younger. The father was a veteran, had come home from overseas to study, work, start a family. His grandparents helped with the down payment on the house and with adoption costs and they were the ones who had paid the reward.

We don't have much, the father said. We have to be willing to take help wherever we can find it.

They didn't have much but they had a family. Kelly sat down on a creaky wooden chair, focused on not putting his head in his hands. Before the small talk was exhausted Kelly stood and again began inspecting the family photos on the walls, tried to imagine the life they suggested. The mother saw him looking, came to stand beside him, touched his arm. He looked at where she had touched him, followed her hand as it left his skin to gesture through the photographs, indicating various ages, after-school activities, the brother playing basketball for the school team, the boy sitting at a piano dressed in the same gray suit.

The mother asked, Do you have kids?

No, Kelly said. No kids.

She said, We wanted kids of our own. And when he couldn't have them, then we wanted to love a child no one had wanted. We wanted there to be less suffering because of our love.

Her earnestness embarrassed him. He turned and looked for the boy, wondered what the boy had heard. The blonde reporter asked where the brother was and the father and mother looked at each other before answering.

He's out, the father said.

We didn't know you would want him here, the mother said.

The blonde reporter needed a family reunited but it didn't matter to her who the family contained. The cameraman shot video of the father and the mother, of the family together, and then the boy by himself. The father put his hand on the boy's shoulder and the boy flinched. On the news the reporter had said basically nothing had happened to the boy. But it wasn't nothing, couldn't have been nothing. Even if he was unhurt now, he had not been unhurt in the basement. He had been *watched* and Kelly knew watching could be its own kind of injury.

The boy had been *left* too, and hadn't he screamed in the dark?

The boy was looking at Kelly and Kelly tried not to stare back. The cameraman maneuvered closer, asked Kelly to sit beside the boy. They were supposed to talk but about what? Kelly had good teeth too but never showed them in pictures because before they'd been bad. He had to keep blinking to keep his eyes from watering. He never paid much attention to his face but the camera made him aware how it was moving wrong.

Kelly wanted to say something to the boy but not in front of these hovering people, not with their hands touching the boy, his head, his hair, his hands. He saw the way the boy suffered under their touch but he didn't know if this was new. After the photographs were finished the father pumped Kelly's hand and thanked him, handed him a check. The worth of a boy, paid for again. Who was the real criminal, the one who took the boy or the one who took the ransom? They treated him like a hero but he'd been acting like a thief and yet here was the payment for the best thing he'd ever found, in any abandoned house.

Kelly could smell the suit he was wearing, his sweat tanging through the harshness of the cheap chemicals used to wash away whoever had worn it last. He kneeled down in front of the boy, touched the boy's skinny arm.

Daniel, he said. I want to see you again.

He hadn't meant to say it so loud but there it was. Conversation stopped and he knew he'd made a mistake. The father bristled and the mother put her hand on the boy's head, pulled the boy away before Kelly could see his reaction.

The parents had been friendly with him but now he saw their truer feelings cloud their faces, suspicion shifting toward accusation. They were happy for their boy's return, had paid the reward, but honestly what was he doing in that house.

The boy was too old for the gesture but now he hid his face in the mother's side, tucked away an expression Kelly couldn't track. Then the boy nodded, his face moving against the fabric of the mother's dress.

If it's okay with you, Kelly said — speaking to the boy's parents, being careful not to address the boy again — I'll leave my phone number, in case you need me.

Need you for what, the father said, but the mother brought Kelly a pen and a pad of paper. An instinctual courtesy.

The father said, I don't think this is a good idea. We want this to be over. I'm sure you understand.

The boy stayed where he was and shuffled his feet, scuffed his dress shoes against the linoleum. An odd smile crossed the father's face and Kelly knew he would be polite enough to wait until Kelly left the house to throw the number away. The cameraman shot more footage but Kelly knew it wasn't the story they'd come to tell and afterward Kelly cried out in the reporter's car, a tremor in his hands and his voice not making the words he wanted to say, not any apologetic noise. The blonde reporter touched him on the shoulder but her touch wasn't what made him stop. He was almost done when she took her hand away, checked her watch, put the car into drive.

By late afternoon, the local news was teasing the story, displaying a ticker along the bottom edge of daytime programming: LOCAL HERO MEETS SAVED BOY. When the broadcast began, Kelly poured himself a tall-enough drink to watch the video of the family together, a video of him and the boy. He wasn't in the first shot, and the second made him look criminal. He had three days' worth of beard, needed a haircut. The suit fit him but its origins showed. How long had it been since he'd seen himself look so naked. You stopped looking in mirrors when you brushed your teeth, you learned to shave by feel and muscle memory, maybe you never had to look yourself in the eye ever again.

He watched the blonde reporter speak, heard something missing in her cause and effect, in the suggestion that he had always been the hero, that the boy had always been the saved boy, their meeting a plan instead of coincidence. The national news picked up the story, reran the report. He'd been invisible for a year but now he was so easy to find. Other reporters called, wanted their own exclusives. A news van parked outside and Kelly called into work, pushed his luck. He wondered if the southern woman saw. He wondered about her boy. How they would not be convinced by the new narrative of his life, despite the eerie parallels. How he would always be sorry for what he'd done, his own worst thing. The collapse within the collapse. How *sorry* wasn't enough, how nothing he could say would be. Always there would be the complete insufficiency of words. On the worst day he had promised not to contact them and this was a promise he would keep. There had been love but he of all people knew love was not enough.

Later a familiar sickness returned as he pushed the cashier's check across the counter at his new bank. How he could have sent it to the southern woman. How he could have given it to her boy.

When he asked, the bank teller said he probably would have to pay taxes on the reward but not until the end of the year.

THE OTHER WORKERS KNEW HE'D been hired to appease the boss's wife, smoked and swore and spat and ignored him. He wanted a reputation as a hard worker but first he had to match their pace. The challenge of the right kind of slow. He wanted to work safely but it was hard to keep yourself safer than the least-safe guy. He said he knew how to swing a sledge, to work a torch, wanted to be inside the buildings putting his skills to use but after the first week Kelly never saw the man who hired him again. The other men showed him where to shovel the debris, told him to move the shattered plaster or concrete into the long red dumpsters in the parking lot, they made fun of his name and he let them. They weren't the first to try.

Once the walls of a building came down Kelly swept broken glass in the open air, breathed hard under a paper mask. Snow fell, made every shovel-load heavier. He wore layers of shirts, long underwear under thick brown pants, filled the layers with sweat and silence. He swept and shoveled and hauled what the others knocked down and it was beneath the skills he'd acquired in the zone. Sometimes he worked straight through the day. More sweeping glass, more dragging splintered rafters and crushed wood paneling. In one building he carried cracked urinals down five flights of stairs in one wing, down six in another. Often someone shit in a toilet long after the water was shut off. The others joked it beat walking all the way downstairs but Kelly was the one who had to carry what they made, had to crouch over and reach around the loaded bowl to back out the four bolts securing it to the wall. Shit on his hands and piss on his shoes, a hard hat on his head and a fluorescent vest fastened around his chest. A mask might keep his lungs from turning black but nothing stopped his stomach turning.

How do you rate, one of the others said, shouldering past him in a narrow hallway littered with broken glass, shattered plaster. My brother used to do your job and now look at how shitty you're doing it.

One day the foreman made him maneuver a fire hose, spraying water over the dust forced free by an excavator. The dust could explode, the foreman said, and Kelly nodded, did what he was asked. The water turned the worksite into a puddled muck, gray water moving fast over frozen ground, thick with floating particulate. The dust rose and he knocked it down. It was a job anyone else might get complacent about but never him. He could never tell anyone about the fire at the plant but he knew some part of him was constantly turning over what had happened. He had worked to make this part inaccessible to the rest of him. This was a diminishment in capacity but so far he thought he was getting along fine.

When the Christian women left, the city watch entered. Five men, volunteers dressed in orange t-shirts and orange football jerseys worn under winter coats, each shaking Kelly's hand, each bearing a name forgotten immediately for some identifying mark instead: the first, big as a linebacker; another white haired and white mustached; another bad toothed, tattooed; the fourth with one cloudy eye, as white as the other eye was yellow, jaundiced. The fifth a former cop with silvered temples, a nose broken multiple times.

We saw you on the news, the cop said. A hero. We want you to come to our meetings.

Kelly balked but opened six beers, dumped an ashtray so the men could smoke. He'd seen men like these men before, in other neighborhoods, had learned to recognize their type, the sunglasses and ball caps and leather gloves, how against their own rules some disguised their bright uniforms beneath dark jackets. The city watch held its own training sessions, invited city councilmen and police veterans and the survivors of horrible crimes to come and speak. If you could tell yourself you were protecting someone else, how much further might you be able to go.

In his apartment, the men told stories and Kelly relaxed into their tall tales, the bravado and the dismay. The volunteers spoke the name of a minor dealer; the name of a raped girl, the name of her child; the name of a minister who fed gang members because he said everyone deserved a chance at redemption. A roll call of scared neighbors they each checked on, of old women living on blocks all their own, their yards growing high and snarled as the streetlights clicked off for good. The last white family living in what used to be a white neighborhood. The last black family living in what used to be a black neighborhood. After both families were gone, only ghosts would remain. And what color were ghosts.

The men drank and the men smoked and Kelly followed along better when they used the names of streets and neighborhoods, the numbers and letters of freeways. In the zone they drove pickup trucks or SUVs, installed brighter headlights, dashboard cameras, did their best for the city they loved. Kelly asked the former cop if he carried a gun on his rounds, and the cop said, Never tell them either way. Don't say you do and don't say you don't.

We don't talk about firepower, he said, but whatever they got, we can match it.

Kelly nodded. He understood but he didn't want a weapon of his own. He had a short temper he controlled by not putting himself in places it might erupt. If he had a handgun in his truck he knew someday the handgun would go off.

Would go off. As if it were the gun doing the work. As if a plastic Glock had its own agency.

He would go to their meeting, he said, but that didn't mean he was joining their cause.

They laughed, clapped him on his shoulders. He'd see, they said. He had saved a boy but the police hadn't found the boy's kidnapper. Maybe these volunteers would.

Kelly put down his cigarette, rubbed his eyes. For a moment he'd had trouble telling one man from another. What was similar was stronger than what was different, their station an ideal better than any individual. He moved his gaze from face to face, trying to match the names they'd offered to the features he saw.

The suspect, he thought. The volunteers were right: he had been thinking about the suspect. Maybe there was something more he wanted done. Or else something he wanted to do.

He wasn't scrapping anymore but nights the girl with the limp worked he drove the oldest neighborhoods, cruised the streets bordering overgrown fields and crumbling industrial parks. He bought a police scanner, affixed it to the dash, listened for arsons and burglaries, domestic violence, the reported sounds of gunfire. Dispatch spoke at a remove, spared the details. Most nights he heard her voice on the airwaves, disappearing fast into a squelch of turning static. Her radio voice was pleasantly dispassionate, speaking from within an unfolding tragedy but without inflection. She narrated codes, directions, the street addresses, and the names of cross streets. Sometimes he went the places she named. If he didn't know how to get there he plugged the address into the dash and then there were two female voices telling him where to go. The satellites pointed him in the direction of her mind. He often beat the first responders to the scene but what could he do next, what else except drive by a burning building and hope everyone inside had escaped the flames.

He wasn't scrapping but it didn't keep him out of the oldest buildings. The night he found the boy he had come home to his apartment and found all his relics uncharged, their thrum dissipated. His life had changed but he didn't want to lose what he'd gathered, needed more. He pry-barred the lock on a door in a house he was sure was empty and walked its rooms, ran his fingers through the carpet, put his palms against the plaster walls. There was a mailbox out front with a series of numbers meant to separate this home from all others. Someone could live here again but who. Someone had owned this house but where had they gone. He listened to the boards creak, waited to hear the way the house held both a whisper and a hush. The absence of expectation: nothing more would happen in this house. The phone would not ring, the kitchen timer would not go off, no one would knock on the door. He'd gotten used to so much quiet but never this.

The boy still appeared on the television but less and less. What had happened to the boy was a crime but who would solve it. The scene had given the heavy detective nothing, thanks to Kelly's obscuring work, his covering of every surface in drywall dust and tracked dirt. He gauged his responsibility, tried to assign fault in right proportion. He tried to imagine what might happen next, if the kidnapper knew his name, the name of the boy. He tried to imagine if the balance of power might be upset, if he could come to know the watcher, the man in the red slicker.

From the relics he'd found in the zone Kelly had learned it wasn't possible to know what the hearts of others would treasure or protect. He was coming to believe that if he wanted something saved he had to save it himself.

THEY ATE COLD SANDWICHES AND hot soup in a diner, split a piece of apple pie for dessert. She told him about her week, rehashed all the stories that made the newspaper. Even worse, she said, were the ones that never would, the lower cries of human misery answered at her terminal every hour of her working day: a mother with her kitchen on fire, a wife with a voice slurred by drink or bruises, a child calling for help from the last pay phone on earth, lost and unable to explain where she was, where she was supposed to be. The car crashes, the slip and falls, the temporary troubles and the irreversible blows. The insane cruelty of chance, the magnificent dangers of the everyday, all filtered through her station.

When I started this job, she said, I thought the voices went right through me. I took each call, passed its information to someone who could help, moved on.

The first month, she said, I couldn't remember the calls by the time I got home. I dealt with them and then I forgot. But I didn't stay uninvolved forever. I became something else.

A salvor, Kelly said. *Salvor.* A word he'd been thinking of ever since the first step out of the basement in the blue house. One possible future.

She said, One day I came home and I told someone else what I'd heard on the phone. I'd never done this before, never talked about the day. The someone else was a man but who he was isn't important. The story I told him was about a boy who had fallen into a sewer opening while playing with some friends. They shouldn't have been doing what they were but their mistake wasn't my concern. My concern was getting the boy out of the hole.

There's always a boy to be rescued, he said. Or else a girl.

Public works, she said. The fire department. Both called and put on the case and when I hung up the phone I didn't know how the case would end but I believed it would be resolved. It was so simple, a boy at the bottom of a ladder, too scared to climb back up, maybe hurt.

She stopped talking, stuck her fork through the pie to scrape the plate below, carving the slice into smaller pieces without taking a bite.

The fire department radioed back, she said. This happens. They need more information than what I've provided, or else the person calling has made a mistake. It's so hard to be accurate in the presence of trauma. The firemen and the men from public works had arrived at the open sewer cover to find the first two boys, the one who stayed and the one who made the call. From the street the men couldn't see the third boy at the bottom of the hole and when they went down into the sewer—it was ten feet down, nothing any man and a flashlight couldn't handle—the boy wasn't there. There was nowhere for a boy to go but the firemen searched the shallow passage, trolled the water, shined their lights across every foot of the sewer entrance, all its holes and cubbies, any place a boy might have hidden.

Why would he hide? she asked. From who? Public works unlocked the gratings at each end of the chamber and a further search was organized. Even as they searched they must have known they wouldn't find the boy, because how would he have gotten past those same grates? At first they thought the boys had made up the fallen friend, but he was real enough. It turned out the friend's parents hadn't seen him since before school. They never saw him again.

She said, Once there was this single mystery, the missing boy in the sewer. Now there are so many. Your boy too. Because you saved him — at last she lifted a bite of cold pie to her mouth — but from who?

It's not the unsolvable that bothers me, she said. It's the solvable unsolved.

She wasn't as emotive as every other woman he'd dated. He didn't know the shapes of all her thoughts, had no taxonomy for her modes of expression and speech and careful withholding. After her third bite of pie he realized he didn't have to respond. As with every other conversation it was often enough for him to be the listener, to remember what he'd been told.

There was a grocery in his new neighborhood but he didn't need more food. He bought a handle of whiskey, a twelve-pack of beer, a carton of cigarettes, a squat spiral notebook, and a package of black pens. Back in his apartment he started at the beginning, listed details, whatever precursors of memory he might be able to tug. What had he seen. What did it mean. Who had hurt the boy. The boy had given the detective only the mask, the gloves, a red slicker; no identifying details, no sure guesses of height or weight. As if he'd been abducted by a ghost or an idea. Kelly could picture someone more solid but the imagined man wore a face born from movies, crime procedurals.

In the notebook he wrote what he had not told the heavy detective: How before he'd returned to the basement, he had tried to pretend he'd never seen the boy. And how when he returned it was for a moment the blankness he'd seen.

He wrote, *The two ways of seeing the room: the scrapper and the salvor.*

The boy was screaming the first time Kelly touched him. He couldn't get the boy to stop. He had tried to pick the boy up because he couldn't see the cuffs around his ankles.

The cuffs caught and the boy screamed again.

Kelly had sawed the handcuff chain but he barely remembered doing it. By then the boy had almost stopped crying. Maybe there wasn't any sound except for the scraping pull and push of the saw, the breaths in between.

Kelly wrote: *The night of the first snow. The night I found the boy. The beginning of my involvement in the case but not the beginning of the case. When had the boy been reported missing? Two days earlier. When had the boy actually gone missing? The day before that. The entire case three days long, the crime cut short by my entrance. My last night as a scavenger. I must have known but I went back for my tools. While the boy waited in the locked truck, down in the dark of the pit.*

The facts of the case, the scenes of the crime: The boy's school, the house where the boy was kept and watched. The car that ferried

the boy. The man in the red slicker. The accumulation of mat-
tresses and foam and handcuffs. The purchase of tools. The lock
on the basement door. The coming and going from the house and
how had no one seen him coming and going. Easy. The complete
absence of neighbors. The total lack of community. The man in the
red slicker and the boy, adrift in the zone, waiting for the first to
find the second.

The confidence it took to take a boy. The confidence it took to park
right in front of the school. Confidence or else direst need. And if the
man who kidnapped the boy wore a mask, then when the boy first
saw my face he must have thought I was the kidnapper, carrying the
same wants into that basement.

What if this wasn't the first time. Then what happened to the
other boys. Then what would have happened to the boy if I hadn't
found him. And if there is this depravity what other depravities
exist, wherever no good man is looking.

What is the responsibility of the good man in the zone?

Is detective *a role or an action. Is* the good man *an action too.*

Can I take on the role of the detective and carry it to its comple-
tion.

Can pretending to be a good man one day make me a good man.

Outside, a great rain filled the city, overwhelmed the sew-
ers. Another hundred thousand homes went without power
and today there would be no work and in the dark of the apartment Kelly smoked and listened to the thunder announce
the lightning and he wrote in the notebook and when he got
bored he did one hundred push-ups, one hundred sit-ups,
sets of one hundred squats, lunges, leg lifts. He thrilled at his
body in motion, his body hurting. He was strong from the

zone but he knew he could be stronger. In high school he'd put on muscle fast, lifted his way into the starting lineup, the top of his weight class. The pride of his father's coaching. County wrestling champion one year, state champ the next. Once he'd been able to run for miles without tiring and he wondered if he could make himself do it again.

5

THE PHONE RANG AND KELLY didn't recognize the number. The phone rang again and he let it go to voicemail. He waited for the beep and then he pressed the button, put the phone to his ear, heard the boy's voice. He listened to the message, listened to it again. Five minutes later, the first text arrived: THIS IS DANIEL CALL ME

Then: THIS IS DANIEL I HAVE MY OWN PHONE

SO I DON'T GET LOST AGAIN

THIS IS DANIEL

Kelly had given the boy his phone number and the boy had put it to use. What could Kelly write back? The one thing he knew.

THIS IS KELLY.

They were strangers but now they would be something else. Kelly couldn't pretend he didn't know what a bad idea was because here they were at the start of one, a mistake amassing potential.

THIS IS DANIEL

WHATS YOUR ADDRESS

I WANT TO SEE YOU TOO

Kelly unbuttoned the top button of his shirt, smeared the sweat from his neck and chest. He put his thumbs to the screen, typed his new address. The invitation had become a trap. He was the sole suspect in the kidnapping and he had shown who he was: someone who wanted the boy, who couldn't keep from asking for more.

HOW WILL YOU GET HERE.

I'LL COME GET YOU.

ARE YOU HOME.

ARE YOU HOME.

ARE YOU HOME.

An hour passed before the phone beeped again. Kelly went to the intercom beside the door and he buzzed the boy in, then opened the door to find the boy in his school uniform, the blue jacket and the striped tie, the khaki pants over clean white sneakers. He wanted to ask the boy why he'd come but it wasn't the right way to start.

Kelly asked, How did you get here?

My brother brought me, the boy said. I told him this was a friend's house.

Okay, Kelly said. Come in. This way.

Kelly pointed to a chair on the other side of the room, took his own seat on the couch. The boy sat where he was told. He had a quiet politeness in his movements Kelly had seen before, known himself, the boy moving as if afraid to make a mistake. The notebook was on the coffee table, folded open. *The case*, Kelly was calling it. *The case notes*. Kelly picked up the notebook, folded the cover around the spirals. The television was tuned to a documentary about whales, whale songs. The narrator claimed whales could recognize voices through a thousand miles of black water but military outposts and underwater fiber-optic cables disrupted the songs, confused the whales, and limited the range of their speech. The sound was below the limits of human hearing and so it took special equipment to know what had been lost. The cost of progress, above the earth and below it and upon the air and in the sea.

Kelly muted the television. The boy asked if he could have something to drink and Kelly appreciated knowing what to do next. There wasn't anything in the refrigerator for a boy so he filled a glass of water from the tap. He had plenty of food left from the Christian women and when he asked the boy if he was hungry he thought it was better if the boy said yes.

But then the boy's voice spoke from closer than Kelly expected.

Kelly turned around and found the boy in the kitchen with him. A mere foot of separation breathing between their bodies. Kelly set the table, retrieved the last of a deli tray from the fridge, a plastic container of potato salad. A bottle of mustard, a jar of mayonnaise. Salt and pepper. He only had enough dishes for two people but there were only the two of them eating.

Kelly asked, How old are you?

Twelve, the boy said. Until next summer.

Twelve, thirteen. What had changed for Kelly in the gap between those years. The arrival of the new body that brought him further under his father's gaze, bought admission into the gym and the mat room and his father's coaching.

Kelly thought he wasn't hungry but he knew better than to have another drink on top of the two he'd had before the boy arrived. The boy grinned above his sandwich and Kelly's appetite awoke. He piled more meat on his plate, more cheese than the bread needed. The boy finished his sandwich first, excused himself from the table. Again the politeness but when the boy returned to the living room he sat on the far end of the couch instead of the chair. The whale documentary was still playing and the boy picked up the remote, fingered the mute, returned volume to the room. The boy watched the whales and when Kelly wasn't watching the boy they watched the whales together.

All slap and splash atop the surface, quiet consumption underneath. Nothing was bigger than the biggest of their number, and their only predators were men and giant squid and other whales. On-screen a whale carcass appeared on the seafloor, lit by an unmanned submersible. Thirty-five tons of gray whale a mile below the surface, crawling with life: the whale had fed off the ocean and the ocean would feed off the whale. The narrator intoned the stages, the eras of the mobile scavenger, the enrichment opportunist, the sulfophilic, spoke over footage of eel-shaped hagfish swimming through the whale fall, through the fallen timber of the bones: Two years of soft-tissue consumption, one hundred thirty pounds of blubber and muscle and organ consumed every day. Then years of unimaginable creatures colonizing what was left. Then bacteria breaking down lipids in the bones for fifty more years, a hundred. The bacteria not needing oxygen to live, not expelling carbon dioxide. Sulfate in, hydrogen

sulfide out. Mussels and clams living on chemosymbiotic bacteria. Limpets and snails grazing bacterial mats, biofilms.

There were many places any one animal couldn't live but
nowhere no animal would not. All these animals Kelly had
never known: the squat lobster, more amphipods, impossible
mollusks. Zombie worms born without digestive tracts. A
name for everything, no matter how strange. So many hun-
dreds of thousands of dead whales crashed into the ocean
floor they created a migratory path, a way for organisms to
move, evolve. If you were a single cell wide, how many cities
might one whale comprise, falling blackly through the black
water? Another exclusion zone filled with rot, shared by other
scavengers. A bowhead whale could live two hundred years,
and one hundred years after it died it might at last disappear
from the earth, dispersed entirely. Off the shore there were
carcasses of American whales as old as America and what did
this say for this past century, for what was man-made and
had lasted only half as long.

When the show ended the boy stood from the couch and
retrieved his backpack, paused by the door. He was nervous
but there was something brave in him and Kelly recognized
this too. He had come through his own troubles with something similar, an unspoken belief nothing worse would happen next.

Kelly asked, Where are you going? It's a long way home.

I'm not going home, the boy said. I'm going to my father's.

Now the boy began to speak, slowly, carefully, his backpack
on his shoulders. At first the boy hadn't noticed his father had

moved out. In the first month of the separation, his father had come back every night for dinner, stayed listening to records in the living room until the boy was in bed. He wasn't there for breakfast but he'd always left for work before sunrise. He'd realized the father was gone only when the father's things went missing. The books stayed on the shelves because the father didn't read but one day there was hardly any music left in the house. Certain kinds of food stopped being stocked. The boy hadn't said anything. He didn't mention every obvious problem he saw. His parents had separated before what happened but afterward they'd reunited for the photo op, made nice for the cameras. The appearance of normalcy for the return of their boy. Now the cameras were gone and the boy's father was back in his apartment, didn't have to pretend to show up for dinner.

This was why the parents hadn't understood he'd gone missing. They weren't speaking and both of them had thought the other had the boy.

I'll drive you, Kelly said. He gathered his keys, found a ball cap and a sweatshirt. He checked his watch. On the way to the truck he called the girl with the limp, offered her a time, then adjusted his arrival into the further future, said all estimates were dependent on weather and traffic. She heard the truck start, asked him where he was going first.

He gave her the details: The boy had come to him. They had spent some hours together. He was taking the boy home.

She said, I don't know if that's a good idea.

Be careful, she said. I hope you know what you're doing.

He gave her the details but what did the details mean. She

was the soul of understatement but maybe she understood. Something had begun in the basement of the blue house and this was how it continued. He hung up the phone, maneuvered the truck out of the neighborhood and onto the freeway, moved the truck into the left lane, kept his foot on the gas. There was a joy to going fast and when a grin broke over his face he looked over at the boy, hoping to share it.

The boy's face crumpled. He cradled his backpack in his lap, hugged it against his chest. He wasn't crying yet but maybe he would. Kelly reached out a hand, put it on the boy's shaking leg.

I'm sorry, Kelly said. I forgot you'd been in the truck. I forgot how it might feel to be in it again.

He waited until the boy was calm again and then he removed his shaking hand, put it back against the wheel. The questions should have been hard to ask but somehow Kelly got them out. The truth at higher and higher speeds, acquiring motion, dopplering through the night.

He said, You don't have to tell me anything you don't want to.

Yes, I do, the boy said. Because you were there too.

What the boy remembered hadn't changed. There was no more or no less story than before, when he told it to the heavy detective.

The boy said, My brother was supposed to pick me up in front of my school. We don't go to the same school anymore but his school excuses first so he's supposed to be there waiting for me when I get out. But my brother didn't come and then there were less cars waiting.

My mother used to pick me up but now she was looking for work. My brother used to be late all the time but now he didn't always show.

I didn't have a cell phone then, the boy said. I have one now.

The boy said, He isn't my real brother. My parents aren't my real parents but I know you know. My parents are separated and they don't talk and my brother uses their two houses as a way to never go home, by saying he's always at the other house.

He hasn't been in our family long, the boy said, putting his head against the steamed window. The boy was quiet for a mile, two miles. An eerie silence complemented his calm speech, too controlled for his age. Snow fell over the pavement, obscured the lines marking the edge of the road. As the miles passed the boy began to speak again. He said he wasn't telling Kelly anything he hadn't told the police.

The boy wasn't confused. This was a repetition of the facts.

He had been waiting for his brother.

He waited until there wasn't anyone else waiting.

When the brown car arrived, the boy thought it was his brother's or else he never would have been so close to the curb. The car was the right color and make and model, the right year, a car like the brother drove.

The boy didn't know if the man in the car was trying to take him or just anyone there waiting. The boy opened the back door, the boy climbed in, sat down, closed the door, and buckled his seat belt. The boy said, The whole time I was doing it, I could see it wasn't my brother's car. It didn't smell like cigarettes and pot. It wasn't littered with fast-food wrappers.

It was spotless and there was no smell and as I buckled my seat belt I saw the man who was driving it wasn't my brother. He was shorter than my brother and he was wearing a red hooded slicker. In the car the man wasn't wearing a mask. It was the only time he wasn't. He wasn't wearing a mask but he was wearing gloves and as I slid into the backseat he pulled his red hood up.

The boy said, The sound of the child safety locks.

He hadn't meant to sit down. He hadn't meant to close the door. He'd been tired or uncareful. Habit took over and by the time alarm arrived it was too late.

Kelly knew this mode too, the maturity in the boy's voice, the flatness of affect: the shock that outlasted the trauma. What the boy said he remembered most wasn't the fear but the confusion. The car was the same car his brother drove. The same color exterior, the same patterned fabric inside. At first the boy had thought the brother's car had been stolen. For a moment, he'd worried about the brother. He couldn't understand why the car thief would pick him up from school. He hadn't realized yet it wasn't the car the thief had stolen but him.

The boy said, The man told me to unbuckle my seat belt, to lie down on the floor. Down where my feet were supposed to go.

I used to call it the pit, Kelly said. When I was a kid.

Yes, the boy said. The pit.

The boy said in the basement he had been frightened of worse but worse had not come. The man made him strip naked so he wouldn't escape, but after he was naked he was given a blanket, allowed to cover himself. The boy was naked beneath the blanket but the man who took him didn't touch him. The man wore a hooded red rain slicker and the man didn't take the slicker off while he sat in the chair beside the bed or while he fed the boy or while he came and went.

Three days passed. The boy not molested or tortured or killed.

The boy merely kept.

Kept and *watched*.

Kelly had entered the low room too. There was *the boy before* and *the boy after*, and at the boy's suggestion he remembered his own feeling of being split by entering the room: into *the scrapper*, perhaps, or else *the salvor*, two new ways of naming this second self he'd perhaps always known, recognized at last after a lifetime of mirrors.

THE VOLUNTEERS WELCOMED KELLY INTO their fold, pressed one of their orange jerseys into his hands, then pushed him to his knees and pulled it over his head. The men laid their hands upon him and they prayed for protection and his wisdom and grace in securing their city until Kelly was one of their number. The taking on of new duties, how immediately the office weighed upon him: He had not intended this. He had not intended any more than the acquisition of the uniform. A mode of access and anonymity, a man dressed up behind a symbol.

The watch met in schools and in churches and in bars, in backyards in the summer and in community halls in the winter, and wherever they met there would be the smell of barbecue and baked beans, piles of coleslaw and bread, all surrounded by men in their orange t-shirts, their orange jerseys and orange caps. They prayed before they ate, they ate before they invited the week's speaker to the podium, and then Kelly was pointed out, made an example: This was the good man, the speaker said, in this bad world.

The speaker said this was the week a mother flushed her premature newborn down the toilet, then changed her mind, calling emergency services in time for firemen to cut the bawling baby loose from the pipe.

This was the week a woman beat her husband with a bat while he slept, too drunk to defend himself, as she had once been too afraid.

This was the week the homicide rate eclipsed the previous year's and there were still six weeks left in the year.

This was the week the mayor cut the police force again, expanded the border of the zone another few blocks, darkened another row of streetlights, abandoned another portion of the city. The volunteers had dedicated themselves to keeping those streets safe when the police could not but they couldn't hide their dismay, let their voices cry out in anger, the opposite of hallelujah, the cursing opposite of giving thanks.

This was a bad year, the speaker said. But this was also the year when Kelly saved a boy.

Like Lot in Sodom, he said. The good man who tries to rescue his city.

Afterward men swarmed to clap Kelly on the back or shake his hand or else they offered some more intricate greeting Kelly couldn't follow or reciprocate. He had done what they had dreamed of doing: he had stopped a crime, he had saved a life. A child endangered, a victim rescued, a hero in their midst. They asked him what it had been like to carry the boy out of captivity and he said he didn't know how to explain it. They wanted a story about a hero but he didn't know how to say he hadn't had the kind of feelings they wanted to hear. He didn't know how to say that what he thought he had felt was *responsible*.

He couldn't tell them about the *scrapper*, about the *salvor*, about the two voices he heard whenever he worked on the case notes. How there was a voice that wanted to punish the guilty. How there was a voice that wanted to protect the innocent.

Or not voices, exactly. Not voices but modes of thought, systems of organization, suggestions for action. Actions themselves, actions in waiting.

There were other support groups for other needs. After hours in a high school classroom, Kelly sat in a circle of chairs and listened again. This time the circle contained mostly women but it was the men he'd come to hear. When it was Kelly's turn, he wanted to speak but the words wouldn't come. He opened and closed his mouth, choked out a sound. The words wouldn't come. *My father. My father, who never took anything he didn't ask for first.* What had Kelly done to hold the words back. What would it take to reverse the damage. He shook his head, studied his hands. An older man touched his knee. The older man had been through something terrible, had done something equally bad. Kelly pitied the older man, the absolute safety of pitying in others what you wouldn't pity in yourself. Kelly wanted to say what happened in his youth was worse because it had not left a mark, because it had not hurt, because he had only touched, not been touched. Because he had been asked to do it and he had agreed and even if it wasn't fair—even if he had been too young to know better— even then what had happened to him had happened out of his own free will.

My father, so big upon his bones. All thick flesh, so that even where he was fat he was hard. In those years Kelly had believed in a world where you could be forgiven for every worst thing but later he threw away his rosary, revoked his right to those comforts, and so the world in which Kelly had passed on his hurt was a world in which his crime would not be forgiven, could not be redeemed or righted.

When he had paid for his vasectomy the nurses made him sign extra forms because of his age, because he was young and unmarried and childless. They asked him again if he was sure.

Yes, he said. He knew he would never have children of his own. Because he would not risk it.

But then the southern woman, who already had the only child she wanted. Then her boy.

How at first he had felt nothing. How he celebrated the nothing, the future he thought it promised. They bought their house, they moved in together, and for a long time nothing bad happened to anyone, for a long time when Kelly looked at her boy he had told himself he wanted to feel only love, something fatherly forming in the accumulation of days.

The collapse changed everything. The loss of his employment, their house. The constrained summer months they shared a single motel room, man and woman and child, when too often it was only the boy's mother who left the room, who had her insufficient work to take her away.

The collapse changed everything but what if it merely sped the inevitable.

Just watch me, he had said, in the hot dark of the motel room, the night he and the boy were alone for the last time. After Kelly and the southern woman had fought again, after the woman took her purse and her car keys but not her boy. And how by then Kelly had loved the boy. How Kelly thought he would never hurt the boy but in his worst moment he knew he had somehow not known the boy's name.

How in his worst moment he had said, Boy, just watch, but the boy had not wanted to watch.

What happened next had not taken long. When it was over Kelly grunted with relief, some clenching softening so fast it hurt, like the aftermath of a cramp. But then the horror of what he had done, what he had set his whole life against doing.

To have for so long restrained yourself from every urge and to have it buy you nothing. To still have to be yourself, everywhere you go.

The older man told Kelly this was a safe space but Kelly shook his head again. There were no safe spaces except those you made yourself. Safety could not be granted. Safety was the absence of anyone stronger or weaker. And always there was someone stronger or weaker, someone greater than, less than. The only true safety was the deepest kind of loneliness and for a time Kelly had chosen it. Now he was choosing something else, Daniel and Jackie, the found boy, the girl with the limp. Now the world's every angle would be sharp with danger, for him and from him, until the case was closed. Until he found the watcher, the man in the red slicker. Until the boy was as safe as Kelly wanted him, as saved.

He gained another five pounds, another ten, stopped weighing himself, promised himself it was temporary, tried to compensate with more calisthenics on the worn carpet of his living room. He drank out of the cupboard and he ate out of the freezer, cleared the least-wanted remnants of Christian charity. There was a limit to how much pasta salad a man could crave but he passed the limit and kept going. Whenever he was alone and he couldn't sleep he sat down at the table, clicked open his pen and began to write, scrawled bits of memory, details about the house where he'd found the boy, the low room inside.

He'd traded away distraction but he had obsession and so who missed it. He started bringing the police scanner in from the truck with him every night, and if the girl with the limp was away at work or in her own bed, then he listened to the scanner in his, fell asleep to the addresses of gunshots, arson, domestic disturbance, animals abandoned, abused. Every human horror reduced to a number, a flattening of fear and disgust into numeric code. Names repeated, last name, first name, middle initial. Say again. License-plate numbers, makes and models. Say again, say again. The ringing in his ears meant Kelly struggled to separate meaning from sounds. The litany of the nighttime city. The squelch and the static obscuring speech, every word so distorted the casual listener might make a mistake.

He was more tight-lipped than anyone else but he still worried he might begin to leak his secrets whenever he shared an afternoon with the boy, whenever the girl with the limp came home to find him drunk and reeling, chair to wall to floor, bed to morning. When the boy wasn't with Kelly he was with his parents in their separate homes, or else with the brother, who sometimes didn't go to school, staying home while the father worked, while the mother worked too, preparing for a life without the father's income, his grandparents' support. The boy put Kelly's name to use, said it into the telephone, when he answered the door, when Kelly picked him up after school. The boy said it was easy to confuse the parents, to do as the brother did to make room between them. The boy's parents were more careful now but the only person they ever checked with was the boy. His phone rang constantly and the boy told them he was wherever they expected him to be.

The boy's brother treated him rough too. It wasn't the first time they saw each other when the boy told Kelly this part of the story but almost. From the moment of his adoption the brother had pinched the boy, twisted the skin on his arms when out of sight of their parents, when in the room they shared, in the twin beds for boys who were not twins. Don't tell anyone, the boy said the brother said. Or else.

Kelly asked, Is that all? Is that the worst of it?

The boy looked away, covered half his face with one hand, tugged at his ear with the other. Kelly tried to take the boy's hand away from his mouth but stopped when the boy recoiled. The boy and the brother hadn't been in the same family long but already Kelly thought the boy flinched where he hadn't flinched before.

You can tell me, Kelly said. What happens next?

Kelly saw the boy often had to prepare himself to speak. The boy wanted to share what was happening to him but Kelly thought it could take all afternoon for the boy to gather the force of a sentence. He didn't push and the next time they were together in the apartment the boy began again, said, It's easier to talk to you, and so Kelly said, Then talk.

Day by day Kelly felt a rough and growing affection for the boy, a swelling knocking about his chest. Sometimes Kelly woke in the night and walked his featureless hallway into the living room, looking for the boy even though the boy couldn't be there. If the boy was there the television would have been on, the boy would be sitting on the floor with his homework spread across the carpet. There would be sound and light surrounding his presence, instead of only the standby hum of the television, the louder drone of the refrigerator. Only voices in the night. Kelly listened to his neighbors, the sounds of scuffling feet, of television and radio, the murmur of their conversations, the noises of sex and kitchen, the huffing slap of bodies and the clatter of dishes. Whenever he was alone he found himself pulling his phone from his pocket to answer phantom vibrations, imagined missed calls. The boy had never spent the night but Kelly knew he would let the boy if the boy asked. It was another bad idea but Kelly was full of them. The important thing was not to ask, not to let your need be known.

6

YOUR NAME WAS NOT IMPORTANT but you believed one day an inquiry would begin, an organized speculation of detectives and reporters asking *who was he* and *who was the real him* and *how was a man like him made*. To refuse these interrogators you scrubbed the name clean, restarted yourself, removed all of the old life's worldly tarnish. You had a past but in the present it was only this you who remained, this you and a boy, one boy at a time. Or so it had been, before the intruder.

At birth you had been given up before being given a name, any name.

Later came the first name, the one ill fit for the child you'd become. Then your second name, the one you gave yourself. You hadn't wanted a last name but the judge wouldn't let you refuse one. The use of a middle initial was a matter of deep ambivalence to the court but at the last minute you chose an X, made to leave no box unmarked.

Someday reporters and detectives would repeat the name chosen, its simple syllables, its known unknownness a cipher standing in place of a man. They would debate the deepening of the mystery by the middle initial standing for nothing, the X in the middle of a name whose whole stood for nothing either, not even to you.

The boy was a phrase that was a moving target. There had been a number of boys but you were careful not to think too often in specifics. The given name: mere words elevated to description, to knowledge of what a thing was. How all the power resided in the giver. How without such a gift an individual could be made a type, how the type specimen could be returned to the herd.

When you were a boy you had been nameless and now you unnamed each boy.

Anonymous then, anonymous now. You were not a name but a watcher, dedicated to a philosophy of watching, of inaction except for where action was necessary, and there was no way to put a boy into a house except by the taking. What else couldn't be omitted? Food for the boy, food and drink. Whatever could be fed from a bowl, served with a spoon at room temperature. Even for yourself you wouldn't make anything more complicated, couldn't see the point of intricacy.

You read but you were not good with books. Every written word was an abstraction instead of the thing. What use were articles, conjunctions, prepositions. The way an adjective or an adverb revealed nothing except a wrong-named object or action. But who could know all the right names against the vagueness of the world, the insufficient exactness of nouns. You didn't want a better system but rather a removal of all systems, the reduction of complex things to their simplest parts. What you wanted was the irreducibility of a centermost point, occupied by a single set of figures. The hollow inside, the blank at the heart of mystery.

The few people who saw you thought you were a mute or else slow, but you could talk, think for yourself. Only in the manner of your choosing. Only at a time of your making. You would talk only to the next boy, vowed silence against all others. Until then you revealed nothing. No one would ever know your names for the gone boys. The story others told about you would not be the story of the boys. For it was always the killer who was remembered, never the killed.

So grandiose: *the killer, the killed.*

You didn't want to hurt the boys. Not until there was no other choice. And with the last boy, the intruder had made sure you hadn't had to hurt anyone. The intruder saved the boy and also he saved you, because when you were finished with the boy you hadn't had to hurt the boy to set you both free.

THE PAYCHECKS DIDN'T COME IN the mail. The office was at the front of a warehouse, a small rectangular room with a glass partition over wood paneling, separating the receptionist's desk from the chairless waiting area. The receptionist was bleached blonde, tanned brown, embraced a certain brand of department-store professionalism. He could stand there grinning all day and still he'd never be invited past the glass, the locked door.

He opened the check in the truck, read the number lower than what he'd expected. The reductive mathematics of taxes, Social Security, Medicare. The bank was closed by the time he arrived but there was an ATM outside. In the dusk and the falling snow he pulled the new card from his wallet, followed the screen's instructions prompt to prompt. He forgot he needed a pen to sign the check, jammed the CANCEL button until the screen reset. There was a pen in the truck, clipped to the case notes. He found it in the glove box, then shut the truck door, turned to walk back.

In three separate movements Kelly saw the gun, the hand holding the gun, the man who owned the hand.

He did what the man with the gun said. At his urging Kelly opened his wallet to reveal small bills ordered by denomination, some faded receipts. Back at the machine the man with the gun lurked out of the camera's eye, told Kelly where he wanted him to stand while he worked the keypad, depositing the check, guessing at his daily limit. The mugger kept a stride's worth of distance but occasionally he closed it for effect, pressing the barrel of the pistol into Kelly's back, where Kelly could barely feel it through the thickness of his coat.

Each time the nub of the pistol's barrel touched him Kelly felt a diminishment of effect. He could get used to anything, even a pistol snug against the small of his back. He withdrew another hundred dollars, watched the worth of his time pass into the mugger's hands.

Now your keys, the man with the gun said. Hand them over.

No more, Kelly said. You've taken what I have for you to take.

Kelly turned. The man with the gun raised the weapon. Kelly wasn't confused about whether or not the pistol was loaded but he didn't think the man would fire it. The bank parking lot wasn't the center of the zone. There were rules here, an expectation of law, punishment. They stood a couple blocks outside the most desperate geography, and maybe distance meant everything. It was dark and snowing but there were cars driving by on the avenue. Someone would witness whatever happened next unless the man timed it right. The police would come. Kelly had to believe this. The girl with the limp would send them, they would come by her voice.

Kelly laughed and the man with the gun started. Kelly remembered the school gymnasium, other incidents in other cities. How once the fight began there might be no stopping him. He took a step forward. The mugger's face swapped expressions. At closer range Kelly could see the details were shaking.

Kelly said, You're what I knew you would be.

The mugger spoke, his voice shifting. What are you talking about.

Kelly said, I would rather you were anyone else. Anyone different.

A surprise, said Kelly. That's what I wish you were.

I'm not giving you my truck, he said. My truck is my life.

Kelly took another step forward and whatever sometimes happened to his heart happened again. All his blood gushing around and he could track every singing pint. Kelly's face dropped its blankness for another expression, something sporting. He told himself it wasn't the color of the man that made him feel this way. There were other factors. Dress and speech and something else, something learned. Greater than, less than. The beliefs of the town named like poison.

They were both sweating, breathing hard through the waiting.

Get the fuck out of here, Kelly said, with such force he thought the man with the gun would run. Instead the mugger slowly lowered the weapon, put it back into his pocket. He zipped his jacket, pulled the hood up, put it back down. It was a cold night but not that cold. Kelly waited next to the truck, fingers clenched around the keys, the metal carving his palms. He waited in the falling snow until the man with the gun had walked two blocks, three blocks, then around a corner. The pounding in Kelly's chest continued, a fist trying to escape its slatted cage. He thought he wanted the feeling to last.

At the bar that night a man called another woman a cunt and the girl with the limp was there to tap the man on the shoulder, to register her complaint. She didn't mind cursing but she wouldn't put up with other kinds of comments, certain kinds of objectification. Her rude body had made her an object of curiosity and she had no tolerance for unwelcome comment. What was happening to her was vulgar but it was also hers.

To the man, she said, You can say what you want but don't say it around me.

When the man called her a cunt too, then Kelly took her by the arm and dragged her from the room, leaving their drinks unfinished, their bar tab unpaid. Some people loved to talk and talk. Kelly didn't default to the right words but if he talked slow enough he might say fewer of the wrong ones. On the way back to her place he tried to grope after the handle of the day's story, the place to open it up, let it out. He was embarrassed by his victimhood. He knew he was angry but he was having trouble feeling more than some numb portion of the rage. He could see the man with the gun if he let his eyes close. She caught him blinking too much and asked if he was okay. He shifted his expression into a smile, made small talk about the new job he hated. The worst part about keeping a secret was anything going wrong seemed to be about the secret. But so little revolved around his gravity, held an orbit. The case was his secret, the mugger too. The latest in a long line of things he had done, would do, had had done to him.

The confusion of past and present and future. He didn't have to share. This was their agreement. They believed there was a certain kindness to keeping yourself to yourself.

He hadn't wanted to reveal his nature in front of her but after she was asleep in her own bed he left the apartment, drove back. He liked the bar and the bartender and wouldn't do anything within those windowless walls but that didn't mean he couldn't wait in the parking lot, huffing steam into the frozen air. When the breather of the insult stepped out toward his car, then Kelly was there—or else not Kelly but the scrapper. The action did not require a weapon. The object of the lesson was instruction and if instruction required infliction it was something he could add with his hands. The language of the bully, put to better uses: the sharp inhales and exhales, the straining lungs following a landed punch, a right hook he'd been missing throwing, the way skull and knuckles split the bruises. How long since he'd last felt this way. The wordless voice of the fistfight, the meaty thudding of flesh on flesh, how even if Kelly had to be hurt too he would never cry out, would keep punching and kicking and dragging the other down into the gravel and the broken concrete and the dust and the dirt.

THE FIRST BOY YOU WATCHED only for short spans, walking twenty paces behind him on the street along the path from school to home, from three thirty to almost four in the afternoon. A pattern so obvious you waited every day for someone else to notice. You thought you craved the voice of a teacher, a school aide, a concerned parent, the *bleep-bleep* of a querying siren and the red-and-blue splash of lights. The tight stretch of action, the gathered potential, the desired flush of shame, suspicion: it walked with you, it walked you down the street after the boy.

The more you watched the more visible you became. Every hour spent walking behind the child was another chance someone might notice. A police officer, a neighbor. A passerby, a bystander. But the child himself would be the first to see you for who you were, although you didn't imagine this possibility at first. This was another thing you learned only in the low rooms, each a new space carefully chosen, prepared, soundproofed, and locked, one room for one boy. On the surface, each face required you to separate one expression from another, from the endless variety of human emotion, but faces were different in private than in public. Faces were different in the dark.

You left clumsiness behind in the first few takings. There

was a lesson in the early mistakes, prompting the cultivation of a care you had never before exhibited. You hid the taking from yourself but you couldn't hide the preparation. The soundproofing and sequester. You liked the houses with names on them the best: names beside doorways, on mailboxes, anywhere. Scrawled into the back of closets.

You became more complex with every taking. In the past you had acted without premeditation but now all your life was premeditated. The difference between the now thought and the then thought: you hadn't known the monochrome of your movements until the first watching busted the seams of the world, filling it with color, movement, a low hum becoming a buzz between the ears. This ringing was what it meant to be a person. You hadn't known, hadn't ever imagined, the dim world could be made so loudly beautiful merely by having someone to watch, to make watch you back.

HE HADN'T HIT THE HEAVY bag in ten years but after the fight in the parking lot he went looking for a gym, somewhere to train. The morning after his first workout he woke up unable to straighten his arms but before work he went back for more, tried to put the same soreness in his legs. It took a long time to lodge the feeling where he wanted it, so close to the bones. His body was strong from work but he wanted it to be stronger. He winced around the apartment, made breakfast hunched over with his arms curled up near his chest. He contorted his body in the shower, found an angle to brush his teeth where the burning in his biceps went away. Dressing became a supreme act of will. He'd done too much but he wanted to do more. The bench press, the lat pulldown, the curls and tricep extensions, these were the beginning, what he remembered without effort, what he could do alone without needing to ask for a spot.

He was the strongest he'd ever been but he wanted to find his limits. He lifted in the mornings and after he lifted he worked, swung the sledge and worked the shovel, drove busted drywall downstairs in wheelbarrows. When he went to bed he suffered through the angry stress of repetition, the lactic stretch of a body growing out of strained muscles, and after the first week he switched gyms, found somewhere cheaper, deeper in the zone, where he wasn't wanted. The manager said he was welcome to try but he wouldn't last. He referred Kelly back to the gym he had left but Kelly shook his head. He wanted to be held apart. He told himself the will to fight wasn't about the color of a man but the otherness and he didn't know how this was different, only that to him it was. He wouldn't have said these things aloud, would have denied them if accused. The case notes had started calling for a man like the mugger and this place allowed him to fight such men. To align his aggression with the image in his mind.

The other boxers' tattoos were different than the tattoos he'd known. He didn't know the subtleties of their speech, the nuanced syntax of their slang. He couldn't always beat the other men—in the beginning, he never could—but he could fight against their difference, could throw himself against what he told himself he was not. In the past, sparring had focused his instincts, forced him to act differently than in bar parking lots. Beyond the greater strength and training of his opponents he was also at a forgotten disadvantage, deprived of many of his oldest tactics, the wrestler's grips and tricks he could use in the gravel and the dirt but not here, between the yellow lights and the cracking mats covering the floor. Out in the world he had counted on the other person having more to lose than he did or at least believe he did. In the ring there were safeguards in the way of total loss and so his pretense of fearlessness had less strength.

These men stood naked to the waist in their padded helmets and padded gloves and they put those gloves together and they spoke their prayers aloud, gave the familiar words new inflections. He'd grown up among people who mumbled their professions of faith, who sang hymns as if a monotone made the sweetest music. These men craved bravery and victory, forgiveness and salvation. They said that to perfect what you were given was to become mighty in your gift. They said a great fighter was a man who loved the body God had made, who loved it with bench presses and curls and squat thrusts and leg presses and the impact of fist on flesh.

The men at the gym had their methods but in the zone he had built his body in another way. It was not a temple. Or if it was then it was one more beautiful for being ruined. His uneven heart, an ulcerous stomach. Manual labor had set predictable pops and creaks into his joints, the telling music of early onset arthritis. He had forgotten the origins of most of his scars but he knew they spoke to other men, suggested a certain hardness. Or else bad luck, some idiocy in the way of his quitting.

Trainers arranged bouts by weight class but after the soreness receded Kelly signed up to spar with whoever would agree. He didn't have the right shoes but you could buy shoes. He wrapped his hands and put in a mouthguard. He'd had to buy equipment but he had the reward money, the promise of more paychecks. He didn't want all this protection but this was the price of arranged fighting.

He put his hands on men his own size but he preferred heavier fighters, the density of their bodies bowing below his blows, each jab like punching a statue made of meat. When their fists connected with his skull he heard memories realigning into new spaces. The shattering of old logic, his heartbeat rising as the speed of thought slowed, consciousness fading not in a subtle turndown but in a series of pulses, a drop in ability ten or twenty or thirty percent at a time.

They weren't supposed to go this far but their honor system said it was up to him to stop the sparring, to wave off the bigger and stronger man. He never gave up, never gave in. There could be blood in his eyes or in his mouth and then he believed he heard it sloshing between his ringing ears, in the low cavities of the body. When he couldn't breathe he spit out his mouthguard to clear his airway, gestured with his gloves that he was coming back for more.

In the case notes the story got more determined as time passed but maybe it remained a fiction. His own past often faded and cracked open, let in white space between fragments of sensible time. If he found he knew too much he stopped trusting what he thought he knew. Some of the pages of the notebook contained drawings, smeared sketches. Some drawings were of the house where he'd found the boy, its doorways and staircases, its blue siding and peaked roof. When Kelly next returned to the notebook he found several sketches of a suspect. He didn't know what the kidnapper looked like and the boy remembered only the mask watching, the rough handling of gloved hands, the red rain slicker—Kelly didn't necessarily remember drawing the sketches but there they were, rendered with his amateurish pen. The faces in the sketches wouldn't have moved anyone else but they moved him: the sketches were of the mugger or else, sometimes, the brother, who Kelly had not met, who the boy would no longer speak of, who he would no longer blame for the bruises Kelly spotted pressed into his upper arms.

Kelly thought the tragedy of love wasn't that we weren't loved but that we weren't loved by the people we'd been given. The problem with seeking revenge was that if he couldn't find the one he was seeking, then who might get hurt instead.

One night, Kelly parked the truck down the street from the green house, the only lit rooms for blocks. In the darkness it would be harder to see out the windows than to see in, and from the far edge of the yard he watched the mother setting the table for a dinner for three. The mother's car was in the driveway but the brother's was gone and Kelly wondered who she was expecting, the older son or the husband. When no one else came he watched from the dark as she called the boy in to dinner, as the boy sat down in the bright room and ate his food silently, eyes cast to the task. The mother's mouth moved but what was she saying. If she was asking questions the boy didn't answer.

Kelly flexed his muscles, hopped from foot to foot to keep warm in the black and lightless air. He was starting to get his step back, remembering how to keep his torso and his head in a constant bob, an unpredictable weave. The painter with the big hands had taught him to fight by never taking the same step twice but Kelly thought a better tactic was to broadcast his every intention and still come out ahead. For now he was making a case. He was glad the boy came to visit. He thought no matter how long he spent with the boy he would never want to hurt him. He was aware of what lurked within and he had made moves to cordon that action from thought, present want. He would stretch his life beyond the mistakes of his past, and for this the boy was both the test and the answer.

The gym posted its rules on every wall. There was a maximum number of times you were allowed to spar in a week but no one kept close count. Most of the others sparred at sixty or eighty percent of full speed but if they held back against him he surged into the space of their hesitance. His head snapped back under jab after jab; in the locker-room mirror, his belly and ribs looked punched in, bruises sprawled over scrawny skin. He wasn't eating again or when he ate he didn't eat right. He was stronger than he looked but he wasn't strong enough. His was a musculature fit for climbing the exposed structures of the zone, for swinging the sledge and dragging scrap. The others appeared molded for boxing alone, for punching into and through a man. Every opponent all veins and teeth, hungry eyes bursting from tight skin, angry under the brow of a padded helmet. They had taken the given and built the desired. He had made what body was necessary for his work and now he sought to bring it to a new task.

He didn't want a trainer, couldn't pay, wouldn't ask. He trained by fighting. By getting hurt. Education by knockdown. Gloved fists pummeled his stomach but the next time a boxer came for Kelly he'd find the same tactics denied. Experience had made him who he was. If he could get hurt he could get better. A man raised his tattooed forearms over his face and Kelly battered his defenses until the man cried out. Kelly liked the way winning was temporary. You earned it but it didn't last. He liked how after he showed his opponent he would give no quarter, then the man spit and swore and came at him senseless, his entire body open to the blow.

When Kelly got his insurance he went to the doctor but he

didn't tell the girl with the limp he went. The doctor measured his blood pressure, listened to the thumping chambers of his heart, counseled him to avoid strenuous activity. He laughed and told the doctor what he did for a living. The doctor lifted his chin, probed around his neck and jaw, put a light to his eyes and ears and nose and throat. His fingers and hands were blacked from work and his body was bruised as rotten meat and the doctor suggested nothing he didn't believe he could be paid for. Kelly had insurance but the doctor said mostly it would only promise that if he died he would die in a bed.

Now Kelly walked the zone like a squared spiral, moving outward from his starting point in a series of right turns, every rotation allowing another block's length to stretch the circle. He bought graph paper, plotted each block of buildings, their various modes of inhabitation. He got to know every boarded house, every chain-link fence. He found members of the city watch in the zone and he signaled to them, offered to buy them coffee. Each questioning began with the necessary small talk, family, children, church, work. The endless sameness of the weather. Eventually they invoked the holiness of their task: if the police wouldn't protect their communities they would protect the city themselves.

Whenever Kelly encountered the volunteer built like a linebacker again, the linebacker pulled Kelly into a headlock or else faked a jab to his stomach. Then to resist punching back. To resist locking his arms around the slab of the man's belly and lifting, trying to put him on the ground. Later the linebacker answered Kelly's questions over coffee, handling his crude maps, adding landmarks Kelly would never have known. The locations of legendary shootings, rapes, hate crimes. The names of families long extinct or fled.

What exactly are you doing here, the linebacker asked, and Kelly shrugged.

I'm looking for someone, he said. Somewhere in the zone, he said, then waved his hands across the graph-paper maps spread out across the diner table. Somewhere out here.

It's a big city to hunt a person in, the linebacker said. You'll need something better than luck if you want to see it through.

The linebacker carried a pistol, a black shape inside a black holster tucked under his jacket. He taught gun-safety classes, he said, helped others get concealed-carry permits. He sold guns out of his house but only to men he trusted.

Whatever you need, the linebacker said, I can help.

The year dwindled. The farther Kelly moved from the center of the good story the more dangerous the story seemed. Somewhere in the zone there would be a space where no one suffered names. He wouldn't ascribe complexity to every actor. The more blank the image the more able to inspire terror, to excuse hurt. He moved through the frigid desperation, a lone striver walking rooms where many had lived, studying floor plans that had housed the generations, three children to a bed, two beds to a bedroom, houses standing through booms unimaginable, eras resigned to the unknown expanses of the past. When he arrived home he added the squares of graph paper to the case notes, tucked them loosely in the back of the notebook. On nights the girl with the limp worked latest he thumbtacked the maps to the walls of his living room, placing each block beside its neighbors, each sheet covered with simple diagrams, streets drawn in a shaky hand, outlined squares and rectangles for houses, filled in black if they were confirmed vacant. He paced the room, poured a drink, considered the spreading stain. In the zone Kelly had seen the lengthy shapes of the world, how what was to come was set down by what had passed, the long story of progress bendable only by degrees. He'd acquire the tools, he'd choose the space, he'd find the man in the red slicker, he'd take him and make him pay.

Because what if a degree was enough. What if the slimmest fraction of a degree made all the difference.

How to press an advantage. How to break through a defense. How to feint and have the feint believed. How to make a man of eighteen or twenty-one or twenty-five worry the peak of his powers wouldn't be enough. How to accept the same when it was your turn to fall. To stay in the ring three minutes at a time, to take the fists upon your head and body until each punch stuck in the meat of your bones. How to stay. How to stay. How to bear anything no matter the hurt. How in another age *agony* had meant *contest*. How there was nothing in the fight not brought there by an act of will. How to take the other's will and push it out of the square. How to have all your options reduced to violence, no way out except to strike or be struck.

He woke up, he trained, he sparred, he put his fists against the speed bag and the heavy bag and against toughened skin. He relearned a forgotten vocabulary, better ways of getting strong, to go past bench presses, shoulder presses, squats, and dead lifts, ways to pack on mass, power cleans, dumbbell snatches, power jumps, ways to pack on speed, explosiveness, fast-twitch muscle. Ballistic movements. There were ways he could train himself, could work out at home too, pull-ups and push-ups, box runs, medicine balls. At night he closed his eyes and imagined he could hear his muscles stretching and in the morning when he woke up he saw he was bigger, so slightly enlarged, cut with a bit more bark beneath the bruises.

The others ate creatine, protein, ZMA, vitamins you could choke on. Some evenings Kelly swallowed pills smuggled from the girl's purse and they thickened his veins until he thought if he didn't keep moving he might turn to stone. With them he saw with some new dilation, how the streetlights glowed big as suns. The buildings never wavered or blurred but perhaps they throbbed. If he saw a man on the street who looked like the man who mugged him, then he raised his phone, took a picture of the man. The phone's digital zoom was useless and as it brought him closer it showed him less: vague impressions, the color of skin, the shape of the skull, a slash or curve of expression. At an office-supply store he plugged his phone into a printer, ran color prints of every face he'd gathered. At home, Kelly taped the prints into the case notes where no one would find them, where the pictures began to color whatever pages they opposed.

Everything he added to his life became another repetition, a way of filling the endless everyday. He went to work, pushed his wheelbarrow down long industrial hallways, carried the broken fixtures from every bathroom, removed everything too valuable to leave for when the machines came to crush the building. The foreman trained him on other tasks, let him get a taste of the excavator. When they cleared one block they found a steel swimming pool dug into the dirt and the foreman showed Kelly the push and pull of the levers, how to reach down to puncture the pool's floor, to crumple its steel walls. Everything they encountered could be removed but Kelly was starting to think about what was closest to permanence. About cement, masonry, stonework. About close enough. It would require new skills but if the need emerged he had time, ambition, the will to learn.

Maybe it was enough to hide the deed between the gaps of attention. To put an action into a space where no one wanted to look.

Kelly made the boy a key so he could come and go as he pleased. He picked the boy up from school and because the boy hadn't eaten lunch Kelly took him out for fast food, filled the table between them with paper-wrapped burgers, red-boxed fries. When they ate together the boy often ate his food out of order: he would start with dessert, not finishing his burger because he'd already had a shake, a paper-boxed apple pie. The inversion of norms, left over from the last time the rules disappeared and so maybe the rules were gone. They sat in a booth at the back of the dining area and behind them was a glass wall cordoning off an indoor playground. Someone had soundproofed the glass so you couldn't hear the children playing. Every time Kelly looked over his shoulder there was another child there, shoeless or sockless, running across the floor, disappearing into a plastic tube. The smallest steps of the smallest children. There were cameras everywhere but the only one they warned you of was the one in the playground, a guardian behind smoky glass.

Kelly raised his phone, snapped a picture of the boy's face, flushed and full over the remains of his meal.

Because you're my friend, Kelly said.

Kelly dropped the boy off at his mother's then returned to where he had rescued the boy to find the blue house demolished, removed. Kelly squatted, graded the ground with his gloves, found nothing except a tenth of an acre of bare earth and dirty snow, not a single nail, a single screw. He knew the basement walls were gone too, torn out in dirty chunks, like he'd removed the swimming pool in another part of the zone. They would have used an excavator to dig a ramp, then sent the excavator to break the walls, the cement flooring. The machine digging into the hard and frozen earth, the house more joined to the dirt than in any other season.

If there was any physical reminder of the boy's captivity it was gone. Kelly lay down in the snow, let its shivery melt radiate into his clothes until his teeth chattered, until his skin burned. Later in the night he dreamed he heard a smile in the dark: a faceless man spoke up in the offenseless volume of the hopeless, testified in favor of his acquittal. There weren't handcuffs but duct tape held sturdy enough in the deep. Despite the mask Kelly wore he understood the man fine as long as he was standing right beside the chair. He was sure the man had had a face but it wasn't visible. He wasn't sure he could hurt the man but how could he let him go.

LATER PERHAPS THERE WOULD BE all kinds of perverse accusations but you didn't think they would be true. Certainly there was no touching beyond the necessary. But if the accusations were true how surprised could you be. You did not know yourself well. You guessed, conjectured. You had urges but not toward the boys. You had urges but you didn't understand where they originated.

In the faces of others you most often saw a certain kind of blankness, neither sad nor happy nor angry. A lack of gladness, a lack of sorrow. You saw on the television a show about people whose brain injuries left them unable to recognize emotion in expressions and you thought you were probably one of those people.

But where was your injury.

The watching was an exhaustion. Of the boy and of you. You had not expected this. You couldn't watch continuously but the longer you watched the greater the unfolding of the boy. It took time to get beneath the surface. You had to watch and you had to be sure the boy knew you were watching. At first the boys were merely confused, unsure of who you were, why you had picked them. There was something you wanted and the more the boy showed you the longer you kept the boy. The best boy had long since come and gone but others

had been good enough. Their eyes couldn't stay afraid forever. There was curiosity. One spoke and told you he would
never forget your face but everyone had forgotten you and if
this boy did not then he would be the first.

When the watching was over you didn't want to see
the boy ever again. There were a few ways to ensure you
would not.

Boys ran away, disappeared for reasons not related to being
taken, to being watched, what came after the watching. The
getting gone. This was why you took boys and not girls. If
you took girls, then no one would ever believe they had gone
missing on their own.

AT THE GYM, THE RELATIVITY of age: the age of a thirty-four-year-old man. How there was almost no one older worth putting your hands on. It was folly for Kelly to be in the ring with these monsters of youth but he wasn't trying to compete, didn't need to ever fight a real match, the nine minutes of amateur spectacle. All he wanted to do was to throw himself against their strength. They knocked him down but he knocked them down too. The ones who refused to spar with him he called names, goading their pride until they split his lips, bruised his eyes, filled his skin with the language of their rebuttals. He turned an ankle at a jobsite and then he had to limp around the gym, push through his disadvantages. In his apartment he imagined filling his tub with ice, filled a tumbler instead, put ice packs on his hands and whiskey in his stomach and vowed tomorrow he would go back for more. Dead lifts, squats, lunges. The seated row, the shoulder shrug, the dozens of pull-ups he'd become capable of again.

His body expanded, screamed at its seams. The bigger the shell got the more obvious its emptiness in the mirror.

The trainers had their favorites and they hired some of the others to fight them. Harmless men with enough steel to fight but not enough to win. There was money in being such a man but so far the trainers had never approached Kelly. Like every job, you got paid for being predictable.

The house he sought would have to be deep inside the zone, at the crossing of all vectors of loneliness, abandonment, loss. He drove blocks he had scrapped, tried to recall each house's layout of rooms and hallways, windows where neighbors might be able to see into the house. If there were neighbors. He wasn't confident in his recall, had to check his street work, his graph-paper maps. There were too many indistinguishable houses, too many similar floor plans. He thought he required a basement but that was only parity. He could make do with any dark room, its windows blacked, its walls and floor and ceiling made dense against sound.

The sound of breaking glass carried in the silent streets but no one would come to investigate. The emptiest streets, emptier for winter. He cleared the glass with a pry bar or a hammer, climbed into small rooms cramped with drop ceilings and the pile of faded shag carpet. He tested light switches and water taps, tried to remember the qualities of the house where the boy had been held. But the boy was what had imbued the house with meaning: it wasn't the structure but what the structure contained. Once a family, then vacancy, then a boy.

The shape of the house he picked mattered less than its proximity to others, its potential to remain undisturbed. He needed a house he could work in for an extended period of time. It would take time to make the necessary preparations, to assemble his tools, to soundproof a room, to be sure he would remain undisturbed until he finished.

It was possible to drug a man but he didn't know how it was done. He remembered choke holds from his wrestling days, thought to put his body to use instead. He asked at the gym and the others reminded him, happily demonstrated: the hardness of his arms putting pressure on a throat caught in the crook of his elbow. The air choke, the blood choke. Compressions of the carotid arteries, the jugular veins, the upper airway. Asphyxia, cerebral ischemia, temporary hypoxic conditions. The health sciences put to harder use.

The reward dwindled but there was enough left for what he intended. He acquired a new set of tools secondhand, kept them separate from his regular equipment. In a steel toolbox heavy as a child he placed an ancient pair of pliers, a pair of scissors rusted at the hinge but sharp along the blade. A selection of blunted chisels. Hammers with splintering handles that'd hurt when he swung. Rolls of duct tape, more than he needed. He had to leave the zone to get some of what he wanted. He purchased a generator, ninety-nine cubic centimeters of engine inside a compact roll cage, twelve hundred watts, nine and a half hours of juice. He had plenty of gloves but he thought he might want a pair he had never worn. There was a welder's mask in the same aisle and he put it in the cart. The mask wouldn't hide his eyes but it might obscure his emotions, put distance between him and the suspect.

The suspect or *the subject,* how one would become another as the process progressed.

He paid cash at the counter but cash didn't mean there wasn't a record. There were cameras in the store, receipts stamped with the date and time. He spread out his purchases, some today, some tomorrow. He bought another LED head-lamp, a handheld high-intensity discharge spotlight with a rechargeable battery. He thought maybe he might want more lights but how easy would it be to carry all of this in, to remove it after. One or two standing lights would be enough for the kind of work he was intending. All he needed was to illuminate a space the size of a man.

The boy called from downstairs and Kelly buzzed the boy in, got up from the couch to unlock the door. The boy had a key but why didn't he use it? When the boy entered he was followed by another, taller boy—the brother, Kelly realized. The brother was still in school, seventeen, a legal juvenile. Kelly didn't know his name, had never heard it spoken. This was one difference between a person and an abstraction. This was the way he wanted it.

This is my brother, said the boy. He wanted to meet you.

The boy's voice was quieter, cowed in front of the brother. For the first time in weeks Kelly looked at the boy and saw a child. The boy was dressed in his blazer and tie and khakis as ever, the brother was dressed the same but wore the clothes in his own way, looser, less what was intended by the public school dress code.

I heard you've been spending time with him, the brother said. Taking him places. Buying him things. Letting him stay here.

Kelly said, He comes after school. He does his homework while I watch television. We share a meal and I drive him home after.

I'm curious, the brother said. Just wondering what a grown man is doing with my brother.

Nothing, Kelly said. It's harmless. Anyway you're the one who brings him here.

The complicity of the brother driving the boy. Of Kelly leaving the boy within the brother's reach so he could come into Kelly's. Kelly wanted to ask if their parents knew too. He hadn't done anything wrong. He had saved the boy and when the boy was with him the boy was still safe. He had to keep reminding himself the brother wasn't the boy's real brother, not the boy's blood. No matter what the brother said. How the brother was cruel to the boy, by the boy's own admission. How the brother had touched the boy or else made the boy watch. How the boy told Kelly this or else it was only conjecture, something Kelly had written in the case notes.

The brother put his hand on the boy's head and the boy flinched and Kelly knew all he needed to know. He'd known the flinch himself. Not an instinct but something learned.

I'm going to stay today too, the brother said, moving his hand to the boy's shoulder. I want to make sure everything's okay. If that's all right with you.

If Kelly wanted to protect the boy he could do so right here. The brother wasn't a man but he was the height of one, could be hurt the same.

When Kelly stood his joints cracked and popped, his strained muscles protesting every movement. He invited the boy and his brother in, pointed toward the coatrack, the couch, the kitchen. The boy knew where everything else was but if the brother wanted something he would have to ask.

Kelly never smoked in front of the boy but he smoked now. The brother controlled the remote, scanned music videos, reality television, the late-afternoon reruns of some past evening's entertainment, sports news repeating without end. On the other side of the room the boy watched the television too, his backpack unopened, his eyes glassy and absent, his quietness doubled.

The brother was here under the guise of protecting the boy from Kelly but this wasn't the relationship the boy had revealed. The brother: Kelly thought he knew how such a person was made. It might not be the brother's fault—not in the ultimate reveal of cause and effect—but wasn't the brother still responsible for what he'd done, was doing. Hadn't Kelly been responsible for the same.

THE MAN UNNAMED, THE BOY unlabeled, the toddler and baby so unwanted he did not merit three words of description, first and middle and last. This was the person they'd say you were but the real self had been obscured behind a series of labels: occupation, race, education, religion, political affiliation. The states, the conditions: you stockpiled canned goods, ate sparingly. Generic brands or worse, the white cans with the bold text, left over from foreign wars, humanitarian aid. Fingering peaches out of syrupy containers. Saving half a slice of cheese in its wrapper. Trying to remember to eat the leftovers before they got hard. Forcing yourself to eat the crust if you forgot. The crusts of bread. A sandwich only needed one slice. Everything open-faced, revealed. Water from the tap, the same glass used repeatedly. The repetition of minor acts. It wasn't difficult to cut your own hair. You never bought your clothes new. You rarely gained or lost weight. You remembered your birthday but never on the right day. Some of your teeth were missing but you'd had the same number for several years. A stability even in decay.

There had never been a pet to call your own. You weren't afraid of dogs but didn't see the draw.

Once a woman threw a coffee at you in a fast-food lobby and you never knew why. Sometimes you found yourself in line somewhere with an erection that wouldn't go away. Then the long bus rides, the hands over the lap trying to hide your discomfort, leaving behind an ache you didn't know how to soothe. Or you knew how others soothed it but you didn't know how you should. It hurt too much to touch it yourself and you didn't know how to ask someone else. In the group home you had watched other boys handle themselves in the darkened dormitory, watched their faces as they moved through the pains of pleasure. One night you had gone to one of those boys and asked for help, had begged for it. The other boy had punched you in the neck and in the ear, had knocked you to the ground and pressed your face to the linoleum floor. There were words to make him stop but who knew which words you screamed were the right ones.

It should have been enough to keep your hands to yourself, to not ask for others' hands upon you. It should have been enough for you to watch. You had not wanted to go further.

This was the self you were bringing into the light: the one who wanted to stare out from behind the mask of new name, home haircut, hooded garment. Who looked at the world as it was and who only wanted to make the world look back.

THE CALL HAD COME FROM her number but it was her co-worker who'd answered. The co-worker said she wanted Jackie to go to the hospital but Jackie wanted to drive herself home instead. Calling him was their compromise. The building where she worked wasn't what he expected but he wasn't sure he'd had an expectation. The life they shared when they were in the same room was all he had of her. No shared past, no shared present outside of her apartment, his, the bars they drank in, the diners where they took their meals.

It was easy to forget. He saw a woman every day, shared a bed and a table until he thought he knew her, until she might imagine she knew him back. But what proportion did he know, what was the ratio between known and unknown. She saw him with the boy but so far the boy was his. She told him about her week but to him her experiences were mostly stories, as distant as the news.

When he arrived he found her sitting pale faced in her cubicle, clutching the edge of the desk as if she might fall out of her chair, the screen before her blank, every emergency in the city redirected. There was medication she was meant to take when this happened but he couldn't remember its progress, if her dilated pupils meant she had swallowed her pills.

What did you say when you couldn't say *Are you okay.*
What did you say when you couldn't say *What's wrong.*

It was impossible to get her into his truck in her clenched
condition so they would take her car instead. First the excru-
ciation of pacing her slow progress, stooped and dragging
toward the exit, because she refused to use her cane at her
workplace, in the company of others. The elevator was farther
than the stairs but the stairs weren't an option. He put his
arm around her and she cursed but as the doors slid closed
she crumpled against him. When the doors opened onto the
ground floor, she shoved herself free, used the elevator's railing to yank herself upright.

In the parking lot, he offered to bring the car around and
she glared again, pulled away.

He said, You can let me help you. There's nothing wrong
with letting someone help.

She scoffed, swore. She said, The last thing I need is you
carrying me to the car. And who are you to talk about needing help.

He stopped walking but she kept going, didn't look back,
didn't speak. He waited but she didn't slow. She limped
beneath the parking-lot lights, her shadow stretching her stag-
ger. He caught up to her, didn't let her walk alone. The attacks
were coming faster now. Long ago she had said there wouldn't
be rhyme or reason but for Kelly there was no denying their
increased frequency. She didn't want him to carry her and
wouldn't take his arm but she let him stand beside her, let him
match his pace to hers. She wouldn't fall this time but it didn't
mean he couldn't promise to catch her if she did.

He started to watch more closely, until every day he discovered some previously secret aspect of her life. Hobbies he didn't know she had. A circle of friends he hadn't met. In their earliest days they were always together and so there hadn't been room for outside interests. He no longer spent every evening in her company and so she had returned to her life before him. He called her and she was out with the other women from work, drinking beer and playing pool. He called her and she was home, watching the hockey game by herself, or else he called her and she was at their usual bar, watching the game in the company of others. She hadn't ever talked about books before but now he often found library books on her coffee table.

He picked up a murder mystery, flipped it over to read the jacket copy. A serial child abductor on the loose, an unlikely detective tasked to take him down. She brought him a beer from the fridge, put her hand on his chest. She took the book from his hands and put it back on the table.

It doesn't mean anything, she said.

She liked the order, she said. She liked the way the evil in these novels was a solvable mystery temporarily unsolved. The guilty could be found, accused, punished. When a woman made a mistake, the woman could redeem herself. The world of her novels was not chaos but merely the appearance of chaos. Instead there were hidden systems, mechanisms that could be uncovered, put to use. The righting of the bad world. A point to suffering, a suffering that improved the sufferer.

Three hundred pages and an expectation that by the end all the answers would be revealed. The transfer of weight as the pages fell from the right hand to the left, an accumulation of certainty.

I fell asleep reading last night, she said, and then I dreamed I was still reading but in my dream the room I was in was too dark for me to see the words. When I closed my book the dark got darker. I left the house, got in my car, started to drive. There was a lot of traffic but it dwindled as the road narrowed. When I passed the last car I realized my headlights were broken, that without other cars there would be nothing left to light the way. And then the last lights went out: streetlights off, moon gone, stars vanished. And I could not stop driving so very fast.

The reward should have made escape possible. He could have gone anywhere else, another city, a town. A simpler place for a simpler life. Now there was Jackie, there was the boy, there was the case, necessary to solve — but also his television, his couch and chair, all his possessions nothing special, only *his*. In the South he had owned a house full of such objects — or he had almost owned it — or else he had been only the completer of paperwork, the mailer of checks. Other people thought escape was something you did but Kelly knew it was an accretion of small choices, an action you earned. He worked and he drank and when he could he drove the streets of the zone, he checked his lists in the case notes, his homemade maps. A haphazard survey of the city no one wanted. More and more he wore the orange jersey underneath his coat. He kept his doors locked, smoked with his windows up, rolled through stop signs if there were men lingering on the corners of the street. Wherever he went he wore heavier layers, t-shirt, flannel, hood and coat and hat and gloves, thermal underwear under heavy pants tucked into insulated boots, but he arrived back in his apartment shaking, his fingers blue, all his skin full of needles and steam.

Whenever he woke up alone in his apartment he woke up afraid.

Where was the girl. Where was the boy.

For some time he couldn't bring their names to mind.

But then *Jackie*. But then *Daniel*.

He wrote down the same details again but not in the same way. He began to call the heavy detective's desk in the middle of the night, calling from pay phones to leave lengthy messages, the disconnected thoughts of the case notes:

I know the past is the past and cannot be changed. I accept this limitation but I do not accept that the past does not end, how I have to live through the past again and again in the present, how the future must contain the same.

How do you see what might take the people you love. How do you understand which of their million hurts is the one that changes them forever.

What other stories are there. What other stories go on and on, waiting for someone strong enough to bend them toward their conclusions.

Kelly never identified himself, hung up if the detective answered with his voice too high pitched for his bulk, asking *what, who, why,* all the investigative cues. And what was the detective doing there so late, working past midnight, past the middle of the darkest hours.

In the last third of the case notes, Kelly wrote version after version of opening the basement door, of releasing the boy's wailing, and as he descended the stairs again and again the bed never moved from the center of the room, but was it always the same bed?

The boy was still the boy but now he knew more.

The chair was there too but sometimes he put someone in the chair.

When he tried to picture the bed as he first saw it he also saw the cuff chain looped around the bedframe but he knew he had tried to lift the boy from the bed before knowing the boy was cuffed to the rail. On the page the boy screamed again. Kelly couldn't have known about the cuffs in the darkness but now he remembered he had. Even as he knew he hadn't.

The scrapper lived within one story. The salvor occupied another. The case thickened with what they added. What bothered him weren't the gaps but their overlap. The many stories where there should be one.

Kelly spoke into the phone, said, *The threat of physical violence is not enough to prevent violence but it is enough to match it. I used to know this. I used to have a savagery lodged within my bones. Once you could have taken out a rib to grow a killer. I haven't been punished but who says I don't want my punishment. I have excuses but I am exhausted by my excuses. Now I want to remove my own rib. To plant it back. The rib is named* the scrapper. *I recognize the arguments. Circumstances have made me uniquely qualified to be*

*this specific kind of good man. An action that is the end that justi-
fies the means.*

The other good man is called the salvor. *The one who salvages.
Because what is there in the zone but ruin. Who is there left in this
blue world but everyone lost at sea, sliding free of the sudden slant
of a sinking ship.*

Whenever he imagined finding the boy, the boy he saw in
the bed became the boy he knew. Not a stranger trapped but
his friend taken, an individual stolen from his care. Memory
shifted to accommodate current emotion: What was he afraid
of then. What was he afraid of now. What was the difference.

He knew so much more about the boy but who was the
watcher, a name that meant nothing, the man in the red
slicker, a description pretending to be a title.

In the absence of knowledge he inserted abstraction. In
abstraction he had always found something easier to fear. It
was easier to see if he put the mugger in the chair. If he made
the man with the gun do the watching. It made him feel less
unsure if it was the brother who sat there, supposedly cruel.

It was not difficult, in his mind, to put either inside the red
slicker.

When Kelly called the heavy detective, he sometimes
wanted to reveal his identity, to ask if the detective would
play his statement back to him. So he could know how it
had changed. Because what he remembered was that the
salvor opened the door and the boy was there in the bed,
whole and ready for rescue. Or else the scrapper opened
the door and there was no boy. Or else the scrapper opened the
door and there was a boy and there was a suspect and you

finished rescuing the boy by punishing the suspect too. A rescue in two parts.

The man in the red slicker, Kelly said, *is he a person or an action? An action that until I found the boy I had never been able to name?*

Sometimes Kelly would look at the boy and also through him. When the boy sat on the living room floor watching the television or doing his homework. The boy didn't flicker but maybe he fugued. Once when the boy was over Kelly looked out his window and thought he saw the detective sitting in an unmarked car across the street but what was the chance. He picked up his phone, dialed the detective's cell number, got the voicemail message. If the detective was the man in the car, then he did not move to answer.

How far back does the long stain go, Kelly asked, one hand opened against the window glass. *How can we assign blame unless we know the original mistake, the first man standing over the first boy.*

Kelly started to forget if the boy was with him. An amnesia of the commonplace. The first time the girl with the limp woke to the boy sleeping on the couch—to Kelly sitting in the armchair, watching him sleep—she didn't say anything she couldn't say with arched eyebrows, a crumpling of the forehead. The tight set of her mouth, holding back all the questions they'd agreed not to ask.

He knew he was making a mistake but he wouldn't tell the boy no. Another afternoon the buzzer sounded and Kelly pressed the intercom button, asked who it was. The boy knew to let himself in but then the boy's voice answered: he'd lost his key, needed to be buzzed into the building.

I'm sorry, the boy said, his voice crackling over the intercom.

Inside the apartment the boy hurried to unwrap himself, hat and gloves and scarf and overcoat and blazer, shivering and anxious.

I looked everywhere, the boy said. My room, my desk, my bag. Everywhere.

The constrained *everywhere* of the young.

Kelly had never seen this expression on the boy's face: the boy was worried he would be punished. As if Kelly were Kelly's father, the boy Kelly's father's boy.

Locks can be changed, Kelly said. I'm sure you'll find it. It's nothing.

Kelly reached for the boy and the boy flinched and Kelly grabbed him anyway. Kelly kneeled down, pulled the boy to his chest, put the weight of the boy's head against his shoulder. He had never dared hold the boy before, had rarely touched him since bringing him out of the basement. He had barely let himself imagine all this heat, all these bones and scrawny muscles, all this need wrapping arms around him too. This amazing gesture, what he'd wanted for so long. Every moment after wouldn't be this moment but this one could stretch as long as it had to, its memory becoming something lasting. A charm, Kelly thought, a reassurance in the dark.

THE WEATHERMAN SAID RAIN ALL day but they walked along the river anyway, her hand in his while the boy skipped ahead, kicked at loose rocks, debris fallen over the footpath. The water's edge was the edge of the city and the edge of the country and on the other bank of the river there was another country because there was nowhere on earth where one nation ended and another did not begin. It was too cold, the end of the year, but it was still forecast to rain any minute and this was the right kind of danger for a man and a woman and a boy. A manageable catastrophe at worst, a story to share. There were other times of day when it wouldn't be safe to be here. For now there was the rain that didn't come and the charcoal sky and the high gusting wind putting new waves in the fast chop of the river. The boy ran ahead but he never failed to turn back, and every time he looked Kelly weighed the tangible substance of the gaze. He smiled, shook his head, pointed at the boy. She squeezed his hand. In the distance there was thunder but they couldn't see the lightning and though they walked all day the rain never came. Ahead of them the boy passed into the darkness of a tunnel under a bridge and though Kelly couldn't see him he could hear the boy's laughter, the surprise at being alone in the dark and yet still safe.

On the way back to Kelly's apartment the boy vomited without warning into the floor mats of Kelly's truck, the cracks and crevices of the backseat. Then the boy vomited again because everyone vomited twice. He apologized softly from the backseat but Kelly waved his apology away. These things happened. It had been a long day or else the boy was overexcited. When they arrived at his apartment, Kelly lifted the boy from the backseat, the boy's soiled clothes squishing against Kelly's chest, the boy's sour breath hot in his ear. The boy was too big to carry far but young enough to sometimes need to be carried and this was one of those times. The girl with the limp shuffled ahead to hold open doors and Kelly brought the boy up the stairs to his apartment and into the bathroom and as Kelly moved through the building the memory of carrying the boy before manifested again: how he had ascended the basement stairs with the boy, how he had taken him to the truck, to the hospital, through the first snow into the waiting light of the emergency room.

Let's get you out of these clothes, Kelly said. Can you do it yourself or do you need help?

The boy could do it himself but he wasn't. In the bathroom they kneeled before him, working together to pull his shirt over his head. The boy's chest so narrow, the unmuscled frame of a child still, his belly a soft roundness over the waistband of his pants. Jackie's got you, she said, starting the shower while Kelly wet a washcloth. He kneeled back down to clean the boy's face, his hair, the crusting vomit requiring a more vigorous method. Kelly never knew the right thing to do so he held the boy's head in one hand and scrubbed with the other. The steam filling the room didn't help the smell but it did change it. Kelly threw the boy's t-shirt in the trash and threw the washcloth in after it and when he turned around to face the boy he saw the girl staring at the boy's back. She didn't say anything but he saw some of what she'd seen in her look, enough to guess. The shower was running loud and the room was thick with steam and she gently turned the boy by the shoulders to show Kelly the ugly markings on the boy's back, a stretched series of pinched bruises riding both sides of his spine.

Who did this to you? she asked — and it was almost Kelly who answered.

No one, the boy said. No one did anything.

Kelly asked too but the boy wouldn't say the brother's name, only cried harder, his body trembling. The shame of being hurt, of being hurt again. And when Kelly didn't move to the boy's side she was there instead, sitting down on the floor and pulling the half-dressed boy into her lap, saying, Jackie's here, saying, Daniel, you're safe now. You're safe with us.

Kelly stood against the vanity, a new kind of uselessness falling over him, another failure to act. In the swelling steam of the room he watched this fine woman comforting this fantastic boy, telling the boy she would keep him safe, sounding so sure she couldn't fail, speaking as if a mother comforting her own child, her soft speech promising the long safety of love, every motherhood's first and most lasting and most necessary lie.

———

The boy's parents were already waiting when Kelly pulled into the mother's driveway, the father and the mother reunited and shivering in the short dusk of winter. What had the brother told them after he visited? Enough that before Kelly opened the door he knew the boy would be taken. As he approached the boy's parents Kelly could barely listen over the ringing in his ears but he knew they would speak all the expected words, all the other words Kelly must have known would one day come: It had been a mistake to let the boy spend time with Kelly. They hadn't known until the brother told them but they should have paid more attention. They too had been the victims of trauma. What happened to the boy had happened to them, in their own way, and in the aftermath they hadn't been the best parents they could be.

The father said, Thank you for taking care of Daniel. It's been a hard year for all of us.

The mother said, We missed him but we didn't know how to be with him. This is our fault, not yours.

The father spoke again, said, We appreciate everything you've done—Daniel's brother told us you've been watching him after school—but I think this friendship has run its course. Daniel needs friends his own age, normal friends. I hope you understand.

What Kelly wanted most was to put his hand on the boy, to touch his head or his shoulder. For it to be as easy as it had been beside the river, as it had been the day of the lost key. Instead Kelly would give the boy back so they didn't have to take him. He would surrender his affection for the boy and he would promise not to see him again, not to let him into his apartment, certainly never to take him away again. A week from now his apartment key would come in the mail, the second key he'd made for the boy, barely used. It would be the mother's handwriting on the envelope but there would be no accompanying note. Kelly knew this and later it came true.

The father offered his hand. The boy stayed beside Kelly, waiting to move until Kelly reached out, took the father's hand. The father released his grip, reached for the boy. The boy didn't move yet but he would soon and in the last moment with the boy at his side Kelly surveyed the family the boy was rejoining: The mother, fit in her sweater and slacks and scarf. The father, bigger bearded than ever, looming in his winter coat, smiling his odd smile. The palpable presence of the missing brother. The boy moved toward his mother, put his arms around her. She would smell the sickness on his breath and know what to do. This was the boy's mother, the boy's father. If they were not perfect they were good enough. It was they who had claimed responsibility for the boy, who had freed him from foster care and group homes, who had promised to give him a better life. Theirs was the first taking of the boy, the best of its kind.

You had to trust, you had to have faith in their goodness.

But doubt. But fear. But how Kelly had always succumbed to the rush toward quicker action, immediate results.

Daniel, Kelly said, the word harsh in his mouth.

Daniel, he said again, softer, more sure.

He's sick, Kelly said, speaking to the parents. He threw up today. He needs you to take care of him.

The mother smiled, ran her hands through the boy's hair. She said, Of course. Of course we will.

Now there was worry in her eyes and for a moment Kelly thought he would tell her. He opened his mouth, closed it again. He could insert himself further into their lives but by what right, at what cost. He could tell them about what he believed the brother had done to the boy but the boy wouldn't admit the brother's fault, and so would the mother and the father believe Kelly or would they think Kelly was the one who had hurt their son.

She said, What is it? Is there something else?

Kelly shook his head. It's nothing, he said. What would the fear of exposing himself to danger let continue, for how long. He wanted someone to tell him what to do next but the girl with the limp was already taking him by the hand, pulling him away. The boy wasn't his boy, she would say. In the truck he shook and flushed and drove away too fast, accelerating through the unplowed streets until the girl objected. It was almost the holidays, almost the new year. A few more weeks. The weather had turned bitter and there was more snow coming. The snow wasn't like the rain. He couldn't smell the snow before it arrived but he knew there were other ways to read the sky. He thought he might at last train himself to suss out such deeper signs, to hear clearly the subtlest speech of the slower, colder world to come.

THE LAST HOUSE IN THE northern city, the city's last boy: always the blue house had been silent and static but that night you arrived to a movement of the air whistling through an open window, to muddy tracks on the floor, boot prints leading from the foyer to the kitchen, upstairs, and then down into the basement.

Remember the powerful wakefulness, every nerve lighting up for the reappearance of the new. You had been bored and had tried to keep yourself away so your boredom might fade and now there was this newness, arrived again, lighting you into attention.

Remember how this boy had meant nothing. How there had been no joy in the watching. How you thought perhaps someone else had watched him first, how the other had removed what you sought, the unnamable portion of a boy the watching could claim.

You took your shoes off in the foyer. You had to kneel to undo the double knot of the laces. There wasn't anywhere to hang your coat so you carried it into the kitchen, where the stove jutted out from the counter, half dragged into the middle of the room. A window hung open, let in snow accumulating on the dirty tile. The walls were opened too, the wiring and piping roughly removed. The basement lock was busted free and the basement door was ajar and no sound came from below.

You should have fled then but you needed to see for yourself. You moved slowly down the rough wooden stairs, descending through the busted plaster and the bare studs, down into the cool damp of the underground. You had a flashlight in your pocket but you didn't use it.

Certainly the dark had never bothered you.

There were footprints upstairs, damage to the house everywhere. An intruder had come for the plumbing and had taken something better. You had known the boy — had almost already been done knowing him — and now the boy and the intruder were somewhere else, together.

In your anger you first thought you would find the intruder, find him and bind him and watch him. But in your fear you fled until one day you awoke in a new city, in the room at the top of this yellow house, into the terror of its absolute dark, its total quiet. The room sealed so tight it stayed warmer than the rest of the house even without heat. Your mouth starched, your tongue thick between your teeth, your heart hammering above the absence of other sound. Every wet noise outside your body dulled by the soundproofing but your licking your lips loud as a scrape of sandpaper across flesh. Your pride in your accomplishment as the movement of the chair against the wood disappeared into a whisper.

There was nothing in the room but yourself and when the boys were in their rooms like this room there were only whatever sounds their bodies could make, all those trapped breaths and thumping bloods, their fickle limitations. What a gift, given to every boy you'd taken.

Outside the yellow house the midwestern winter hung, cold and blue and uninviting. In every city in the country you believed you could find a place such as this, an uninhabited zone full of empty buildings, rooms waiting to be repurposed into function. You walked the long blocks from the yellow house into the brighter parts of your new city, the busy streets where you watched and waited and looked for the right boy. The yellow house was readied for the taking and yet perhaps it would not be enough. Perhaps the intruder had changed the terms of your watching. If you made any mistake in the blue house perhaps the mistake was in the fleeing. You could have waited for the police to arrive. Did you want to hear what they would say, once they could see you? The explanations of who you were, of what you had become? The great curiosity of the why. The question you had never answered even for yourself. Your captors would have tried to see the evil in your face and they would have been disappointed. No matter how long they watched they would never see what they wanted. Because you had already looked and whatever there was inside you it was nothing you could watch no matter how brightly the light shined upon the mirror. Because it was only in a boy you could make yourself seen, only in a perfection of fear you could reveal the name you most desired being called.

KELLY FOLLOWED THE LINEBACKER INTO his house, a squat building of brick at the end of the neighborhood's last occupied block. Inside, a television voiced a repetition of sports news and on either side of the set there was a dog behind bars, in a cage barely wider than its shoulders, their animal smells swamping the crowded living room. The dogs barked at the sight of the linebacker, who swore in their direction, kicking at one of the cages but absently, without malice. Kelly didn't recognize the dogs' breed, imagined some combination bred cheaply together, a mix of incompatible angers, canine functions.

My girlfriend's dogs, the linebacker said. I could take them or leave them. He asked a question, had to repeat himself before Kelly answered: What kind of caliber, what kind of stopping power?

Kelly said, I would like something the sight of would make a man do anything.

The linebacker said, There are certainly guns like that but they aren't free. Have a seat.

The linebacker returned from the second floor with a logoed duffel bag, its two zippers padlocked together. He pulled a key ring from his pocket, separated out the right key from the clump. Inside the duffel were individual objects concealed in bubble wrap, their danger sealed away.

The linebacker chose three of the bundles, peeled back the masking tape across their folds, laid out the contents on the kitchen table.

Each weapon was black, unloaded. There were some differences in ornamentation, some spread of calibers, stopping power. The smallest pistol was heavier than Kelly expected but immediately he knew he wouldn't want anything lighter. If he was going to carry a loaded gun he wanted to know it every step. If he was going to hurt someone he wanted to carry the burden of that hurt across a great distance. The act might be a surprise to the killed but he thought the killer should know its weight. He put down the smallest pistol and picked up the biggest. He couldn't imagine doing anything but killing with it.

He asked, What would the recoil be like?

Magnificent, the linebacker said. Like holding a stallion in your fist.

The safety was on but Kelly gave the trigger a pull anyway, explored the short range of motion the safety allowed. He put the pistol down, asked how much.

The linebacker laughed. That's it? Five minutes ago you didn't know what you were looking at and now you know exactly what you want.

The linebacker laughed again. The sound filled the room, overflowed it. Somewhere above them a baby started crying. Kelly had forgotten there was an upstairs. He hadn't even known about the baby. A woman's voice could be heard comforting the child. Kelly made an awkward apology. He wanted to leave but not without the pistol, its halo of deathly want. The linebacker named a price and Kelly opened his wallet. The linebacker sealed the pistol in the bubble wrap, reaffixed the masking tape, searched the kitchen drawers for a plastic shopping bag. Upstairs the baby cried and cried. As Kelly walked out of the house the dogs kept their silence, cowed in their cages. He wanted to get down on his hands and knees and growl into their faces but the linebacker wanted him out of his house. Upstairs, the baby continued to cry and the woman's voice lost its whispered comforts, rising harsh and frustrated as Kelly stepped out into the snow.

On the last night of the year they made love carefully, bodies angling against each other in the dark, their motions unhurried. Her cane was beside the bed, her nightstand full of muscle relaxers, creams, lubricants. It was up to him to find the proper approach, to move them through the stations of their sex, and now he did so easily, knowing what she liked best. Or else he thought he did and she let him think it. She was vocal in her desire in a way he had not previously known. He had preferred a certain roughness but this was good too. He'd never known any tenderness within himself, had only briefly approached it in the past. The way a child supposedly rewrites its parents: he'd craved this, thought he needed it. Even though the child wasn't his own he had wanted the child to make him new.

Afterward they lay naked beside each other, waiting without talking for the end of the year, and in the quiet dark preceding the midnight hour he didn't speak the sudden sadness she couldn't see. The new year came and went and at first he said nothing, instead thinking about how distant all the other years he'd known had become, how everyone he'd ever loved then had been lost to him, their faces gone dark, the smell of their skin faded from memory. Now here he was in the zone, in a new year, living some new life. But every new affection bred its own fears. Because anyone you loved became a responsibility. Because to be a good man meant taking their protection seriously, meant removing every danger it was in your power to remove, no matter what the consequences.

Because any responsibility taken far enough inevitably risked an atrocity.

He could only rarely speak openly but now he turned toward her, tried to tell her what he felt for her, how he wanted what he felt to last. But as he spoke she moved closer, then stopped his mouth with hers.

No, she said, pushing herself up on one elbow, her pale body lean and luminous in the streetlight descending through the window. This is all temporary. I won't last. Sooner or later the attack that ends all this will come.

He shook his head, denied the obvious truth. He said, I am with you either way. I am with you no matter what happens.

Temporary, she said again. Everything you love about me is temporary.

Her hands pushed upon his stretched chest, lifted her body atop his again. He was so much bigger than her, the difference greater than ever before.

She said, I think you are temporary too. I think you believe you know who you are because of something that happened to you a long time ago. You haven't told me but I know. But there's always a choice. You could be this person or you could become someone else.

There is a good man, she said. There is a good woman. We could become those people. Sometimes it feels so easy to choose.

FLORIDA

THE KILLER WAS NOT AFRAID. The killer knew who he was, how he had been made, made himself: The killer almost joined the marines. The killer almost remained a Catholic. The killer almost had a successful insurance business. The killer almost earned a criminal justice degree. The killer almost went to jail for threatening his then fiancée. The killer almost went to jail for shoving a police officer. All this in the almost-distant past and now the killer was almost thirty. Now the killer rented his home but he almost always thought of it as *his*.

The killer did not think of himself in the third person but there almost wasn't enough of him to justify the first. The killer was living a life of *almost* but surely *almost* had not made him afraid.

The killer was not afraid. There had been four hundred police responses to his neighborhood in thirteen months but still the killer was not afraid and because he was not afraid he had placed fifty of those calls himself.

The killer was not afraid when he made his complaints:

This loud party, he said; *This garage door left open; These unbearable potholes; These children playing in the streets, where they might be hurt.*

The killer was not afraid when he reported suspicious persons, loose dogs.

The killer was not afraid when he said *Burglar* into his cell phone, when he said *Thief.* Even if he had not seen any actual burglaries, any actual theft. Only *almost,* the potential of.

When the dispatcher asked him to describe the suspicious persons, he was not afraid when he said he was almost sure they were black males, when almost every single time he said they were young and black and suspicious.

The killer was not afraid of the suspected burglars or the suspected thieves. The killer was not afraid of the thugs he thought he saw, their dark shapes moving from house to house, looking in windows, eyeing flat-screen televisions and surround-sound systems.

The killer, who did not know he was a killer yet, was not afraid of meeting one of these thugs while he patrolled the streets, in command of the neighborhood watch.

Why not? Because the killer was not afraid.

Surely the killer was not afraid behind the wheel of the car, with his pistol on the passenger seat. Not just because it was raining and hard to see. It wasn't the weather the killer wasn't afraid of.

The killer was not afraid for his home.

The killer was not afraid for his wife.

The killer was not afraid because he was there, watching and waiting.

He would not let *them* make him afraid.

Even though he couldn't say who *they* were.

The killer was not afraid when he dialed the emergency number.

The killer was not afraid when he said into the phone, *There's a real suspicious guy here.*

When he said, *Walking around in the rain. This guy is up to no good or he is on drugs.*

When he said, *These assholes. They always get away.*

The absence of doubt. The pushing back of *almost*. This was what the killer wanted. To be sure. To be right. To be righteous.

The killer was not afraid of what he knew. *These assholes.*

The killer was not afraid when the dispatcher said, *Stop.*

When the dispatcher said, *We don't need you to follow him.*

When he said, *I'm not afraid.*

The killer was not afraid because he knew he was in the right. The total absence of doubt. The end of *almost*.

These assholes, said the killer. *They always get away.*

The killer was not afraid when he drew the gun from his waistband.

Because at that range the killer couldn't miss.

Because there was nothing to be afraid of.

Because all he had to do was close his eyes and squeeze the trigger.

The killer was not afraid because squeezing the trigger required basically nothing.

The killer was not afraid of the sound of the shot. He could barely even hear it, the blast muffled by the body.

These assholes. They almost always get away.
Not always. Not this time.

The killer was not afraid.

The killer was not afraid when the police arrived.

The killer was not afraid when they cuffed his hands behind his back or when they asked him if he needed medical attention or when they pushed his head down as they helped him into the back of the squad car.

The killer was not afraid when the ambulance came for the body.

The killer was not afraid when the news vans arrived.

The killer was not afraid when the squad car drove him from the scene in front of their cameras.

The killer was not afraid when the detectives questioned him at the station.

I stood my ground, the killer said. *I saved myself first.*

The killer was not afraid when he walked out into the lobby of the precinct, when he saw outside the protesters already gathering their anger against him, or when his wife appeared to take him home, when he saw she knew she was the wife of a killer.

The killer was not afraid because he had kept safe his family, his home, his community.

These assholes. The killer did not think in the first person except when the killer thought *us* and *them.* And so what if the kid had been living there too, if he had been a part of their community. Because inside a community there were other communities.

The killer was not afraid when he watched the television news, where the reporters and the pundits called him a killer for the first time. Nor when the pundits asked themselves who the killer was because if there was anything the killer knew it was this, *who he was*. He had almost been the killer before. Now there was no doubt. The law could quibble over whether he was a murderer but forever he would be a killer either way.

The killer was not afraid even during the lengthening nights in the dark of his house, where in those endless hours he lay unsleeping, listening to the charged noise of the street outside his house, listening to the steady clock of his heart while he thought about the spot blocks away where he had killed, where *these assholes* had made him kill.

Even now, deep in the aftermath, the killer is what the killer was. Surely this has not changed.

Because surely the killer was not afraid.

Surely the killer was not afraid then or ever again.

Surely the killer was not, is not, will not ever be made afraid.

PART THREE:
THE LOW ROOM

7

THE PLANT BECKONED AGAIN. A year later and it was still merely scheduled for destruction, hunkered in all its crumbling glory upon the famous avenue. One January afternoon Kelly drove his truck around the front of the buildings first, then into the back alleys, parking along the frozen and rutted mud of the broken roads. He walked across the rubbled yard and into the vast vacancy of the plant, moving through rooms whose shapes loomed differently than what he'd imagined, with ceilings that climbed and swelled or else sagged and fell, with floors cracking and curving away from the level. In other places the reinforced concrete held, looked ready to last another hundred years, and in the interior there were places where no sunlight penetrated and in those dark halls he used his headlamp to peer through piled debris, followed a patina of mold and rust through doorways without doors, the wood long ago rotted, the hinges pocketed. But what was on the other side of any wall was never so different than where he'd come from: a similar kind of cold, better lit or more dark, scavenged or else cluttered with trash, the unmaintained grandeur of open space, everything useful carried away.

Inside the plant he followed the sun's dappling path, the hours of the day clocked by its transit. It took longer to cross the building in this slow fashion but it was something to do with his body, its newly inexhaustible muscles. As he walked his cell phone rang and voicemail notifications beeped and though he rarely listened to the messages he never deleted them. He let messages pile into his inbox, let voices remain upon his device, caught between satellites in the sky and servers buried in the coolness of the earth. He was well acquainted with how anything might happen. If he wasn't careful he could lose the people under his care and he feared then he would forget them so fast. This was the cruelty of the linear life, its adaptations: not that you would move on but that the moving on would obscure the past, bury it deep.

Once he'd thought he would never forget the sound of anyone he loved but now he couldn't remember his grandparents, his mother, his childhood friends. The southern woman was gone only a year and it was as if he had never known her voice.

He could see her boy's face but could he hear her boy's speech?

Such a quiet son. So little conversation between them, even at the end when they were always together. More and more all he could remember was his error. All the good destroyed by what he'd done wrong. How he'd stood beside the boy's bed in the night, how after he'd undressed he had thought he had not been naked but instead dressed in *father*, as he believed now his father had dressed in his own father's skin, a trick of black magic for the blackest hours.

When he closed his eyes he could see the southern woman and her boy speaking but he could not hear their voices, their images keeping company among all the other silent faces, all motion, no noise. People he'd loved, fading toward the abstract. There were grids buried beneath the earth and floating above the sky and threaded up the bellies of skyscrapers and from them he would delete nothing. The machines would hoard it all. He didn't love the modern world but he loved this. If the girl with the limp died tomorrow then he would listen again to her last messages because to keep her alive in memory would be to keep her alive. Because one day there would be no one living who remembered the form of your face or the sound of your voice and on that day it would be as if you had never existed. This was the final death of the unremarkable. No record, no remembrance, no one to carry your speech and your image forward into the future. It would happen to the memory of others because you couldn't always be vigilant against it. You would not know when it happened to you.

He arrived at the location of the fire not from the outside but from within, from above. It took hours but he knew the general direction through the plant, climbed the floors as he walked until he emerged onto the roof at the edge of the building. The fire was a year old but he thought he could smell the blackened earth somewhere below him, beneath the snow, the bent steel moved aside for the extraction of the bodies. He remembered: How the fireball unfurled as every alight mote of dust lit the next, the distance of air so slim and the fire traveling easy across the gap. How he'd watched the fire engulf the building, the company of men. How he'd put his back to the fire and fled. How as he had he'd imagined the better man who might have stayed, the brave man who might have called for help, who might have heard the voice of the girl with the limp months earlier, when he'd needed it most.

How different this past year could have been.

He might be dead, consumed in the secondary blast bursting after he was already far enough for safety.

He might be in prison and then there would be no girl with the limp for him to know.

The boy would not have been found, at least not by him.

Memory didn't require remembering to exist. Memory could wait dormant, metastasizing in silence. What he had forgotten might dismantle or appropriate what surrounded it. A mass of loaded neurons fired across gray matter, set off a squelch of wet distortion and biofeedback until there appeared these nameless men lost in the fire, lost as from a safe distance Kelly had stared helplessly into the scorched place of their anguish, their screaming and flailing.

Next came the boy, lost already, who was always to him the boy he became after his captivity, never again the same boy he had been before. It was an agreed-upon fiction that he could be made so again. This was the creed of parents, teachers, therapists, that there was a previous state the boy could be returned to. As if a boy were a fixed quantity. As if the quality of a boy were not a thing in flux.

Then the southern woman, then her child, her own boy, their names he couldn't bear to speak.

How the nightmare of time was that time was not linear but simultaneous.

How everything that had ever happened to him or from him was still happening, even if he couldn't always remember the cause. Even if he wouldn't always admit what he remembered.

How what he'd done meant that he was still his father's son. How he had become the man the father had been to him, that he thought the grandfather had been to the father.

Their inheritance: Once a killer, always a killer. Once a victim, always a victim.

And could the good man be made to last as long.

Now the fading twilight of the midwestern winter: the site of the fire lay below but whatever he thought he saw wasn't lit by anything but memory. He had wanted to finish climbing the plant during the day but when he looked around him all he surveyed was the deepening gray of the zone, stretching as far as he could see. The streetlights extinguished, the roads untrafficked for long stretches, each set of headlights a mere wrinkling of the dark. In all directions he saw fewer windows lit than the architects and city planners had intended, than the first citizens of these blocks had hoped.

His headlamp illuminated almost nothing in the open air but if he pointed it at his feet he could see where he might go next. He took a step out onto the central girder leading across the open span of air below and the metal received his weight without movement or sound or other complaint. He put his arms out to steady his walk and then he took another step. Somewhere above him he heard the passage of a passenger jet but he didn't look. Everything peripheral became unnecessary distraction, increased the danger of forgetting the necessary forms of attention. From this height he could see more headlights moving in the street around the plant, lone cars making lonely traffic. There was a tightness in his chest but it was only more fear. There was a ringing in his ears but there was always a ringing in his ears. He was sweating but couldn't lift his hands to wipe his face. His legs didn't start to shake until he was past the halfway point but then his heartbeat came unbound from expectation, set its own rhythm. There was the starting a task and there was finishing what you started and he was making the move across. The air freezing around him and above him, and in the zone below the air was black beneath the furrowed winter sky, and almost everywhere he looked there was no light. Only a single length of glass blazed, a fluorescent banner stretched at street level some blocks away: a storefront church, holding a late service. The power of prayers he had believed in, caught brightly behind distant glass. The girl with the limp believed there were good men and women in the city and as Kelly looked out across the architectural darkness of the zone he wished those secret saints would come to their windows, wished they would each lift to the glass a single lit lamp, a flashlight, a flame. For his sake, he wished they would make themselves known.

The place where the fire had burned waited closer than

ever, a short plummet to the ground below, where in his nightmares he'd dreamed of the dirt mixed with concrete and dust, the char of bone, the flaky remnants of skin. A single breath gathered, enough to let out one or two words, no more than several short syllables. His body was moving forward as if disconnected from his mind but if he could retouch the connections he would begin to speak. What he wanted to say might have been *Help me*. It might have been *I'm sorry*. The cold slid through his layers of clothing, found purchase in the holds of his body. He had saved a boy but what other goodness could he do, alone in the zone. He blinked and when he opened his eyes the light had changed again and he was closer to the other side of the beam. When he thought he couldn't take another step he reached up and strobed the headlamp, moved the switch back and forth, the lamp's flashes lighting the nearest bricks. He noticed he was only wearing one glove, the skin of the bare hand blotched and rashed. He closed his eyes, wavered on the beam. This was the purest manifestation of alone: the cold, the dark, the absence of anyone to hear what he meant to say, the way he moved his mouth around the words. The cold grew absolute, its deep numbness a weariness piercing muscle and organ and bone, but he imagined there was a colder cold farther down, the permanent freeze, where movement and breath and heat would all cease. For a moment he saw around him every wrong thing stilled, slowed until he might step outside their wrongness. He knew who he was, who he had been becoming, what he would have at last done to himself if not for the girl with the limp, for the boy. How now he had something to live for, found in the zone where he had not expected to find it.

He took the next step. The step after. He wasn't sure he believed he'd make it but with every step less of the crossing remained and into the abridged remainder of the dark he spoke the words he was most afraid to say, the admittance of his failure to find the man in the red slicker, the splash of color he sought surely moving somewhere within this muted world and still somehow nowhere to be seen.

8

F THE INTRUDER FOUND YOU again it wouldn't be in any basement. All the boy could give the detectives was the brown car and the black mask and the red slicker and you had left the car and the mask and the red slicker behind. The intruder couldn't know where you'd fled but every night you imagined him finding you inside this upper room readied for a boy, readied for listening to his muttering, for watching his face, the tiny movements of a boy, the tiny features, the eyes, ears, nose, lips. The opening and closing of the hands. The little hairs tall on the arms but nowhere else, not yet.

When you were inside the room with a boy the only noises would be the boy breathing, the words the boy spoke, if there were words—and there were always words, small phrases, beggared queries—plus all the small exclamations of the body and of the shifting room. In the new city you began to have dreams of a new and better boy but you remembered the dreams best in the little room, inside its small measurements made smaller by mattresses secured to the walls, the carpeted floor thickened and deadened with more carpet, remnant scraps. Upon the carpet there was the bed and the chair, the bed prepared for a boy and the chair meant for a man, and in your dream the boy stayed in the bed, cuffed to the bottom rail, and in the bed the boy aged: first the age of the taking, then the ages after, one year after another, and at every age the boy was naked on the bed, too big for his first clothes and without you offering to find him anything else.

I'm hungry, the dream boy would say, his voice huskier now. Or he would say, I'm thirsty.

The boy would grow but not by getting bigger, he would age but he would shrink against his bones and you would shrink with him. Your bodies slimmed to skin and thin muscle. Hair falling out. Teeth, toenails, fingernails. A complete lack of nourishment but never pain or diminishment or death. You were tired but you wouldn't sleep. Both your tongues so large in your mouths, those disgusting organs. You not clothed either. Your bellies distended, plump with absence. Your penis collapsed, your scrotum hanging loose between skinny legs, your bones resting atop the wood of your chair, which by then you wouldn't have left in decades.

See the bowl and spoon from the boy's last meal, eaten years ago. See the flies, many seasons past. Their husks moving with the dust. The boy staying a boy as the years pass. Heartbeats louder without muscle between heart and skin. Ribs so soft without nutrition. The rubbery thud of the body, the papery rasp of breath.

One day the boy would be as big as you or else you would be as small as a boy and the boy would slide his emaciated ankle through the catch of the cuff and stand up beside the bed. Then he would speak or not speak, then he would stay or he would leave. If the boy went from the room you would follow. If the boy stayed, then you would stay too, content at last.

You were in the upper room when they entered the house. You heard their footsteps on the floorboards, their voices loud but casual. They were not the ones who were afraid. Whenever you were caught you hid and you were already in the best room for hiding, the last room with a lock, one you'd installed yourself. A padlock latch for either side of the door, for whichever world you occupied.

You closed and locked the door but what was a locked door but an invitation.

Inside the soundproofed room you couldn't hear their movements. Time passed but how much. Impossible to tell. All the sound in the room the sound you made yourself. The huff of breathing, a nervous wheeze through weird teeth. Perhaps they were dismantling the bathroom, ruining the walls to get to the pipes. Probably they were tearing the wiring from the bedroom or the living room. There was a kitchen without appliances but there was more wiring, more pipes. There was a basement and there was more metal downstairs in the dark. Surely they wouldn't need to enter this one room, the smallest room in the house.

But what was a locked door but an admittance there was something worth hiding.

You counted your breaths. You lost count, counted again.

The impossibility of knowing how much time passed inside a clockless room.

Then the door bucking in its frame. The dampened sound of a body thrown against wood. The return of motion to the air.

Then the door bucking again.

The door would not hold. Nothing in the wasted house would hold against such men. The door opened.

The heatless sunlight from the hallway windows flooding the room.

The silhouettes of the men, pausing only momentarily in the doorway.

You turned on the flashlight, caught white eyes and white teeth rushing into its beam of light and even though there were two men, didn't you think *they* were *him*? The one you had been waiting for, ever since he took the last boy. *Your intruder.* Didn't you think he'd somehow split into two men, each with slightly different reasons to want your blood?

Your intruder remained in the other city, the city you left, the city where all the gone boys were buried, but where it was no longer safe for you. What happened to you next had nothing to do with him or the last boy or anything else you'd done.

This was only the terrible randomness of the world.

You lifted the chair as the men with white eyes and white teeth charged, swung it once before it was taken away. They started in with their fists, a hammer. The men held you to the ground, opened your pockets, found your wallet, pulled your coat over your head. There was blood on the floor and when was the last time you'd seen your blood. Maybe never but there it was. How you'd assumed what was inside you was so different than what was inside everyone else. But you'd seen this mess before, inside the gone boys. How your last conscious thought was to renew your belief that you were at the center of a story — but then here was your premature ending — and outside your soundproof tomb the story continued without anyone even once having spoken your name.

9

B Y THE NEW YEAR, ONLY one fighter stood out from the undistinguished rest and Kelly thought of him as the contender.

The others named the contender Bringer, a name that was an action, fit for cultivation into legend, this man a myth in the making, forged before the deed, taller than Kelly by six inches, every pound of his flesh corded and bulged even under a sweat suit, his skin covered in tattoos scribed in a script Kelly could never read, his footwork quick and sure and his reach like something out of prehistory, made for bringing down the megafauna. It was only the contender that Kelly avoided, by never approaching him in the locker room, by ceding weights and machines at his advance, giving up the speed bag, the heavy bag, the sparring ring itself. Kelly thought the contender was the only boxer in the gym who would escape the zone, who might one day earn his way out of the city by the strength of his blows, the steel of his skin, his endless will.

The contender's trainer was younger and taut too, different

than the other trainers, the aging men dressed in tracksuits, bellies barely covered, questionable primes long past. The contender paid no attention to Kelly but Kelly saw the trainer watching whenever he sparred on the mats at the center of the gym. Kelly's punches would send another man reeling and in the gap the trainer would appear, standing beside the mats, his hands shoved deep into the pockets of his shorts, his eyes bright and scanning with the kind of gaze that lit you up to yourself.

Kelly, almost half past thirty and without an honest future, in this world or any other, but still strong, angry, willing. The human body as perfectible tool. The other men thought Kelly was without fear but in the trainer's eyes Kelly saw a more honest reflection, how he was almost nothing but afraid, afraid in every straining muscle fiber, every sliver of bone, every gush of blood, bile, marrow. The fear sweat from his body, stained his clothes, broke his skin with every blister and bruise. What the trainer saw would make him want something from Kelly and one day the trainer would ask. And when the day came Kelly would not deny him. It was the man who was most afraid who needed to put his fear into someone else. There had been so few people who had seen Kelly for who he was and now when he met one he wished only to say yes.

His activities began to jam against one another, a tectonics of overlap and damage. At the gym, he lifted heavier weights, lifted to forget, heaved the loaded bars over his shoulders again and again, probed the limits of his endurance. He was getting stronger faster than ever before and he took his new strength into the ring with him. When he sparred the men he fought were like ancient golems brought to new life by his want for opposition, their muscles carved of rock, their fists hard as the oldest earth. They knocked yesterday's booze out of his flesh and the breath from his chest and if he found he couldn't win he thought he'd at least bloody a lip, bruise an eye.

The world could destroy him but first he would become a destroyer too.

Now he watched the contender sparring, the contender's trainer watching too. If any of the others were boxers going anywhere he couldn't tell. He didn't know how to measure a man's quality except to throw himself against the man. A more personal metrics. The others had names but Kelly wouldn't use them, kept to *guy* or *sport* or *champ*. They called each other words he wouldn't repeat. He wasn't ignorant and as they exchanged punches he hoped they knew. He respected their difference, wanted to see it preserved. There was no equal ground anywhere but the ring was close. The body the most personal tool, its absolute lack of any privilege you didn't make yourself. Fists like meat mallets thudded against his skin and he felt the muscles beneath wearing thinner, he no longer had any fat on him so it was like their fists were striking his bones. He went down on one knee and the other man didn't stop swinging because another time Kelly hadn't either. There was a frustration in the others at his insistence on standing again, asking for more. They weren't supposed to be going this hard but Kelly always forced the blow.

At work he carried gunmetal gray file cabinets to stairwells on his broadening shoulders and dropped them down two or three or five stories, let them crash off banisters all the way to the ground, where they'd wait in the pluming dust to be dragged out across the ice. He worked with other men but they had their own tasks and he barely saw them, acknowledged them less. Every possible friendship had ended before it began. The other men just pale shades of the better men he'd known at other jobsites, separated from him by a veil of disinterest, their comradery living in a world he could see but not touch.

In the absence of time and charity his meals with the girl with the limp reverted to meat and potatoes, everything starch and protein. Winter vegetables, carrots and beets, frozen foods. Cans of beans and cans of soup. They let the hockey games play through dinner so often they only spoke during the commercials, their voices loud over the volume of Budweiser, Labatt Blue, Molson Ice. One night she looked surprised as she reached out to touch his beard, his temples—he was going gray but you couldn't tell until he got a haircut. He had stopped buying fresh food, stopped replacing his clothes. He was getting ready to leave again but he wasn't leaving her, he didn't think. He had started to notice how much more space he was taking up on the couch, the way his neck stretched the collars of his t-shirts, his thighs pulling his jeans tight into his crotch whenever he sat down. He knew how to throw a powerful punch without breaking his own wrist but he couldn't stop his skin from splitting across the knuckles. She picked up his hands and frowned at the damage she found.

Is this from the gym? she asked. Don't you wear gloves?

He said, Gloves and helmet. Mouthguard. Hand wraps and taped ankles.

He said, The gloves protect the other person. Not the striker but the one struck. Every punch you throw opens you up. You have to be willing to hurt yourself.

Be careful, she said. You're not young anymore. We're not young together.

She said, What will happen to me could happen any day and I can't do anything to stop it. But this is something you're choosing.

She wasn't wrong. He had begun wearing the watch's orange jersey underneath his other clothes, its mesh scratchy against his skin, under flannel or sweater or sweatshirt. He hadn't expected there to be so much power in the bright fabric but its intention clung to its flesh, authorized his vigilance. Now the jersey stunk no matter how he washed it, its material discolored under the armpits and around the neckline. He rinsed it every night in the sink but too often he put it back on before it was fully dry, wrapping himself in the smell of laundry soap, unscrubbed sweat.

He hid the jersey from the girl, felt more naked than ever when he removed it in the secretive dark of the bedroom. She was worried enough, already had her reasons. There was a space growing between them, the case shortening his days and nights, constraining the chances for him to be with her, the attention she received. He thought he would make it up to her soon, ask her to move in or to move to a new place together, somewhere they'd have no previous history. A new beginning. He would ask her soon but not until he closed the case. He wanted to be with her but he didn't want the case to come along.

How to protect yourself from the blow you can't see coming. This was what the other boxers talked about, beside the mats, in the locker room, while lifting heavier quantities of dull-black weights over their heads, straining thighs and calves and backs and shoulders. Chalk everywhere, on their hands and arms, the floor and the benches, and always the same topic: how to protect yourself from the invisible blow. Because it was the blow you couldn't see coming that knocked you out. If you stared into every punch you could never be put down. The illusion of control. Self-determination in battle. Kelly didn't believe in anything else he'd once believed in but he thought he might believe in this. To stop escaping what was coming. The recognition of the inevitable, the way a boxer's knees might be buckling before the blow landed, the eyes rolling back, the mouth slacking open to utter some last dumb sound.

In the morning the trainer approached Kelly in the locker room to pitch the fight, Bringer's first. The trainer said he would train them both, with his assistant serving as Kelly's corner man. There was no conflict of interest because no one—not the contender, not the trainers, perhaps not even Kelly—actually expected or wanted Kelly to win.

I think you're wrong, Kelly said. I could beat him.

No, the trainer said. But I want you to think so. I'm betting on you believing.

Kelly shook the trainer's hand, saw how the trainer knew the truest shape of his heart. His ability to keep fighting even after he'd been hurt. How even if he knew he would be hurt badly it didn't mean he wouldn't fight back, wouldn't push against every fist in the world. Always he had left behind what he'd done by giving up the portion of himself it lived within. With enough versions of himself he might compart-mentalize anything. Diminishment could be a path to action and if Bringer did nothing else he might diminish what little resistance remained.

THE BOY WAKES UP IN the middle of the night. A nightmare. He's back in the blue house, back in the basement. But this time it's not the man in the red slicker in the chair. This time it's the brother.

The boy's ankles are handcuffed to the bed. He can move but he can't leave.

He is naked but there is a blanket covering him. His body exposed but hidden.

He waits quietly. This is the brother. He is not in danger.

But then the brother says, Watch me.

The brother says, Watch this.

He says, Boy, just watch, and then the boy watches. The brother walks away from the bed, into the dark corners of the room. He's looking for something but the boy can't see what.

But I can. He's donning the red slicker, slipping inside it one arm at a time.

When the brother comes back into the light the boy starts to scream.

And then whose dreams are these.

The man in the red slicker — is he a person or an action? An action that until I found the boy I had never been able to name?

Who do I see when I picture the kidnapper?

Anyone I can put inside a red slicker.

Once upon a time the brother claimed a calendar's worth of extra-curriculars but I cannot find the evidence. If the brother was on the basketball team, then there would be practices, games, public places to surveil from within a crowd. But if these events existed they were without schedule or record.

Despite these mysteries, the brother is not impossible to track and so I track him.

I follow the brother's brown car, memorize its license plate. The same model as the man's in the red slicker, an accidental overlap with dire consequences. The boy's false schedule buys him freedom behind the wheel, access to all the city from school's end to curfew, eleven on the weekdays, midnight on Saturday. The brother's friends are not indistinguishable but at this distance I know them only by their grossest types: there is the fat one and the tall one and the thin one, each more similar than distinct. Always the brother drives, the others fighting for shotgun and the losers crowding into the backseat.

Together they visit certain houses in the zone. The brother stays in the car while the fat one goes inside. I hang back but afterward I roll by the houses again, scan the metal screens over the windows. The game the brother's playing isn't basketball but I think I know the rules.

The brother and the brother's friends drive the neighborhood closest to their school, stop to pick up girls from front porches. They smoke in the car, keep the windows rolled up for blocks before letting the world back in. I think I can hear their laughter but I know I'm not close enough. I never had these kinds of friends but I was once young and dumb too, know the story, know these girls with bad taste.

I watch while the brother and these others get high in his car, get high in lots between abandoned houses, then high in the houses. At first I maintain my distance, stay down the block in the truck. The brother knows my face but the brother never sees me. The obliviousness of youth is all the cover I need. I leave the truck behind, walk into the small trees circling the house the boy and the friends and the girls have found, approach it from the back. I can't get close enough to look through the windowless walls but I can hear the sounds of laughter from the first floor, then the brother's voice upstairs, then the sounds of him with one of the girls. A girl, yes, but a girl is not adequate cover. Not proof of anything. There had been girls for me too. There is a girl now and I know better than to believe it means the past is ended.

The brother going to school but not staying all day. The brother cutting out early, leaving at lunch and not coming back. Or else not going at all.

The brother sitting in the fast-food restaurant where the fat friend works, hanging out in the backmost booth. Not buying anything. Sitting there drinking a soda. Thumbs on his cell. Bored but nowhere to go.

The brother at the mother's house, turning off the light in the boy's bedroom.

The brother at the father's apartment, where they have to share the second bedroom.

The brother in the dark with the boy. The brother hurting the boy. Because the boy is in the room. Because the easiest victim is the one at hand.

Before he was taken from me I let the brother bring the boy to my apartment. *The brother driving him there even though the brother skipped school. A certain amount of normalcy necessary to retain access to the mother and the father, their separate homes.*

There were ninety minutes between the end of school and when I arrived home from work and some days the boy was there, let in with his own key, and some days he was not.

On the days the brother didn't bring the boy, where did the boy go?

The boy told me the brother took him home but now I know this wasn't true.

I have to be waiting outside the boy's school if I want to follow so I leave work early. It's easier if I don't ask, and the jobsite is big enough I can just wander off. I'm there on the street when the brother pulls up in the brown car. It's like watching a reenactment, every time.

The brown car pulls up. The boy gets into the car. The car takes the boy away. And if the destination is harm for the boy, does it matter who's driving?

What I want to ask: Is he your brother or isn't he?

What I want to hear: He is and he isn't.

I would say, I would never want to hurt anyone you loved.

He is and he isn't.

But I would hurt anyone who hurt you.

He has but what if someone hurt him first. What if he could learn to stop, like you learned.

But I didn't learn. But look what it cost when I failed.

The night of the brother's birthday party, I am there too, watching from the evening gloom through the windows of the green house, its lonely outpost upon this neighborless block. Inside the house, the boy attends the brother's birthday dinner, father and mother and sons reunited again. Chocolate cake, presents, a video game and a pair of sneakers. The celebration ends, the father leaves. I was inside just the one time but I know which window is the boy's. I shiver and shake and watch for him to appear in the glass. Much later I am sure the boy is asleep but still there is a nightlight burning somewhere in the room. He never told me he was afraid of the dark — a ward, perhaps, against what else he had to fear.

The brother, eighteen at last — but despite his age you had to want to call him a man.

The next week the brother moves out of the mother's house and I watch him go. He wasn't their real son and they'd never become close and what other options were there. The mother helps him carry his boxes to the car, hugs him goodbye. At first I don't know where the brother will go but it isn't hard to tail him to his new place, an apartment with the fat friend in a worse part of town. I sit in the parking lot and watch his windows, try to imagine a scenario where this is how the case ends. Because if the brother is out of the boy's life forever, then maybe there is nothing else to do.

The next day I watch as the brother picks the boy up from school. I follow the brown car as the brother drives deeper into the zone, back to the house where he had gone with his friends, his friends' girls. From a distance I watch the house, watch the silhouettes of the brother and the boy move window to window, climbing to an upper room. It's not the same room as when he was here with the girl. They're on the wrong side of the house and I can't see anything more, can't hear what is being said or done.

What I want is an excuse, a reason to let the brother go.

Certainly I admit there are blanks in the records.

Certainly I fill in what I can't prove.

I speculate. I deduce.

I make connections.

What I want for the boy is an end to fear but first I have to leave the boy in danger a little longer. Another crime, like closing the basement door one last time before returning with the hacksaw, before rescuing the boy from the dark of the low room.

I say I want to protect the boy but to do so I cannot imagine any action that is not violence against someone else. And is this limitation found in the world or is it my own most obvious flaw.

THE HEAVY DETECTIVE APPEARED AT the apartment door, flashing his badge to gain entrance. As if Kelly could refuse, as if the detective believed he would.

You again, Kelly said. The detective.

Kelly invited him in, waved him toward one of the two chairs seated at the kitchen table. The hockey game was on the television but Kelly made no move to turn down the sound. He lit a cigarette, held out the pack to the detective. The detective waved away the offer but removed his own from the inside pocket of his jacket.

Sanchez, the heavy detective said. My name is Sanchez. And today is the three-month anniversary of you walking into the hospital with Daniel in your arms. Ninety days without any new evidence means the kidnapping is officially a cold case. I'm supposed to stop working on it.

Daniel. How long had it been since Kelly last heard the boy's name spoken aloud? The day he'd given him up.

I didn't know, Kelly said.

You've been seeing him, the detective said. He comes here after school.

Kelly smoked and maintained eye contact and waited. The detective had not come to tell Kelly things Kelly knew, unless he had come to tell Kelly he knew as well. There was something the detective had come to hear him say but Kelly didn't know what. These weren't questions, required no confession.

Daniel's parents mentioned it, the detective said. They said they're not concerned but I am. I'm concerned about why the boy comes here, about what you do when the boy comes. I'm concerned because there are no clues in this case except you.

The boy is my friend, he said.

Daniel is your friend, the detective said. And my name is Sanchez. Detective Sanchez.

Kelly said, Yes. Detective Sanchez.

But that's not how you think of me.

No. It's not.

It was simply a guess. A deduction by a detective. And anyway, he wasn't wholly correct.

Never *my boy*, Kelly said. *The boy*. I think of him as *the boy*.

Yes, that's right, the detective said. That's the way you say it, the way you've said it from the first time we met. The way you said it when you made those phone calls where you wouldn't identify yourself. As if it could have been anyone else calling. So tell me: What does it mean when you call him *the boy*?

Kelly didn't answer. It wasn't anything so crude as a clue. As a child he'd learned how in the beginning there were the animals, nameless in the Garden, nameless and without knowledge of their uses. The first man, the giver of names, subjugating the beasts into a system of kingdoms, phyla, classes, and orders: thorny-headed worms, wheel carriers, claw bearers, all the rest. It was an impossible task to name all of creation but in the task there existed a chance to own the world.

And so what did the man who named nothing own.

He's not my boy, Kelly said. He comes and goes as he pleases.

It's a mistake, the detective said. That's what I came here to tell you. You are the sole person of interest in this case. You have placed yourself at the scene. If you are innocent of an unsolved crime, then it is a mistake to continue to associate with the victim.

He said, You have made yourself a suspect.

But he's gone, Kelly said. The boy has gone back to his parents. I don't see him anymore. Didn't his parents tell you? They've taken him back. Cut off contact. Whatever might have happened has already ended.

The detective stared, waited for more. The case notes were in the bedroom, in the bottom drawer of the nightstand, next to the stacked mattress. Kelly could give them to the detective, free himself of their burden. He had failed to find the man in the red slicker and he could be released of the charge. He was not a detective. No one was expecting him to solve the case but he had tried his best. He was still trying but in the end he had to admit the paltriness of his notes. The lack of conclusiveness. All the pages were filled with his script but reading them again had left him more afraid than ever. The difficulty of premeditation. How long had he known his course? He was either in or he was out. Ever since he found the boy he had been telling himself a story and it was important that at the last moment the ending became its own inevitable answer to the world.

The simplest version of the ending to come: he had promised to protect the boy.

Kelly thought he could stop everything if he could give the case notes to the detective but he knew he couldn't, not without explanation. Because he wouldn't explain himself he sat in silence, let his face sag blankly, waiting for the questioning to be over or for the blow of something worse. Thoughts followed, but nothing he would say without prompting. The heavy detective continued to talk but Kelly stopped listening. He didn't notice when he closed his eyes but when he opened them the detective was already walking out the door, shaking his head.

The blonde reporter was on the news every night and in his apartment Kelly watched the broadcast until he had seen her and the weather. The forecast was always for clouded skies and snow and whenever the reporter appeared she wore a series of pantsuits and power skirts, blue and black and light and dark gray. He watched every night but he never again saw the tan skirt, the knee-high boots. As if the outfit had been worn for his benefit.

On-screen, she stood beside a median over the west-east freeway, drive time passing fast behind her, the last gasp of quick movement before the nightly slowing of traffic. This was the day of the shooter on the freeway, each shot coming out of a moving vehicle, fired across the median. No one had been killed but the blonde reporter said a wounded man had tickets to the hockey game. The home team lost and the man got treated for a bullet wound and this was the city they lived in. Now the blonde reporter spoke over a photograph of a cracked window, the bullet hole intact in the middle of the glass. Kelly lifted his own loaded pistol from where it sat beside him on the couch, raised it to the screen. Aimed its barrel at the bullet hole.

The blonde reporter's voice was speaking but he seldom listened to her words. He steadied the pistol. He mouthed the word *bang* until the bullet hole was gone, replaced by a map of the lower half of the state, covered in fluorescent clouds.

Snow again, the weatherman said, and temperatures dropping ever closer to zero.

Kelly picked up his cell, called the blonde reporter, the number on her card pasted in the case notes. When she answered Kelly said his name and waited. When she didn't respond immediately he said it again, growled a question. Did she remember him or not. Would she see him again. Could he buy her a drink.

The case notes were in his hands now. He said, There's something I need to tell you.

I'm married, remember? she said.

I do remember, he said. The ring's fake.

Not anymore, she said. She'd met a man, engaged him. Now her ruse was her reality.

But you're not married, he said. Only engaged.

Engaged to be married. It's the same thing.

Nothing is the same thing, he said. There are no equivalencies.

Kelly liked how when you hung up a cell phone there was no dial tone after. Just the ending of sound, its trailing absence.

The next morning the reporter called back, said she could interview him again. The sports anchor had told her about the fight, about Kelly versus the contender. Bringer was someone who mattered, who viewers could be convinced to cheer. More human interest. The accidental hero versus some future greatness of the sport. A feature story, the blonde reporter offered, a way to close the loop, to connect the finding of the boy with the battle of man versus man.

As mornings passed the preparations for the fight took on a fated aspect: if Kelly were hurt or killed in the fight, then without him the target would go free. He threw himself recklessly against the bodies of the other men, sought a stance to bring them hardest against him in return. What could he say or do to them to remove their hesitance, their resistance to the possibility of lasting harm? He jabbed, circled, jabbed, and moved in for a clinch, a chance to push his forehead into the face of another man, a chance to lift a knee into a thigh or kneecap. He fought dirty, sought to anger, bragged in the locker room to anyone who would listen. There was no difference between the amount of force necessary to knock a man out and the amount necessary to kill a man and he invited whatever might come, wanted to taunt it out of his opponents. They shied away, left him alone in the shower room. He told himself they were practicing for an exhibition and he was preparing for something real, outside the ring. Not the representation of battle but battle itself. Every injury became an exhumation by exhaustion, until there would be nothing hidden, nothing buried, nothing left, and when he was nothing but bruises he would carry his blood in his skin and what was trapped within him would be brought to the surface.

The trainer stopped him in the locker room, handed him a paper-wrapped package. He smiled as Kelly tore the paper to uncover the necessary ceremonial garb: a new pair of red gloves, the red-and-white shorts, the hooded red robe.

A gift, the trainer said. For your first and only fight.

Now the scrapper. Now the salvor. Until the duty was done.

Now the deep winter. Now the blue air and the slow cracking of concrete against the frozen and immovable earth. Now the streets ever more vacant in the zone, all Kelly's knowledge of their topography blurred by constant snowfall. Now the unbroken clouds hiding the pale and heatless heart of the sun.

Now Kelly returned to the neighborhood where he'd found the boy, circled the missing house, read the street's graffiti as prophecies, premonitions, threats. THE GREAT HOPE, he read. ONCE AGAIN spelled ONCE AGIAN. Words he couldn't read, words in Spanish and Polish and Arabic, other scripts he couldn't identify, mangled senseless by ornamentation. THE ONLY AGE. A dead raccoon crushed in the street, tagged with blue spray paint, the photorealistic face of a child stenciled onto a brick wall, bracketed by birth date, death date. He rarely saw another person outside but he saw their evidence. DEAD SERIOUS. AMOS, LIED TO. He saw snowplows moving through some blocks but more of the streets went unplowed. There were streets where he wasn't convinced there was one human soul remaining and those were the blocks he searched the hardest. The longer the walk the braver it made him. The boredom of being alone, walking below the many names of the Messiah scrawled in spray paint, the higher the holier. More names everywhere, names falling down, and when the names were gone what city would remain.

This was his last chance but what was the chance the man in the red slicker was wearing the same clothes. What was the chance he looked anything like what Kelly had imagined. Kelly didn't know, kept moving house to house, block to block. He opened gates, walked up to front doors, tested locks and knockers, and in every entranceway he wanted to yell *Hello*, to yell *Is anyone home*, to yell out some right name.

In one living room he looked around at the frozen carpet and he said, If I knew a name I wouldn't be here.

In some kitchen—the sink thick with the petrified shit of some animal, a cat or else something larger, wilder—he said, I want to be the one who stops this but I don't know if I am.

The zone was bigger on the inside than on the outside, the interior spaces of houses each yawning blanker than Kelly had ever imagined. Even without the case notes he made new guesses, inferences, imprecise triangulations. When he was tired of driving he parked the truck in front of nameless bars, their windows lit by neon signs advertising brands he'd thought extinct. He ordered whiskeys until he slurred his questions and then he backed down to beer. Other men drank from tall cans and low glasses and they watched the aggressive way Kelly moved his growing body and he liked the way they watched. In some bars there were nothing but men. All of his responses became inappropriate, crossed up. Once he got so angry he got most of an erection. In a parking lot he broke an offending nose with his fists, put a boot into the wheezing man's ribs before stumbling off to vomit into the gravel. He said, This wasn't an investigation but an interrogation — but later he couldn't remember who he had said it to.

The reporter sent him clips from their filming, private links to web-hosted videos Kelly loaded on his phone. In her email she apologized, said the news loved weird but this was too weird to air: the fight hadn't happened but they were done filming. The phone's screen was three inches wide and so he saw himself in miniature, a homunculus moving through a blighted landscape, the monochrome of the midwestern winter. A certain kind of starkness, the elemental bleakness of a man astride a wilderness of concrete and steel, acid rain and brick and rust.

The word *homunculus*. Where had it come from. What documentary, what book.

She was trying to get promoted, her email said, not fired.

His teeth were still firmly seated but he worried other connections in his head were loosening. He watched the clips and he tried to remember their context. In the first clip he saw a house he had scrapped before finding the boy, where the cameraman and the blonde reporter followed from outside the frame so Kelly appeared to be talking to himself. The walls of the house were opened, and on-screen he kneeled beside them, explained what he might have removed from where. He couldn't recall being so knowledgeable but here he was describing the kinds of pipes the wall had held, the old copper, the discarded technology of the wiring, knob and tube everywhere in the house. Single-insulated copper conductors, he heard himself saying. Joist and stud drill holes, porcelain insulating tubes, porcelain knob insulators.

The insulating sleeves pulled through the walls were called *looms*, he said.

In this house the looms were made of cloth, he said. Other houses, rubber.

In her email, the reporter wrote, *Please do not contact me again. Please consider getting help. Best of luck to you in your recovery.*

One of his ears was swelled and bruised, an ugly organ. He strained to hear over the ringing. The second clip showed Kelly at work, silently shoveling swept debris into a dumpster. His face was blank, his eyes distant. There weren't any other people in the frame and this shot was lonelier than the last. He was in the parking lot in front of an abandoned motor lodge but you couldn't tell from this angle. He could hear an excavator but not see it. The whole block was being leveled and this was one of the last structures. The space around him swelled, swallowed him up. The camera angle widened to better show the absence of nearer structures, the length of the remaining building, a sign bearing some of the letters of the name of the motel. The latest in a line of such signs, partial namings. As if a part of a word did you any good. As if you could half name a city, a country, the world.

The third video showed Kelly at the gym in sweats and a t-shirt, Kelly bigger than he had ever seen himself before. Heaving steel weights over his shoulders until every part of him bulged. A look in his eyes Kelly didn't recognize from any mirror. Then his fists on the heavy bag, too slow, his movements looking stunned and stupid but delivering enough force to shudder the bag out of the grinning trainer's grip.

The final clip opened with a close-up of Kelly, seated before the camera on his couch, his living room splayed in the background. All the familiarity gone. How anything could be rendered alien by the camera. He took the phone into the living room, sat on the couch, and pressed PLAY, then stood, walked around the coffee table, kneeled where the cameraman had kneeled.

It was like watching through an instrument of magic. He could look above the phone and see he wasn't there but through the screen he saw himself sitting in his usual spot, talking about scrapping, about the weight of things, the relative weights. Car batteries were worth so much a pound but they were so heavy, so dirty. Still he took one where he could find one, he said.

Steel was heavier than a lot of things, he heard himself say. A mass of aluminum weighed less than a mass of copper or iron.

The slow terror of his heartbeat. He didn't remember saying what he was saying on-screen. Now he seemed to be reciting the weights of various mammals, various birds. *A wolverine,* he seemed to be saying.

What is the weight of a badger? he said. Twenty or twenty-five or thirty pounds.

He was a little drunk watching but how drunk had he been when he said these words, when he let them tape him saying them? A condor is a heavy bird, he said, and he looked so exhausted saying it.

The video was less than halfway over but he didn't think there was anything else except more of this. The species and weights began to come faster, with less commentary. The weight of the hummingbird and the seagull and the common rat. The weight of the hyena. The weight of the buffalo — *the bison*, he slurringly corrected himself — and the weight of the spotted owl.

Where had he learned these things. What long-forgotten encyclopedia, read by flashlight so his father would know he wasn't asleep, because his father would only enter after the room was dark. The accumulation of so many useless facts a by-product of a childish defense.

In the video his face was utterly serious but more animated than ever. His hands sat in his lap, atop his spread knees, one hand limp across each thigh. He spoke the weight of the white-tail deer. The weight of bears, the male, the female, the cub each a different weight. The weight of the whale and the squid. He was slurring worse, exhibited a strokelike stutter. If Kelly had been watching someone else he would have thought this was a man dying delirious.

If Kelly had been watching anyone else he would have been happier than he was watching himself.

The video ended. The phone was not a magic window.

There was not another Kelly here. The Kelly he had seen was the only Kelly he was. He saw again how he didn't have access to all of himself but no matter what was revealed he did not believe he could be made to quit the story or to turn from its end.

CONCRETE EVERYWHERE, CEMENT EVERYWHERE ELSE. Gray clouds and gray snow and gray earth. The destruction of the plant had advanced since he was last there or else he was more aware of what was gone. There was heavy equipment parked on-site, long red trailers for scrap and garbage. He couldn't come during the day anymore, wouldn't risk being seen by credible witnesses. He searched the plant at night, moved his light through the shattered rooms. As he walked he imagined finding a chasm in the floor of a building, and beneath that hole a great staircase spiraling into the earth, each landing another hallway full of rooms, locked and unlocked doors. Instead he found a tiny aperture secreted into the ground, a break in the surface wide enough to fit a man. Underneath, an uneven descent led to a single set of stairs, a single door. Beyond the door waited a hallway, its first span barely intact, the rest collapsed ten or fifteen feet in, and at the end of that hallway there was another door giving access to a small square room, a space sufficient to the task.

The enumerating of possibilities, the weighing of costs, the sharp rise toward a cliff of certainty: this wasn't the easiest way but for every action there was a right space. Whenever the variables increased he tried to back up, to rethink. In his apartment he loaded the tools into two duffel bags, each meant for athletic gear but put here to different use. Their weight strained his new shoulders, curved his back. He loaded the truck with the bags, returned for the generator and the lights, everything else hidden at the back of his only closet, buried behind his few outfits. As he worked he heard from some cave within his chest the salvor, unopposed by the scrapper one last time.

He could always abandon the tools, he heard himself say. There was still a choice to be made.

It was enough to have saved the boy, he argued — but then he had to ask, Was the boy saved enough?

The salvor and the scrapper were not exactly voices, more urgencies, rushing gushes of suggestion, potential actions. At first hearing them had required a diminishing of Kelly's own personality through alcohol or exhaustion. Now he heard their urges in every moment and either might make him move.

Underground there was no difference between day and night but he could only risk arriving in the night. He drove back to the plant, found the building again. Everything looked different in the dark but he was careful as he carried the duffel bags in past the shattered outer walls, over dumped trash, blown debris. There were long hallways leading into the plant but he knew which way to head. Inside one room there was the hole and the shattered slope of floor and at the bottom the door busted out of its shape.

Past the door there'd be no way to see him from the surface. There was a certain deepness he wanted, a certain distance from the ground and the city and the sky. Any violence there would be a private act: *A man and a man went into a dark room and only one of them came out.* A terrible fairy tale the length of a sentence.

When Kelly was finished he took the case notes from his back pocket and he placed them on the floor, their pages thickened with pasted maps, poor photographs, the weight of ink and frequent handling. He took his lighter from his pocket and because he didn't need them anymore he set the case notes on fire. The flames of his confession didn't last long but for a time they lit the blank cave of the room with their flicker.

There was the cave down within Kelly too and now he had made that cave this room.

He left the plant but he wasn't ready to go home. The girl with the limp wasn't at work but he knew he wasn't ready to see her, not in this mood. The boy was lost to him and there wasn't anywhere else he was wanted. As he drove the streets he passed the storefront church he'd seen from the top of the plant, the bright glow of the prayers within. When he parked the truck in front of the windows to watch the dancing prayer inside he caught the eye of some apostle, the leader of the congregation. The apostle held a plastic sword in one hand, lifted the other to beckon Kelly in. A gesture of ecstatic welcome. As if it were so easy for a prodigal to return to the fold.

THE CIRCLE TURNED AND THE congregation turned around its hem, the apostle leading his followers, their feet dancing behind his feet, tracing the invisible circle his steps circumscribed, a geometry of belief cut across the stained concrete floor, the blackened squares where the rows of washers used to be. The circle contained and guided them and as they turned they lifted toy swords and crimson banners, raised voices toward tongues. The folding-table altar held the speakers and the speakers were containers too, containing cheap electric crackle and the salvation of the congregation, which did not require fidelity, only volume, the voice of the spirit technology-amplified, extracted out of the fire and the dove and magnetized onto tape and uttered upward at decibel strengths born of the far end of the dial.

There were ways to take the air out of a room and this noise was one conceivable method.

Along the edges went the chairs, the buckets lined with plastic bags, ready for the vomit and the retching and the casting out. The congregation used to unfold the chairs into rows but now the chairs were rarely used. Let the faithful sit in their houses. In God's house they would stand and move to his Word. The spirit needed space to churn but the apostle wasn't fancy about smells, walls, former tenants. Any empty room could be a space for the spirit to move a miracle and the apostle and his ministers were there to work the deliverance, to cast out the demons of anxiety and shyness, the demons of addiction, the demons of obesity and fornication.

The miracle was that the swords were just imported plastic, made from recycled soda bottles and lead paint. It was the symbol they needed, not what the symbol was made of.

The miracle wasn't how you were cured. The miracle was how God was willing to cure you again when you fell.

There were at least one hundred eleven ailments a deliverance could cure and the saints could name them all. When the apostle told stories, he encouraged people to take notes. A reminder of what could go wrong. Tattoos drew demons close. Piercings revealed the promiscuous. A woman with a stud in her nose had opened herself to wantonness. When the microphone squealed it was the demon *Bling Bling*. It wasn't a biblical name but most of the demons weren't so named. The enemy bred them from scratch in every age, improved his technology. Anything new could bear his sigil.

The apostle had seen third-degree burns take on cloaks of baby skin, seen cataracts leeched from eyes. Mending lame legs was old and easy work that started in the circle, with the dancing, the music so loud it could shatter eardrums for the spirit to heal. The will was tied to the flesh. You had to get the body exhausted so what ailed it could be drawn free and broken by the Word.

The apostle clapped, asked for a volunteer: Who among you came to be delivered?

Now someone unfolded a chair, placed it before the two

ministers in heavy sweaters and slacks flanking the one to be delivered. Everyone else shaking plastic swords in the air, howling in tongues, spinning the circle. From the street passersby could see what they were doing, through the floor-to-ceiling glass meant to show off the mechanics of laundry. Some of the storefront churches smeared their windows with paint or covered them with paper but the apostle left them clear, kept them clean. Some nights he saw a face pressed to the street side of the glass, leaving the smear of the curious, but inside the church they weren't doing anything needing hiding. He wanted the dark streets to see the bright work being done beneath fluorescent light.

The one to be delivered stepped forward, took his seat. The apostle could see what was inside him, could reckon all his failures, the demons obvious but the bad choices visible too. Because not every impulse was the enemy's and this man had as much free will as any other.

The one to be delivered shook at the apostle's touch, recoiled from his voice. His boots stamped the floor, wrung more sweat free from his jumping body. It was darkest bluest winter and the man was dressed for the weather, had kept his coat on the whole dance. The look in his eyes, the exhaustion, the fear, his and not his. He named some of his demons at sentence length, readying his voice for story, but the apostle stopped him.

Demons aren't complicated, the apostle said, smearing a thumbprint of ash across the other's forehead. No need to confess their every title. Just give us their names.

Give us *Grief*. Give us *Sorrow*.

Say the names *Abuse, Abuser, Abused.* Say the name *Suicide.*
If it's drink, then name it *Drink.* If it's drugs, then name
it *Drugs.* If you're a thief, then you've got a thief inside you,
named by his action.

Name the killers, the apostle said. Speak every name of
every bedeviling thing. The music boomed. The members
of the congregation held their swords up and they spoke
their high speech and at his command the apostle saw the
angels filling the room too, their winged glory summoned,
their pale and dark faces. God had made an angel for every
shade and an office to obliterate every shadow and they were
in the room too, ready for the one who was to be delivered
to call out the names of their opposites and as he did so the
expressionless angels stepped forward and put their flaming
brands to what was called. Someone set a plastic-lined trash
can in front of the one being delivered and he filled it with
retch and when the sickness was out of him the two ministers on his sides lifted him to his feet, wrapped him in their
embrace, a new brother.

Say what you've come for, the apostle said, and the one
delivered answered.

Sanction, he said. *Protection.*

The one delivered was wobbly on his feet but the ministers
added him to the circle again, got him back in step, pressed
a dollar's worth of plastic into his hand. There were others
to save and his voice would help the saving get done—a
charge, a commission. The speakers offered loud directions
to the body, and if the one delivered couldn't speak right yet,
it owed to how he opened his mouth. He could mimic, work

out some call-and-response until he earned his own voice, his own universal manner of speech. The apostle hollered above the noise, danced with his feet high, lifted his knees and kicked up his robes, promised tonight they would all sleep sweet dreams, and the one delivered heard this, considered. The apostle said it was hard to sleep with the lights on but it was impossible to rest without the light within and by the end of the night they would all have their light renewed. The apostle said he would preach until dawn if it delivered them all. The apostle said he was sixty-two years old and if it took forever to put all these waiting angels to work then he planned to live forever.

10

THE EVENING OF THE FIGHT Kelly awoke with ashes on his forehead and his heart thudding wrong—a scuttling, a shallowness. In the bathroom he listened as his heartbeat drummed louder, the blood jerking. He locked his hands over the ache in his chest, pressed hard, as if from outside the ribs he might hold the jumping muscle still. When he turned on the shower he didn't wait for the water to warm, just sat down on the edge of the tub and let the cold water fall. Afterward his eyes jittered in the mirror, bloodshot and blank. There was a slackness to his mouth he hadn't seen before. He brushed his teeth, scrubbed the night from his skin, ran a comb through his hair, forced the part. When he dragged the razor across his face the coldest skin resisted, begrudged. He moved carefully across the floor, water everywhere underfoot, slicking the tiles. He fed his body broader commands, noticing every step of every action, thinking of the parts of objects. He smoked before he brushed his teeth and then he dressed, an undershirt, underwear and pants, the watchman's jersey under heavy flannel, thick socks and the worn boots, the impossible loops of the laces.

While he dressed he watched the news and on-screen the blonde reporter said this was the week ten new homicides were reported inside the zone. Ten homicides including two triple killings. Ten homicides including five men and four women and one child. The names of the victims withheld pending notification of the family. The names of the killers withheld pending arrest and arraignment.

This was the week a burnt and decapitated body was found inside a closed and shredded elementary school, found in a hallway with torn ceilings, with busted tile, without locker doors or lockers left.

This was the week a suspected arson killed a man and a woman and a seven-year-old girl at one thirty in the morning, their bodies falling through the collapsing house, drowned in the smoke and the fire.

This was the week a woman was shot dead in her driveway, still sitting in the driver's seat with two other friends in the car. The shooter *a man in dark clothing*.

This was the week a clerk and two elderly customers died at a check-cashing center in a strip mall, the clerk shot despite the bulletproof storefront. There was a buzzer she had to press to let customers in but how could she know who was dangerous before they were standing at the counter.

This was the week a charred body was found inside a trash can behind a bar and this was the week the spokeswoman for the medical examiner's office said the body was burnt beyond recognition but at least they had his teeth.

This was the week a woman was killed by a neighbor when she knocked on his door, her face bloodied and cut, seeking help after a car accident. This was the week the homeowner opened a locked door to fire a shotgun at the color of her skin.

This week was the week it always was.

What would it have taken to make this week different.

She wouldn't come to the fight because she didn't want to see him get hurt and for Kelly there was no one else. Before the appointed time arrived the trainer came into the locker room, sat down in the corner where Kelly was resting, his eyes heavy, hands wrapped and gloved and ready. Kelly wore the red shorts and the red shoes and the orange jersey of the watch, considered his color-draped bulk in the mirror across from the bench. He lifted his eyes at the trainer's approach but didn't stand to meet him. Whatever had happened in the circle of swords had taken everything he had but he hoped his energy would return before the fight began. The effects of the late mass lingered, the lifting of the swords, the turning circle, the loud thunder of the boombox, the ashes streaked across his forehead, the presence he hadn't felt in many years. Perhaps imagined, he didn't know. In his youth he had craved this feeling. He thought he did not believe in God again but he did still believe in that feeling, the absolute and temporary lack of doubt.

You're not wearing the robe, the trainer asked.

No, said Kelly. Is it time?

Not yet. Soon.

I'm ready.

Soon. Make it a good show and you'll get your money.

I won't fall for nothing.

You will.

I won't.

I wanted you because I knew you'd think so.

I won't.

He'll hit you. He'll hurt you. Bringer will punch you until you go down or the referee makes him stop and you will have no chance of changing this.

This isn't what's going to happen.

Like I said. I knew you'd think so.

It was nothing but bravado speaking. Kelly hadn't come to win but to lose in the right way. He'd never understood the scoring, didn't want to keep score. He only needed to understand if he didn't plan on forcing the knockout.

When Kelly entered the gym he saw the lights turned up, a spotlight over the center of the mats inscribing a glowing circle in the center of the ring. The crowd wasn't large but there were more people watching than Kelly was used to, more noise. The chatter before the spectacle, the boredom muddled with expectation, the crowding of bodies in the motionless air, the gym the hottest room Kelly could remember, sweat already wicking his skin.

The trainer walked out beside Kelly, lifting the ropes for Kelly to climb into the ring. He spoke to Kelly's corner man, then took his place on the opposite side: the contender assigned the blue corner, Kelly dressed in his gifted red. The contender not coming out until Kelly was set. Making Kelly wait, trying to shake his nerve. At last the contender ducking under the ropes, arriving tall and sleek in his corner, his body in motion even before he dropped his robe.

The revealment of the boxer hidden beneath the garment, the contender's name on the lips of every spectator: *Bringer. Bringer. Bringer.* This man Kelly did not know but that he had agreed to hurt, to be hurt by. An abstraction of the deadliest order.

Kelly pulled the orange jersey over his head as the referee began to speak. The call to the center. The expectations of a good fight, a clean fight. The gloves touching gloves. The bell ringing and the contender not waiting for Kelly, coming at him faster and stronger than Kelly had imagined but in both men there existed a matching will to hurt, to be hurt, the suspension of the man outside the ring for the man within, for the contest, the agony, the two words that once meant the same thing.

The contender loomed a foot taller than Kelly but Kelly moved in on him, ducked low under the contender's sprawl. Kelly was comfortable in the clinch, tried to nullify the difference in reach, but the contender was fast on his feet, technically skilled in a way Kelly would never be. The contender landed a first punch harder than any Kelly had ever suffered and at first Kelly couldn't find a way under the punches that followed. He took a step back, another. Another punch landed and Kelly thought of the tightrope beam above the plant, the impossibility of walking it backward like the total ineffectiveness of Kelly's defense, the sudden uselessness of raising his arms, of trying to ball up against the contender—at last the

real violence had arrived, the end of the simulation of sparring, the absolute terror of a fighter born to fight — and by the
end of the first minute Kelly was forced to embrace his inability to defend himself, the muscles in the shoulders numbed
and dumbed by the contender's fists.

Kelly pushed back in, swung wildly, fought against the
gaining lethargy. He crossed his feet, made other mistakes. For
the first time in his life he felt his true age, the accumulation
of injury obvious in the face of the contender's still-limitless
youth. The gap between them only a few years, a slim fraction
of a life. But enough. More than.

The bell rang, the round ended. The water bottle, the towel,
the encouraging word. The fight a third over and who knew
what the score was.

The bell rang, the next round began.

Kelly knew someone should stop the fight but his trainer
was the contender's trainer and what the trainer wanted was
a knockout. One of Kelly's eyes was shutting, the swell of his
brow collapsing his vision on the left side. The contender
jabbed, jabbed again, followed with a hook, a cross, more
punches Kelly couldn't track, couldn't count. The number
of punches fewer than you might imagine. Kelly had made
himself strong but strength alone wasn't a strategy. He had
made himself tough but toughness wasn't enough.

With every strike his quiet mind exploded into sound.

The cacophony, the choir: thought, voice, memory, the
simultaneous swarm.

Bringer drove a fist through the side of Kelly's head and
for the first time Kelly's knee touched the mat. The brain

suddenly a size too big for the shell. Sparks flooded Kelly's eyesight as he pushed himself upright but a grin grew around his mouthguard, a wrong-shaped expression easily mistaken for a grimace.

What Kelly saw: the way the contender rushed in, the way he could be goaded.

The bell rang, the round ended.

The water bottle, the towel, the bell ringing again so fast.

The third round began. The contender uninjured, undaunted, moving fast toward Kelly's corner. Encouraged by the damage he'd done. Kelly protected his face, protected his body, let the injury come. This was the way. Not only to turn the cheek but to offer the entire person. He took one blank step, then another. He was afraid but the fear could make him stronger. He would act out of his fear but first he needed to be scared enough to move.

The contender landed uncounted punches, each one accompanied by a grunted exhalation of angry breath. Their breathing grew sharp, strained. The contender tired now too. Every fighter exhausted in the third round. You could win and still injure yourself with the effort. Kelly dropped to a knee again, invited the overeager rush. It took everything left to stand into the next blow, to take one more punch on his way around the contender — and the gorgeous punch broke every last resistance, exploding a sound inside Kelly's head, a tearing of some supporting structure twisting free of the skull — and for a moment Kelly found his advantage, its fantastic temporariness, the contender's body turned sideways, his flank exposed for mere seconds.

Kelly filled those seconds with his fists, held back nothing. There was no future to his strategy, only a winnable present. He heard the dulled and distant roar of the crowd as he drove the contender to the mat, nearly punching him all the way down, as he stepped away from the falling body and into the rising sound.

The old ringing in his ears. The sound of the fire. The sound that existed long before the fire. He spit out his mouthguard, found the name caught behind his teeth.

Bringer, he said. Stand up.

The referee counting: one second, two seconds, three.

Bringer, Kelly said. Come on.

Now the contender standing into the same noise, the cries of the crowd, their vocalized belief in the possibility of his defeat. Now the contender left with no choice, now the outcome requiring a knockout because nothing else would satisfy the crowd. Now the trainer howling ecstatic, in love with his orchestration of the disaster.

Kelly raised his gloves, jerked his fists toward his body, called in the blow. *Thou shalt not kill* suspended for another minute and a half. He didn't have any legs left but he raised his gloves and with them he said *Kill me* and when Bringer came carrying the killing punch across the mat Kelly surrendered into the absolute absence of doubt: If Kelly died the target would go free. If Kelly lived he would take the target. If Bringer struck him right he might never experience doubt again, instead only this fear perfect enough to swallow him whole, a whale of fear, and from inside its black body he saw more darkness, and from the dark he watched Bringer's last punch leave the shoulder at speed, bringing with it the first pinpricks of light appearing somewhere in the black, stars come to see him home, constellations lit for no one else.

When the punch arrived Kelly felt every higher function stall, his body tumbling, feet turning under softening ankles, calves collapsing, the knees going sideways, the stupid body crashing like a carcass from its hook. The judder of the mat coming up to meet him. Behind closing lids he tried to protect the memory of the impossible thing he'd seen: the knockout blow you were never supposed to see coming, how as it had moved through space to strike his body Kelly knew he would never die. It was as if the match had not actually ended. Before the knockout *Thou shalt not kill* had been suspended and for as long as the injunction remained absent Kelly might do as he wished.

When he opened his eyes the contender was already leaving the ring, the trainer and his assistant both by the contender's side, the crowd heading out into the night satisfied, high on the simulated destruction of a man. Kelly was alone upon the mat with the ringside doctor, who checked Kelly's open eye, pronounced him concussed, guided him to the locker room. The doctor tested his reflexes, listened to his breathing, bandaged a cut atop his bruised cheek. Kelly measured the tightness in his chest, the numb ache in his limbs, said nothing. He was seeing two different rooms, one out of the closed eye, one out of the open eye, but he didn't describe either to the doctor. He hadn't eaten a meal all day but his stomach felt full, bloated. He'd known it could come to this but he kept quiet, wanted the ticking clock in his chest left untouched.

Or else not a ticking but a thudding, the wet slop of uneven blood forced through the centermost chamber of his body, a wet clock counting down to calamity.

After the doctor left Kelly opened his locker, found the promised cash waiting for him in an envelope folded into the back pocket of his jeans, the envelope thinner than he expected but the money all there.

Outside in the parking lot Kelly fell asleep behind the wheel of the truck, the engine off, the cab cold. He woke up, turned the key, put the truck in gear. The engine rumbled to life, the dash lit, its dials incomprehensible enough Kelly knew there was more damage. Or else his life had become a dream, because here was the impossibility of numbers and letters in dreams. He was tired but even tired he was strong. He thought something was punched loose and he thought it would let him do anything. There were a certain number of hours of night left and they would have to be enough. It would be over by morning or else it would never end.

11

H E HAD PRETENDED HE HADN'T built the body for this purpose but here was the powerful body in perfect motion: The target stepped out of his car, turning to lock the car door as the left fist struck his head twice, as the other arm snaked around the head, catching under the chin with the crook of the elbow, the same hand catching the opposite bicep. The right hand gripping the back of the skull, pushing forward. The elbows brought together, a steady pressure, the free hand squeezing the hold shut.

After Kelly let go he had to mind the seconds, work fast against the count. As soon as oxygen returned so would the world, beat by beat: the parking lot outside the apartment complex, the lit rooms above, the television glares and radio bass. He picked the dropped keys off the pavement, opened the trunk of the target's car, lifted the groggy target inside. The body heavy and already stirring so he had to strike the target again, every movement nervous now, less controlled, until Kelly landed a punch across the side of the face disorienting enough to let him get the target's hands behind the back, to

get the wrists taped. The legs were stronger, took longer spins
of the tape. He didn't want to suffocate the target but he had
to cover the mouth too, ran the tape around the head once,
twice, trying to keep it below the nose but working fast.

Kelly shut the trunk, got behind the wheel, locked the
doors. He checked his phone, considered the time remaining.
It was late but there was plenty of night left. Had anyone seen
him? Most of the apartments he could see were dark. The rest
were lit by televisions, monitors, the eyes inside the apartments pointed anywhere except the windows. If you lived in
a place like this maybe you tried not to look at it.

Now the black plant rose again before Kelly, some beginning
and middle and end all contained within the plant's long
decline, its still-undemolished structure. Kelly navigated the
plant's expanse of concrete and brick, its streets that would
have been strange in the uninhabited deep of the night even
without the new snow falling wet and heavy, the slush on
the road making the unfamiliar car harder to handle. He
parked the car in a brick alley, close to the entrance to the
underground. He stepped out into the falling snow, opened
the trunk, waited until the target's eyes found him before
displaying the black pistol. He gave orders, explained next
steps: How the tape around the ankles would be cut. How
the target would get out of the trunk but not run. How running was the biggest mistake the target could make. How
they would walk from the car through the open wall of the
nearest building. How inside the building there was a broken floor, an aperture beneath which he would find a subtle

path down into the basement. How you had to know to look for it. How in the basement there was a hallway that led to a room. How inside the room a metal chair waited. How the target would sit down on the chair.

When the tape was cut the target tried to run but the pistol was there to strike the back of his skull, to prod his stumbling in the right direction: the entrance to the building, the closed door, the collapsed floor, the pitched descent. The gun held the target steady while Kelly worked the padlock installed at the door, then again in the low room, when the target couldn't find the chair where he'd been ordered to sit, instead reeling around the dark like Kelly had in the ring, the world he'd believed he inhabited having ended so violently it was as if it had never existed.

A sweep of his headlamp revealed the low room as he'd imagined it, untouched since he'd last visited, its square space separated from the world above by a difficult distance. A home for spiders but not much else. Even the rats gone for ages. When he turned off the lamp a stratum of darkness filled the vacuum. He listened to his breathing, listened to the other's, the crying and the heaving. There was enough tape around the target's body to make it hard to move, hard to breathe. The crying a nasal wheeze, signaling disbelief in what was happening. Kelly was having trouble too. Both of them together now.

The stale room burst with human activity. Kelly started the generator, let its hum fill the two heavy lights set facing the target. Now there was a darkness where Kelly could retreat, a space beyond the light the target's vision wouldn't be able to penetrate. Kelly had forgotten to don the mask but he did so now, the welder's shield heavy upon his swollen face, burdening his skull. He returned in silhouette, palmed the target's bound face and pushed it back, applied some pressure. The muscles moving the bones, the teeth and the tongue trapped behind the tape, everything he touched young and healthy, no sign of sickness in the body.

Kelly had waited, watched for borders, thresholds, a birthday. He'd had to make the target a man so he could hurt him like one.

Not a man but a bully, he heard someone say. The face of a bully.

The mouth below his hand was trying to speak too but the words were muffled by the leather of the gloves covering the face, the duct tape beneath. Kelly pictured the head of a horse, then a wasted ape. Something dumbly animal. But who was he picturing. And was it ever the victim who stopped feeling human first.

He used a pair of scissors to open the target's shirt but he finished the cut with his hands, ripping the fabric to expose the target's chest, the belly, the arms, the back, the skin swallowed in hurt, heaving with sweat. He was having trouble seeing the target through the harsh glare of the lights but by their glow he knew his own body's recent unfamiliarity, the largeness of every part of it, the way his straining muscles had stretched over his frame. He was the heaviest he had ever been, possessed a certain enormity he hadn't imagined possible. Now he thought the deep gravity of the world dragged upon him, the way that gravity grew the lower you sank, the way his hands were not any larger than before but their thickness increased. His thighs squeezed into his pants, feet squeezed into tight boots. His neck a widening trunk for his heavy head, his head lean and strained with veins but weighted with memory begetting action, weighted with the mask and its slim slot of vision. All of it another mistake. As if improving the body were the same as improving the man. As if physical strength made moral right.

When the flesh was exposed he opened one of the duffel bags on the floor, empty except for one last folded item. He shook out the folds, then draped the red robe around the target's shoulders, pulled the hood up over his head. The target tried to throw off the garment but there were ways to stop his struggling. What was done to the boy couldn't be undone. Kelly could punish the people who hurt him but it would not rewind the clock. These things happened and somehow he couldn't help them happening again. He had lived a life meant to avoid the problem and he had slipped once, had sworn off children of his own, but had loved a woman with a child, had loved the child. Then love had not been enough.

Understanding required argument. The scrapper thought the sound of fists was one place they might start their speech. His hands already aching. His theologies had grown muddled but he said he believed even a single crime could charge you. Everything was equal, every action and word that crossed over from intent to occurrence. The scrapper needed to transfer the fear from one body to the other. He put bruised fists to use, he moved through the tools. He kicked the chair, then righted it again, its frame heavy with the target's taped weight. Perhaps there were deep rituals in the world but he was making this one up as he went. The sound from behind the tape turned his stomach but didn't unturn his hand. He wondered at the words, trapped inside the other's mouth, tasting of the tack of tape. The lungs full of beggared screams, unable to push them out. He heard his own voice speaking but he struggled after the words. There was a certain lack of comprehension he had grown accustomed to but how quickly this encounter had moved beyond any previous threshold.

Are you a boy or are you a man, Kelly heard the salvor ask. Because if he was a boy, then what different crime was this. Age was not enough. Age was hardly fair.

What if something horrible happened to you. What if some years later you passed it on. How long did your guilt indict you. What was the lasting effect of having been younger, of having been unhappy, of having been made mean and dumb in your unhappy youth.

Kelly knew he wasn't different. One day someone might come for him too. An angry child grown stubborn and brave or else a champion sent on the child's behalf. But first anything to protect his boy. Not his by birth or his by the law. His by the saving. His by the carrying up out of the earth. His by the *taking*, the better but not dissimilar version of this act.

The other had taken a boy and watched him. Now Kelly had taken a brother and hurt him.

It was a cheap escape to already render the act in the past tense. He rejoined his thinking to the present: He was hurting the brother, between some times of not hurting him. How far could he go and remain Kelly. How much farther could he go as the salvor. How he could go much farther by giving in to the scrapper. How he thought the scrapper could go all the way.

Beneath the lights Kelly watched the glassy eyes, the fading consciousness. There was blood trickling from the tape around the mouth and how long had it been there.

Kelly shut off the lights, removed the mask. He went into the far corner of the room and spit up into the dust. He took off his coat, the heavy flannel beneath, left the orange jersey sweat slicked against his skin. The low room wasn't warm but his body was. When he returned to the front of the chair the target was awake, choked against the tape, his eyes wide and panicked. The target knew where he was again. Who he was with.

The man in the red slicker. Kelly's father, his grandfather, himself. He could change roles with the brother and there would be no diminishment of what happened next, no matter who was in the chair.

A voice spoke, asked a question. Another spoke next, answered.

Because you hurt my boy.

The sudden appearance of the possessive. My girl, my woman, my boys, all my children I couldn't risk. My parents, wasted and devoured. Myself, who had made nothing lasting and good. A person who couldn't even speak the names of the people he loved. Who once prayed for the shapes instead of the persons within. Who saw the faces falling through his prayers and could not give them the names to lift them back up.

His father: Kelly remembered his face but not like he used to. The vague sheen of some last memory fading. It would have taken a picture to bring back the color of his father's eyes but Kelly could still remember how it felt to hold his father's gaze.

The scrapper remembered nothing. The man of action was a house of empty rooms, a city of empty houses, a nation of emptying cities. Dirt from end to end, from black to black. A dead land where there was nothing left to feel, no one to tell you how you had stopped trying. A place where you could do no wrong because you could do no right.

It wasn't a place you found but a place you could make.

The salvor was not afraid of the dark or the deep but they were not his first elements. He was meant to descend, to take what was valuable, to return to the surface without harm. Past this point in the taking there was almost nothing the salvor could do. There was no redemption in suffering, no correction in violence. Just diminishment and death. A bad thing happened and then another bad thing and another and another until you broke.

Kelly removed the tape and the target began to speak. Kelly wasn't confused by who was in the low room but still it took some time to recognize the soft voice. He had spoken to the brother only once before. The brother had been an idea more than a person but now here he was, his personhood everywhere, leaking in the low room. All the titles merely symbols for what had a better name. *Estranging* did not mean to make someone a stranger but Kelly did not know another word. Whatever he did next would be the final act of his friendship with the boy. He could hurt the target worse. He could let the brother go. The action was close to complete but nothing was yet irrevocable. To have free will was to be both good and evil. To have free will was to choose, moment by moment, one or the other.

The salvor interceded, spoke for the last time. Kelly heard the words, voiced them into the low room. To the brother he said, What if you could become a good man. What if there is good you might do still, what if there is a good man who could be salvaged, someone better inside you who could be brought back into the light. What if the longest story is the story that bends toward the gravity of the good.

Kelly said, What if the greater crime isn't what we've done but that in trying to end it I stop some better you coming after?

But what if I let you go, he said, and you hurt the boy again?

With the tape removed the brother could at last speak in his defense. The brother's voice was strained by a panic Kelly couldn't bear to hear. He paced the dark stretch of room before the chair, clenching and unclenching his fists as the brother claimed unexpectedly familiar grievances: What if it wasn't the mother's house the brother had moved away from but the father's. What if the boy and the brother had the same father Kelly had. What if their mother was his same mother, a kind woman but a woman who would say nothing, do nothing. Who accompliced herself by looking the other way.

The brother kept talking, faster now, less intelligible. There were more words coming but Kelly wanted to already be past them. He howled, grasped for the table, missed and crashed into it instead. The solvable unsolved arrived again, taunting. The table shuddered, scattered whatever little remained. The clatter of tools, the sound of wood and metal impacting concrete, the zone's most common refrain. He hadn't known what he was looking for until he came back up with the pistol. He couldn't see the safety in the dark but he thought he could work it by touch. Even after the brother stopped speaking Kelly could hear him breathing, could hear all the small involuntary movements of his body. Kelly took a few steps back, waited for his blood to slow. He wanted to see what was behind the blackness, wanted to hear whatever was at the bottom of the sound, the new confusion echoing in the dark.

When nothing was louder than the ringing in his ears, then Kelly raised the pistol, lifting its heavy weight against the drag of the black air. Each time he fired the blast lit the room, light and dark interchanging so fast that all Kelly saw was a staccato sort of nothing. In the blindness that followed he put the pistol to his own chin, found the trigger. Nothing. Nothing and the smell of gunpowder. He put the pistol in his pocket. He took the pistol out of his pocket and placed it on the ground. There were new smells in the air and it was harder to hear with the ringing louder than ever. He stepped forward, moved toward where he thought the chair was, toward the body in the chair. With his hands outstretched he found the body gasping, speaking in syllables Kelly couldn't understand, a tongue of one. He put his hands on the body, searching for the wound. When the body recoiled unharmed, shaking in its seat—all breath and voice, all blood and muscle moving beneath clammy skin, strong jumping flesh draped beneath the red hood—then Kelly stepped back disbelieving, fled the brother's barking pleas until he tripped over some fallen object, its length sprawling him across the floor, smacking his face against the concrete.

Kelly lay quietly on the floor, breathed the disturbed dust of the century. Somehow all the rage had gone out of him even though the task wasn't finished. What was left? Only an anxious regret. When he stood with the sledge in his hands he felt tricked. The arrival of grossest inevitability. The limit between one life and the next. The way the blow you never saw coming pushed you over. The land of the living, the land of the dead. Not one and then the other, but one nested within the next. When had it even happened.

The building would stand until one day someone claimed all that yet endured: they would tear it down with machines, they would break the bones of the buildings and rip the last of their guts from the ground. A mechanical reckoning, a recycling of the late greatness. A city collapsed, its citizens driven out, its halted factories left to linger. Thieves in the ruins, murder below the earth.

All the metal in the zone would one day be removed, forgotten, reset. Dental records could identify the body, forensic evidence might find Kelly, but metal had no memory. He'd left the red robe behind. Surely other stains would last. In the grayer light of the hallway he took off his gloves, ran his hands over the door, the doorframe, every surface impossibly cool beneath the earth. He would take his chances with the fingerprints he wasn't supposed to have. Either a detective would catch him or else a detective would not and he would let his worn hands decide. He trudged up the stairs, toward the surface of the world. Already the event began diverging and he recognized this quality of his thought for what it was, not a flaw of memory but an enhancement, a way to believe in a better life than the one he had lived, some good world without a past. What was wrong with him included a way to prepare for an aftermath. How *aftermath* wasn't necessarily a pejorative. How he had lived with the version of himself that had made possible every bad thing he could remember doing, by damage, by weakness, by choice. But surely somewhere within there must still be another man, one who had never done anything wrong, had never hurt anyone, who had been loved back by everyone he had ever loved. But what was this man's name, by what title could he be called to appear.

Back out in the blue air of the zone, Kelly put his mouth to the cuff of his coat, sucked hard, tasted the crackle of sweat and grit. The visible world shuddered and the shuddering came in waves. He wanted to vomit again but the vomit was not coming out. He pressed his hands against his stomach, pushed his fingers and thumbs into the bruises he found. He gagged against the pain but nothing else came, only the familiar throb of overexertion. He sank down to his knees, rocked back on his heels, placed his hands on his thighs. He kept waiting to catch his breath and it kept not coming. Something had broken. His fingers were numb and if there had been anyone to call for help he knew he wouldn't be able to work his mouth, wouldn't be able to hear his own voice over the awful increase of the ringing in his ears.

The car had been parked close but not close enough. He tried to walk, brought himself to life by the effort. Every ache and strain shouted its blame. He heard a sound like a blur, watched a throbbing cross his vision as he tried again to stand. The alley where he'd parked the car loomed emptier than he expected. Paper trash caught against the bricks, lay buried in the snow. The flotsam of a city. He put his hand along one wall, moved forward through a weariness so encompassing he hoped it couldn't have originated within him. Air as exhaustion. One eye was bruised closed and the other so badly diminished his eyesight refocused uselessly as he sorted the blearing scene: something was gone that was supposed to be present and for a moment he couldn't place it.

He began to laugh when he understood the car was missing. A horrible, humorless sound, a high-pitched alien laugh that did not, at first listen, seem to belong to him. A loon, he thought, a bird of his childhood, a spirit bird announcing its flight. It was hard to know exactly how he was harmed, even when he had done the harm himself. Somewhere in the distance a horn honked, a warning or an exclamation, a horn honking and honking, panic and alarm but not from him.

PRIPYAT

EVERY YEAR HE THOUGHT HE was as thin as a man could get but the next year he woke up thinner. Now he knew the name of every rib. His eyes jutted far enough from his skull he thought he could see one orb with the other. The endless dryness of his tongue, how for decades it had been a fat animal and now it was small and black and useless, a worm inside a toothless cavern. When his last loneliness began he'd stopped speaking in sentences and now as he moved mutely through the forest it was only external sounds that broke the silence: the sound of last dogs and last birds, the sound of wind, the sound of creaking wood and straining metal and flapping fabric. The whispered threat of more snow falling, of winter forever.

Now he was awake again. Grief never ended but it faded, went ambient. He took what he wanted wherever he went. It wasn't much. None of it was his but who was he stealing from. No *we*, no *us*, but still *him* and *them*. Same as it had ever been. The other people left lived in the day while he lived in the night. Or else he lived in the distance.

He didn't covet what others had, where they were. He stayed where he was and everything he saw was his or close enough.

Chain-link and razor-wire fences ran around the perimeter of the exclusion zone, contained Chernobyl and Pripyat and the forest and all this was for the best. Those who wanted to be part of Ukraine could live outside the fence. Those who wanted to be part of Pripyat could live within. He had been a soldier once: that was how he had come to Pripyat the first time, to the plant. Years later he returned, arrived at the gate, subjected himself to questioning. He was done with Ukraine, he said. Ready to be apart, within. The first time they had given him a white robe and a white cap, a shovel to clean the dirt down below the melting reactor. The great heat everywhere, the awful unknown of the danger. The feeling in the darkness that anything might happen next, that this was the beginning of something new, a lasting unknown. When he came out from beneath the earth he had watched the others climb the building, cleaning the roof of the reactor. They had called these soldiers the storks but now all the storks were dead, the real and the named. Surely the earth and the dirt ate the birds too, when at last they grew tired of flying.

In Pripyat there waited ten thousand rooms he could sleep in but none of them were his. Not anymore. He walked the city streets on moonless nights but he did not have a home or else the forest was his home, the small caves in the forest where he might build a fire, fight for warmth in the endless winter. He would not kill for food but did not need much, could live off whatever he could gather.

It had been seven years since he'd moved to the forest, since he'd last spoken to another person. Seven years since he'd spoken to a man or a woman. Longer since he'd seen a child. Everyone he'd ever known was either dead or gone and the ones who were gone were likely dead too. Seven years or close enough. Much of his life had been ruled by such numbers. Seven years in the army. Seven years between leaving the home of his parents and finding his wife. Seven years before their first child, then seven more before the child died, before they came back to Pripyat. Then seven years living here, in the house his wife had been born in. The garden, the stucco walls, the eventually shining everything. Now seven years lived in the forest, where there was no wife, no house or neighbors. Where there was no church, where there was no priest.

Once he'd had sins he wanted to confess but now he thought, If there are no people, are there sins? Who was left to sin against?

As he dug for wild tubers or edible roots in the hard and frozen ground he thought he heard an old voice answer, saying, *God.*

But there was no God. No God and no church and no priest. Only death.

And death did not care for goodness or badness. Death was uninterested in anything we pretended to be.

With his hands he scraped back the snow and the soil. There had been food in this place before and perhaps there would be food there now. He did not need much. He was not hurrying toward death but he would not live much longer.

God was dead too and death reigned and if there was evil left in the world then it was a kind of radiation living in the earth, invisible, without scent or touch, and in this place men had multiplied that natural evil, added their own part. They said a dog could sense radiation and he knew a dog would bark at a bad man and maybe they were part of the same seamless cloth. The radiation in the ground and in the air and in the water didn't make you sick in any one moment and he didn't think evil did either. It crept in, got stuck in the hair and the skin and in the bones, in the fatty tissues, the lower organs. You did things. You allowed things to happen. A child was born. A child was born but without everything a child needed. Your daughter, so different from other children. Different from the birds, from the butterflies, from everything that wasn't her. A child died. You forgave yourself or else you allowed yourself to forget. You lied. You pretended you were a good man until one day you were dying of this hot glowing blackness everywhere inside you.

But evil wasn't a matter of physics. Evil existed before we knew the atoms by name. Man came out of the Garden with the names of the world tripping off his tongue but what had the naming changed. Now nameless dogs barked at everything. Now there were no pets left in Pripyat. Everywhere you saw a dog you saw ten, lean and scarred and fur torn and running headlong across the cracked streets, searching for something. Unnamed dogs, unloved dogs, wild again. If it was evil they hunted they would never see it. Because the only kind of evil that existed didn't look like anything.

What he pulled from the earth did not resemble the potatoes

of his youth. Here in the forest they grew strange, pale skinned, thickened with unnecessary eyes, the flesh unimprovable by heat or any other method. Wanting for salt was only a memory of better days but if he could taste salt again then what else might he be able to remember.

Seven years alone. No one who knew him before would recognize him now. The body changed. The mind moved slower than ever, thoughts arriving not by the seconds but by the quarter hour, the half hour, the hour. A meditative pace. In fifteen or thirty or sixty minutes more he would have a new revelation. Everything remarkable arriving at the pace of revelation. Everything more banal allowed to go unnoticed, unremarked, unremembered. He would see the exceptional remains of the world only after the rest was discounted.

Seven years. He remembered everything before but he had let much of these seven years pass through him. Perhaps memory was like the radiation too. Memory and radiation and evil. The invisible accumulating substances of a life in Pripyat.

No man who believed was ever truly alone. Who had said this to him?

His wife, perhaps.

And was the inverse true? Was any man without belief doomed to be alone, even in the company of others?

He'd had a wife. When she died he took her to the cemetery where her parents and her grandparents were buried. He buried her on the grayest day of the year but after she was in the ground the sun came out and shined so brightly he thought the sun was saying to dig her up, to take her home.

That she would live again. He had to throw his shovel into a stream to stop himself. The water would make you sick if you drank it, if you bathed. He didn't need the shovel anymore anyway. There wasn't ever going to be anyone else to bury. He'd found other shovels since but the urge to get her out had passed. Death was death. There wasn't any coming back. No afterlife, only afterdeath, and the afterdeath was in the dirt.

The earth would eat us all but until then he would eat potatoes.

He'd had a knife then. He had the knife still. Sometimes when he walked the forest he took out the knife he'd had when he'd had his wife and he carved her name into the trees. He wasn't afraid to forget it but it was good to read it, to have the letters make the sound in his mind, to hear it spoken. She had been in the world. Her name was in it still. As long as the trees lasted he knew he'd carved enough trunks he wouldn't ever go too long without her.

What had her voice sounded like?

Seven years since he'd heard her last words. She was the one from Pripyat. This had been her home. He had met her the first time, had taken her away, had brought her back. By then she was sick and he thought he would be sick soon too. But she had died and he had lived.

They had come back together but sometimes he remembered it differently. In his memory he had come back alone because now it was hard for him to imagine doing anything not alone. And what was memory but imagination girded with fading truth.

When he returned to the cave he found the coals of his

fire gone cold and empty. If he wanted anything from Pripyat it was matches but there were other ways to start a fire. Dark would fall soon and the cold would increase and as he gathered kindling he knew that what he was making was no home, only a hole, a burrow for a man who knew at last that he was an animal like all the rest.

He had wanted to do the right thing for his wife but she was gone, they were all gone, and he didn't know if he still believed in right or wrong. He supposed he was no longer a moral creature. The earth was death and the earth radiated with evil and the evil soaked into your bones. He wasn't born a moral creature but for a time he had been made one by motherland and marriage. A righteous task could make a righteous man but all he had left to do was live or die. The evil burned in the ground and it came up into his skin and his lungs and when it killed him he would go into the ground too, become one with it.

The good man in the bad world. He had believed once but now he knew the world was neither good nor bad. The world was death and against death there was no sufficient goodness. And what did goodness matter if it couldn't change the world.

He walked among the trees of the forest, gathering what dead wood had fallen since the last snowfall. It hadn't snowed in days but there was snow on the ground, thick and crusted and long from melting. Everywhere he went there were tracks but not footprints, never footprints again. Only the mark of wild boar and wild deer, of wild dog and wolf. Everywhere the marks of beasts and on the trees the marks of his knife, her name, the name keeping him company, the last company he craved.

He couldn't remember her voice. He couldn't call her last face to mind, not the false face she'd worn at the end. He liked seeing her as he'd met her, young, fresh, smiling. Even then full of the radiation killing her but without a hint of its effects. It would take so long for the evil to have its way. Long enough they could believe it never would. Evil got inside her but he couldn't see it, but it didn't change who she was. So kind and joyful, an antidote to himself, to who he knew himself to be. He had never known joy before her. When she was alive he'd thought he would never lack it again. But then the birth of their poor daughter. Then the wages of radiation, of dirt, of the pitiless earth.

He would live but he wouldn't live in joy. There would be no more gladness. He was a thing running its course. Empty as a river. Moral as a river. Until the earth opened up and swallowed it whole, spring and source and the carve of its route.

A man living in the forest. A man who had lost everything he'd ever loved. Somewhere in the distance Pripyat waited outside the future and somewhere beyond that the plant did the same. All the Soviet architecture, Stalinist development plans. Districts of brick masonry, wet-stucco walls. Cities designed to last forever. The glory of empire. Pripyat, the ninth atomograd, the ninth nuclear city. Once fifty thousand Soviets strong and now who was left. A few stragglers, a few returning refugees.

A story of perseverance but against what? The Soviet world

had ended. Pripyat endured, the evidence of its failure. What
the Soviet world had wrought. Was there anywhere else on
earth, the last man wondered, that had ever indicted a nation
so fully? Did every other nation contain a city whose failure
cast such fear, such wide and lasting doubt?

He dropped the kindling onto the snow, fell to his knees.
The old grief was heavy upon him again but he couldn't stay
there long. The cold only killed you if you couldn't keep moving. When he stood he took his knife from his pocket, placed
its blade against the flesh of an unmarked tree. He remembered her name into its bark, carved the crooked memory. In
his youth, he might have carved a plus, might have carved
an AND. He had been so sure then of his name, of who the
man so named was, would become. Now he was not so sure.
Or else he would not admit who he was. Only the last soul
living in this frozen forest. Nameless to any who might see
him, any beast or man. Walking, gathering, surviving. Reading everywhere the name of the woman he'd loved. The best
thing he'd known between birth and death, between the air
and the ground. Her name, of which too much was asked.
Because what was a name. Because what was a name, even a
name you could see in the skin of every tree, against the color-
less evil of the earth, of every inch of dirt.

DETROIT

THE ARENA HAD SPECIAL SEATING for the handicapped and their caretakers, designated entrances. Kelly showed the parking-garage attendant their tickets, then followed the attendant's directions to push the girl in her wheelchair out onto a street named for one of her heroes. When he said the name and pointed at the sign, her head didn't move but he thought she might have shifted her eyes. They had lived together for almost a year now and he had spent the first months learning the new range of her expressions, had started to recognize the small differences between a good day and a bad day, slight shifts in her mood and movements.

In the handicapped section he cataloged the previously unimagined configurations of men and women, their varied dependencies, the results of age, disease, awful chance: An old man with an oxygen tank strapped to his walker, linked armed in arm with a woman who must have been his daughter. Another woman in a wheelchair, her limbs distorted, her age impossible to determine through her deformity. A teenager ancient in his seat, his head wobbling, mouth open, full of soft teeth and dumb sound. All of them dressed in the same red jerseys as anyone else, loose over their differences. The other wheelchairs decorated with stiff flags, bumper stickers for the team, the city, other abstracted allegiances.

The game hadn't started yet. There were twenty-ounce beers available for nine dollars twenty feet away but he didn't want to take her with him to get one, didn't know how to ask someone else to watch her. There wasn't much she needed but he wouldn't leave her alone. To not leave her was the rule. There was a backpack hung over the back of her chair and it contained most of what she might require. Whenever he remembered he kept one hand on her shoulder, let her know he was there. He talked more now than ever before. She couldn't talk but she could make some sounds and he applied certain kinds of sense to each. There wasn't as much hunger in her as before but she was putting on weight, acquiring a sedentary sag to her flesh. They didn't have sex anymore but one of his tasks was to lift her naked in and out of the tub, to rub soap and sponge over her sore skin. Up close there was still something sexual about her body but sooner or later he stepped back.

He was thirsty and he knew caretakers left their charges, took breaks by stranding them in other rooms. Maybe it wasn't right to leave your charges behind when you went to the store or the bank but sometimes it seemed impossible to bring them along. The caretakers learned how to be alone again, despite the work. When and where, even with someone else in the room. You took money from the government for caring for your own disabled person but presumably you loved the person too because the money was shit. Nothing given ever replaced what was given up.

He didn't care what anyone else did. He never left her behind, took her everywhere with him. They were sharing a life and this was it. At home he lifted her out of the chair and into the bath, out of the bath and into the chair, into the bed, into a recliner in her living room, into the passenger seat of her car. Twice a week she went to physical therapy where the therapists moved her muscles like she was a coma patient laid out on a mat in a room of the similarly injured.

The doctors said this was the best it would ever be again. They said this to him and he asked them to talk to her. She was the patient. They were her doctors, not his.

She had asked him if he understood what was coming but he couldn't believe either of them imagined this. The difference between being told and being there. At first he'd thought what had happened to her was his fault: an eye for an eye, a pound of flesh to pay a debt, the taking of the girl for the taking of the brother. But this only was the old belief talking, the remnants of childhood, the holy before. The world without doubt. Even if she had never met him this was going to happen. He wasn't the center of anything. Nothing revolved, nothing was attracted or repulsed by his command.

Every day he told her another secret and the knowledge didn't make her any sicker. He was careful to pace the telling, to make it last. There was only so much of him left.

He wasn't sure what she heard. Or if she heard, did she understand? Her eyes were alive and expressive enough but it wasn't like he saw words in her gaze, it wasn't like there was actual conversation happening between them.

He told her about the low room, how he had named it and prepared it, how he had hurt the brother there. He tried to tell her why. He wouldn't think the brother's name but the brother's last face lingered still. There was a photo the news showed but it wasn't the face he'd seen in the dark. This was another person entirely, someone with parents, a school to attend, a future requiring having left the room. He'd made the brother something different, an abstraction in the dark, he'd hurt him to protect the boy, to remove a single danger from the boy's world.

Time and distance might have done the same work. He'd chosen to accelerate it. To not let a harm he could prevent continue even a single day longer.

I lied myself into belief, he'd told her, in the first days of the wheelchair. It was a crime of impatience, of wanting to ensure causal effect. I was impatient with the good acts of others, he'd said. Because I knew the good was nothing anyone could see enough to fear. Goodness alone stopped nothing.

But then the lie's comfort had deserted him in the last moment. By the end the lights had been off and he had worked in the blackness, imagining whatever he couldn't have seen. Now every night he remembered that imagining, relived it again.

He had been questioned when the brother was reported missing, again when the brother's car was found stripped a week later. Sanchez again, bulky as ever but now smaller than Kelly, the detective diminished by Kelly's new size. But there were no suspect fingerprints and without a body Kelly didn't have to tell the detective what had happened next, how after Kelly left the low room he walked from the blackened buildings of the plant out into the fading hours of night and into the predawn of the city, to a certain house in the zone, a certain driveway in a devastated block where he had left his truck overnight, where the brother had taken the boy the last day he had followed him, the day Kelly finished the case notes.

When Kelly talked to Sanchez he had wanted to tell him about the boy's father, about the brother's last accusations. He had wanted to say that if he could have found the man in the red slicker he would have taken him first. But instead he had told himself the brother had not spoken in the low room and now he was no longer sure the man in the red slicker had ever been real. Now it was impossible for Kelly to see anyone else but the brother in the low room's chair.

There hadn't been running water in the house but in the truck there was bleach. He'd known it wouldn't remove everything but it would remove enough. In the dark basement he'd stripped, scrubbed his hands, his face, his neck and chest, twisted against the burn of the bleach. He lit another fire, sat on the basement steps and shook while his spent clothes smoldered on the concrete.

When he'd arrived at her apartment she was already on the kitchen floor, slumped away from the counter, her feet splayed awkwardly, her face awake but her tongue stilled and her body turned out of sensible position. The burner had been turned on high to boil water, the apartment filled with steam long after the pot had emptied, its bottom blackened and starting to smoke. She'd been wearing slippers and one had fallen off her left foot.

Almost morning then. The city waking up. There had been alarm clocks bleeping through her apartment walls, then the first sounds of breakfast, television news. She'd been making dinner when she fell, had lain there on the tile all night.

Her cell phone was in her pocket but she hadn't been able to reach it, couldn't have opened her hands to work it if she had.

She couldn't talk anymore but her eyes found him, set him to action. He shut off the stove, moved to simplify her posture, untangling her limbs and laying her flat.

He'd spoken in a low voice, spoke slowly in the careful and culled language of apology. He needed to call for help but he couldn't call the way he looked. He had scrubbed his skin with snow and gravel and bleach but it was hardly enough. He wondered what she'd seen: he was her only hope but look at the condition he'd arrived in. Clean jeans and a t-shirt over skin roughed with grit and gore, bruised and battered from boxing and worse, hair streaked with bleach. He didn't know what he'd looked like but he knew how he'd felt and he hadn't felt like himself.

But *himself* had been a shifting thing then. Later the scrapper receded, sated, leaving something else behind, the remainder of Kelly, the broken salvor. He'd done something far from the irreducible center of the supposed law and what did it mean? Just another chink in the universe, another proof of its senselessness, its rules that did not reach all the way up from physics and chemistry and biology to define the right path of human action.

Into that gap he had put his guess.

The jersey was gone and with it all its borrowed symbolism. The gun he'd left in the low room, the sledge beside it. He'd never started praying again so there wasn't anything to quit. Something had happened in the circle of swords but after the low room he let that feeling fly away, and as always when the last angels fled they left their ringing behind.

The morning in the girl's apartment he'd arrived knowing the boy was safe. Then he'd found his girl was not. Now protecting her would require a more ordinary violence, a killing of the moments to come.

That morning Kelly had spoken to her in slow tones, tried to explain. He needed to know if she would die if he took a shower. He needed her to know he was going to leave the room but when he came back he would get her all the help she needed without anyone asking questions.

It was harder to clean away blood than you expected. It took so much longer than he wanted it to take. When it was done he knew he would never do anything worse. In the low room, in its aftermath, he had found the furthest expression of his corruption. Now there would be no more waiting for the blow, only this unforgivable relief.

The national anthem played and Kelly sang along, a swell of patriotism catching in his chest, how no matter what he did wrong he would always be an American. The game started but they were far enough from the ice that he had trouble following along without the girl's constant commentary. The last greats of the past age were retired or retiring and she had mourned the passing of her giants, would have spoken in favor of their legacies, their place among the endless, the names and numbers memorialized on uniforms hung in the rafters. He watched her gaze flicking back and forth across the ice, wondered how well she could track the puck. He held a water bottle to her mouth, let her suck the straw as long as she wanted. He reached down with a thumb and wiped the corner of her mouth, dragged the cloudy spittle across the leg of his jeans. It wasn't only her expressions that had changed. There was plenty of makeup in her apartment but he didn't know how to apply it to her new face. He'd thought of trying to practice with her but couldn't bring himself to do it.

There were steroids for the spasms, amphetamines for fatigue, sedatives to help her breathing. The doctors prescribed an antidepressant but somehow Kelly got the idea she didn't want it, stopped helping her dissolve the pills on her tongue, started taking them himself instead.

She didn't speak anymore but when agitated she laughed, a yelp, all rasp. At night Kelly might lie in their bed with his head on her fading chest, listen to her breath shallow, then recover, shallow again. The shortness of breath might be pain related, the doctors said, it might be the continued loss of involuntary systems, and one night her breathing would stop, the last breath impossible to name until it wasn't followed by another.

The doctors kept telling him to talk to her, that her mind

was sound. He said he knew, said she was the same person he'd fallen in love with. He'd promised not to forget. It was an easy mistake to make. It was a hard mistake to stop making.

He tried to say her name more often. To force it out of his stubborn mouth. It wasn't her name he loved but he didn't know what else to call her. Of all the things she'd lost he doubted she missed the limp.

On the ice a fight broke out and he watched the way fighting on ice was different, how it required a different kind of agility to stay up on your skates with your jersey pulled over your head and fists thumping down on your back and neck. The crowd cheered and he cheered too. He wasn't going to the gym anymore, hadn't sparred since the fight. He didn't plan to ever fight again but he didn't want his body to go to waste so he kept working out at home. He lifted her from her wheelchair into her recliner, got down on the floor between her and the television, did long series of push-ups, sit-ups, squat thrusts. He installed a pull-up bar in the doorframe between the living room and the hallway, rotated her chair to face him so they could look at each other while he did his grunting sets, shirtless and sweating.

It seemed improbable but he was still growing. He looked taller too but taller was impossible. In the bed he took up more of the space, the covers, the air in the room. He thought often about buying a bigger bed or else another one. In the mirror he often saw he wasn't as big as he imagined but he was big enough. This was how you stretched the limits of your frame, how you pushed how much muscle you could pack onto these bones, how you learned how much more could fit inside the shell, more again once the human was mostly gone.

When he didn't know what else to do he plucked her from her wheelchair and carried her around the apartment, being careful not to strike her head against lamps or doorframes or walls. When the weather was better he would take her for walks outside, carrying her up and down the sidewalk, going farther every day. When she started to burn from the sun he smeared her face and neck and hands with sunscreen, found her sunglasses so the light wouldn't hurt her eyes.

Despite his protests to the doctors she wasn't exactly the same person she had been before, not the girl with the limp. That person never would have let him carry her, never wanted anyone's help. But what choice remained. She made noises he interpreted as agreement or disapproval but mostly he was guessing.

At last a whistle blew. The referees separated the fighters, securing them for an agreed-upon number of minutes, the penalty box the punishment for bad behavior, the power play the reward for someone else's. Every game a microcosm of a longer one. Kelly thought he would wait a long time for his punishment, had already decided he would not fight it when it came. In the meantime, he would be with the girl, sharing her life. It was what he had told himself he wanted, even if he'd never said he wanted it like this.

At intermission, he saw the group of boys before he saw Daniel emerge from their number, walking with the others in their blazers and khakis, shirts and ties. Coming up the stairs and then past, into the concourse, laughing and talking with his friends. Daniel inches taller, his face leaner, a teenager at last.

Kelly knew he should let Daniel pass without acknowledging him but he didn't think he could help calling out. He couldn't leave her behind so he backed her away from the railing, pushed her out into the concourse where the boy would see them.

When the boy passed Kelly said *Daniel* but the boy didn't hear or if he heard he didn't turn. And for a moment Kelly saw not the boy passing but the brother, saw how Daniel was growing to look like the brother even though they were not blood.

The boys moved as a unit through the crowd, followed one another into breaches in the confusion, then clumped back up in open spaces. They were moving faster than Kelly could, loudly weighing options for food, souvenirs, talking about the game, the chances for the next period. They cheered for the home team, applied all their boyish arcana, the percentages and statistics and strongly held opinions gleaned from televisions and fathers.

He thought he wanted something else from the boy but what. He couldn't want thanks and hope to get it. He couldn't want a relationship with the boy because those days were done. He had been brought into the boy's life to do something for the boy that the boy couldn't have done himself and now the deed was done. Now he only needed the boy to see him. He needed the boy to look up at him and see this new body, the spent man within, maybe changing again. But what he wanted to believe had changed him most was not what he had done in the low room but what he had done in the first basement, where he rescued the boy. That despite what happened next it was from the first the salvor he'd wanted to follow.

What he wanted to ask was if the boy was at least safer than before. If *safer* was enough to be worth the cost.

The boys moved forward faster, slipped away through the cracks in the movements of the crowd. When Kelly pushed at the crowd most of the crowd moved for him, gave the wheelchair room. Others balked, hesitated, looked too long at her, at him, their new bodies, her loose limbs, his logoed t-shirt tight, how the team's wings and wheel stretched taut over his immense muscles. When he couldn't maneuver the chair forward through the crush he picked her up into his arms, left the chair where it was. Her body was so soft, limp against his chest, she was lighter and he was stronger. She started to make some noise and this time there was no ambiguity whether she approved or didn't approve.

The boy, he said into her ear, her cheek beside his cheek. I have to see him.

Daniel, he said. I want to see Daniel.

He could pretend her sounds were *no* or *yes*, *stop* or *go*. He could pretend whatever he wanted. He stepped forward and the crowd parted. Someone asked if she was okay and he kept walking. He was attracting too much attention but what were his options. There would be a man or a woman who would retrieve the wheelchair and push it after them and he needed to find the boy before this person arrived to force him to play his part. The girl was mumbling into his ear, something repeated, a pattern of sounds, a prayer, a speaking in tongues. Other times he'd shushed her but here he wanted it, wanted it all, wanted her to fill his head with her sound so they might share its nonsense together.

No matter how fast Kelly moved, he couldn't find the boy again, couldn't spy a single blue-blazered friend. He wanted to be winded, exhausted, but there wasn't the slightest need to set her down. This was what this body was good for. He kept walking. People were yelling but he could barely hear them. The ringing in his ears was back again, loud as ever, and Daniel had not turned when Kelly said his name. And no matter how long Kelly looked he knew that had been the moment he'd lost the boy forever.

Back home, Kelly lifted the girl's cradled form, raising and lowering her as if baptizing her in a river of air, until she began to talk in her fastest speech, so she would give him all the noise she had left, all the sounds at once. That night he took her out into the parking lot, onto the sidewalk, carried her as far as he could. A block this first time. Then on another day two blocks. Then one day ten. The neighborhood they lived in had a name he couldn't remember. He carried her around its streets, walked past her neighbors, said hello if they said it first but did not stop.

Her neighbors were the people who had known her but with him she was going away, becoming someone else. Someone new, someone new as him.

As he got stronger they went farther, past the bounds of her neighborhood, into the first circles of the zone. He knew there were men who carried their crippled children in triathlons and he thought he could outdo them all. He carried her past those abandoned houses, those shuttered buildings, all the shattered glass and bent steel, burnt wood and broken brick. The same few elements everywhere unresolved. They couldn't walk at night, not because it was dangerous but because every week there were fewer working streetlights.

The farther they walked the fewer people they saw but he didn't think they walked to be alone. There were dogs in the street, birds overhead. The power lines were electrified but you couldn't get the power down on the ground. The rare car went by filled with staring faces but there wasn't any aggression left in him, wasn't any fear. Fear required hope to live and he believed he'd put his last hope into the earth. One day the rest of the steel and concrete would collapse overtop it. Everywhere they went they went into the painful past. These places where people had lived. Inside some remainder unrecovered. Their old posters of extinct pop stars, assimilated brands. Old uniforms hanging in closets. He knew what men and women had written on the walls, all the countless forms of goodbye. He'd see a pickup truck pass with a bed full of twisted metal and know it was the future being sold, never merely the past carted away. Every address was a reminder how this pasture had been a home. There were good people living in the zone but he no longer hoped to see them. Seeing the possibility of goodness would make it harder to have done what he had done, to have become what he was. He had come to the zone to escape the past. Then he had discovered the past was all the zone was. The city watch had given him its colors but now he was quitting the team. He had done his grim service. He wanted only to be a spectator again.

Now he thought he knew who he was. Not a name but a task. Not a name but an action. His capacity for distance grew. He carried her a half mile then a mile then five miles. He would carry her forever. She was the one he should have protected. He had promised. He would take her the length of the earth, he would never leave her behind, together they would keep moving until he was exhausted, until his muscles were stopped with salt, until his bones bent beneath their combined weight. Until neither of them could move. Until on their lips they tasted their last words. It would have to be far now. They would have to go so far that when they arrived at the center of the city they would be so exhausted they would not ever be able to make it back. When they arrived at their exhaustion he would kneel down upon the ground of the zone, cradle her in his arms, and press his lips against her ears. He would speak to make her believe he knew who she was. He would whisper her name.

ACKNOWLEDGMENTS

THERE ARE MORE SOURCES THAT inspired and informed this novel than can possibly be named, but the following deserve special mention:

Thank you to the anonymous photographer behind Detroiturbex.com, whose incredible images and historical research were crucial to the writing of this novel, and whose generous guidance during a final research trip to Detroit in September 2013 was both invaluable and unforgettable.

Similarly, I might never have written *Scrapper* without Heidi Ewing and Rachel Grady's short documentary *Dismantling Detroit*, which appeared online at *The New York Times* on January 18, 2012. Somewhere in that five and a half minutes of footage was my first glimpse of Kelly, of the world he'd come to inhabit.

I also owe direct debts to Svetlana Alexievich's *Voices from Chernobyl*, as translated by Keith Gessen; to Yasiin Bey, who subjected himself to the force-feeding techniques used at Guantánamo Bay for a striking video released by the human rights organization Reprieve; to the work of Lars Svendsen and Michael Ignatieff, particularly Svendsen's *A Philosophy of Fear*; to the short film *Old Glory* by Will Eno and Shevaun Mizrahi; to the *Detroit Metro Times* article "Kick Out the Demons: Exorcism Detroit-Style" by Detroitblogger John; and to *On Boxing* by Joyce Carol Oates, which — along with too few boxing lessons with Jodi Coolman and Quincy Russell at JAB Boxing Club in Marquette — helped shape the novel's depiction of that sport.

Thanks also to my wife, Jessica, whose constant support made this and every other book I've written possible; to Northern Michigan University, whose support for my research aided the completion of this novel; to my editors, Mark Doten and Rachel Kowal; and my agent, Kirby Kim; to my copyeditor, Susan Bradanini Betz; to my first readers Jamie Iredell, Amber Sparks, Roy Kesey, and J.A. Tyler; and to Kyle Minor, who — during a meal we shared in Detroit several years ago — asked me when I was going to write a book about my home state.

This novel is my answer.